Murder with a Twist

a novel by
Kay Velarde

 American Q

www.Am

The American Quilter's Society or AQS is dedicated to quilting excellence. AQS promotes the triumphs of today's quilter, while remaining dedicated to the quilting tradition. We believe in the promotion of this art and craft through AQS Publishing and AQS QuiltWeek®.

Book Editor: GINA SCHADE
Proofing Editor: ADRIANA FITCH
Graphic Design: CHRIS GILBERT
Cover Design: MICHAEL BUCKINGHAM
Director of Publications: KIMBERLY HOLLAND TETREV

Additional copies of this book may be ordered from the American Quilter's Society, PO Box 3290, Paducah, KY 42002-3290, or online at www.ShopAQS.com.

Library of Congress Cataloging-in-Publication Data
Names: Velarde, Kay, author.
Title: Murder with a twist : a novel / by Kay Velarde.
Description: Paducah, KY : American Quilter's Society, 2016.
Identifiers: LCCN 2015045553 (print) | LCCN 2016001742 (ebook) | ISBN
   9781604604139 (pbk.) | ISBN 9781604603385 (e-book)
Subjects: LCSH: Mothers and daughters--Fiction. |
   Murder--Investigation--Fiction. | Quiltmakers--Fiction. |
   Tennessee--Fiction. | GSAFD: Mystery fiction.
Classification: LCC PS3622.E434 M87 2016 (print) | LCC PS3622.E434 (ebook) |
   DDC 813/.6--dc23
LC record available at http://lccn.loc.gov/2015045553

Acknowledgments

I suspect it might be difficult to be my friend so I want to give special thanks to the people who made the effort in spite of my shortcomings. Torsten Sponenberg is always there for me with unbounded enthusiasm and endless generosity. Her many talents greatly improved the manuscript. To Renee Ryan, a gifted writer, who taught me the rules of good writing and allowed me to enjoy her close family, and Kathy Chadwick, also a gifted writer, who taught me to write with emotion.

Thanks to AQS for creating an outlet for fiction that includes quilting fun. Special appreciation to the dedicated publisher as well, as to Kimberly Tetrev, Elaine Brelsford, Adriana Fitch, and Gina Schade.

Thank you with love to my family and friends: Elizabeth Anne, Jane, and Kathy and crew, as, well as Phyllis and Kate.

And in memory of Tom,
a Southern gentleman, if ever there was one.

Front cover: Photograph of the Sewanee Natural Bridge at Cumberland Plateau in the South Cumberland State Park, taken from a vintage hand-colored postcard circa 1920. The postcard was published by the University Supply Store, Sewanee, Tennessee.

DEDICATION

For Barry, my greatest adventure and the
best husband ever. *"The store closes in ten
minutes. If we hurry . . ."*

CHAPTER 1

"Gibb! I can't hear you. Did you say you arrested Mom?" The only answer to my question was the stuttering static of a bad cell connection. My younger brother Gibb was the sheriff of the small town of Sewanee, Tennessee, our hometown, but why would he arrest his own mother? Was he playing some kind of bad joke on me? This was late October, not April Fools' Day.

"Gibb, you're breaking up. What did you say?" I yelled into the phone.

A tinny voice came through the speaker. "Murder . . . locked room . . . he's . . . unbeliev—"

"Wait, Gibb." My voice climbed another octave.

"Just topping . . . Sewan . . . Mount—" Snippets of words were all that reached me until the call magically came back to life. "Okay, Sis. Can you hear me? I'm on top of Sewanee Mountain now." My brother's voice was back to its usual strong tenor. "I'm driving to the courthouse."

"Gibb, for a second I thought you said you arrested Mom for murder." I wheeled my chair away from my desk and stretched. My neck and shoulders had already been in knots from racing against a work deadline, and now something was wrong back home. But I had to have heard Gibb wrong.

"I did, Stella. That's exactly what I said. I arrested her this morning for murder. Had to."

My little cubicle began to spin—family photos tacked to partition walls, half-wilted ferns in too-small pots, and a bookcase jammed with reference manuals all swam in my vision. The usually too-cool air conditioning suddenly felt like a hot desert wind. I mopped limp bangs off my forehead.

"Stella, stay with me," Gibb said. "You know how you get. Take deep, even breaths."

I sucked air past the lump in my throat. "Was it old Mrs. Fleck? Did Mom finally do her in?" A picture flashed in my mind of our mother finally losing her sanity when trying to deal with her longtime nemesis, the town librarian. I imagined Mom diving over the check-out desk to strangle the old biddy. "Oh, wait," I said, "Otis. It had to be." My mother, a vegan, regularly tried to convert the man who was the butcher at the grocery store. They'd had several loud arguments in front of the hamburger patties. "Or—"

"No, it was Tom Billings." Gibb cut off my next guess. "Mom and one of her guests found him this morning in Mom's office with her good scissors buried in his back. And the door was locked. Mom's the only one with a key. She admits that."

Something wasn't right. As I tried to pull my thoughts together, I blurted out the first thought that came to my mind. "Was it Mom's good gold-handled scissors? Oh no, not the pinking shears." Finally, I focused. "Wait. Guests? Quilt camp isn't supposed to start until this weekend," I said, trying to remember if today was indeed Thursday. I glanced at the computer screen to see that, yes, I had it right.

"She's hosting some kind of quilter's annual meeting. Mom said a few of the women attending are even staying over for the start of class on Saturday."

Our mother made her living teaching quilting classes out of her home. Over the years, the business had become quite successful with her biggest moneymaker being several quilt camps lasting five days each. She was always busy doing what she loved so that, as she said, it wasn't really work.

"How's Mom?"

"Mad."

"Mad that Tom Billings was killed in her house?"

"No, course not. You know her. I mean, she's plenty upset Tom is dead, but she's just as unhappy about the disruption to her business."

"Gibb, Mom didn't—I mean—she didn't do anything wrong. Did she?" I bit my lip for asking the question, but the word *passionate* barely began to describe our mother. She did, however, prescribe to peace and respect towards others. How often had I heard those words when I was growing up?

"Stella! No way. Of course, no way. Mom says she didn't do it, and that's good enough for me as her son, but as sheriff, well, I've got to do my duty. Listen, just get down here quick."

"Of course," I said, but only to the hollow sound of a broken connection.

I tossed the cell phone amid the normal clutter on my desktop, knowing it would do no good to try to call my brother back. Evidently, Gibb was serious as sin, and I needed to get home fast.

I hoped the situation wasn't as bad as it sounded, but my stomach knotted with fear. What was going on with Mom, and when was the last time I'd been home? I ticked off the pages of the calendar in my head, counting to five months before I stopped. Normally, I made the trip at least every two months, staying over for the weekend. Sometimes I saw Gibb, and sometimes it was just Mom and me. Occasionally, I visited friends, but usually I was content to sleep late, take walks with Mom, and curl up on a porch rocker with a book.

Since I'd been named a team chief at work, I had been too busy. Friday evenings I settled in front of my home computer, and the work continued on through the weekend.

With a sigh, I let my head drop back and pressed my palms over my eyes.

From behind me I heard Kathy, my best friend, pedaling her chair, crab-like on its casters, across the aisle from her cubicle to mine. We visited each other several times a day like that, but she'd probably overheard my conversation and was coming over to see what was going on. Probably everyone in the office had heard and now knew that my mother had been arrested.

"You okay?" Kathy whispered, peeling my hands away from my face. "What's up with Cele?"

"Who knows? This is unbelievable. Did you hear it all?"

Her head bobbed up and down, shaking blond curls. "I know Cele can get herself into some crazy situations, but there's got to be some mistake. Right?"

It made me feel less guilty to have Kathy, who'd met Mom several times and heard some of my stories, ask whether she might have gotten herself into trouble. We both laughed at the thought.

Kathy answered her own question. "No, Cele wouldn't murder anyone. Remember when I went home with you that weekend? We're talking about the woman who caught the spider that was in the kitchen and put it outside."

"Yeah. I still do that, too, like she's looking over my shoulder."

"What are you going to do?"

"I'm going straight to Mrs. Howard's office and tell her I need to leave right now, and I don't know when I'll be back."

Kathy pursed her lips. "The Wicked Witch is going to be very unhappy. You are like the only one who knows all the parts of this grant proposal. Stella, she is not going to let her team leader have an open-ended vacation."

Kathy was right. We both worked for a large university teaching hospital in the grant-writing department. Proposals were long, tedious projects that sometimes took as long as a year to pull together. My boss was going to be an angry woman in about one minute.

I shrugged. What other choice was there?

CHAPTER 2

It had taken less than thirty minutes in my apartment to get ready to leave. I had a few plants, so I left a note on my next-door neighbor's sliding glass door asking him to water them for me. Checking the refrigerator, I found the remains of a salad, which I fed to the garbage disposal. There was a heel of bread in the pantry. After spreading it thickly with peanut butter and strawberry jam, I munched it while aimlessly wandering through the rooms of this place I'd rented for over five years. That took about fifteen seconds as it was only one bedroom with a galley kitchen off the living room.

A gloom settled over me more heavily with each step. Where was the bright and lively décor I'd intended to surround myself with? *Buried beneath my work schedule.* Stark white walls, empty of prints or photographs, stared back. The couch was one I'd bought and shared with a roommate my last year of college. It might be comfortable, but it had seen better days. In the bedroom the spread over the bed was the last straw. Why had I bought anything so drab? Then I remembered it had been on super sale.

I popped the last bite of my sandwich into my mouth, wiped my hands on the corner of the bedspread, and jerked the fabric printed with muted greens from the bed. Rolling the cheap cover into a ball, I held it under one arm and hoisted my overnighter onto the other shoulder. With my tote balanced on the rolling suitcase, I was ready to leave. On the way to my parking space, I stopped at the dumpster tossing the bed cover and the kitchen garbage bag over and in. Now I finally felt ready for the two-hour drive south to Sewanee.

At the end of the entrance ramp to the interstate, I goosed the gas pedal of my little station wagon and wedged it between a van and a pick-up truck carrying an ATV painted in a camouflage pattern. There was bumper-to-bumper traffic for a few miles, but it started to thin as soon as I hit the south side of Nashville. Summer was over, school in session, and the holiday shopping season had not yet geared up. The tourists were taking a breather. The Grand Ole Opry was not quiet, but the twanging was just a bit slower.

The car radio blared country. I held to the philosophy that listening to any other music while living in the Capital of Country was grounds for treason. Garth Brooks kept my foot tapping and my mind off the trouble that awaited me back home. Breathing the fresh air from the open window, my spirits lifted, and I refused to think about anything depressing while wheeling down the highway.

With some effort, I focused my gaze on the gray ribbon of road that met a hard, blue autumn sky in the distance. The land around the city was all rolling plains of subdivisions and strip malls, which soon gave way to crops—tobacco, corn, beans, cotton. In about sixty miles those fields would disappear as the hills tentatively raised rocky heads. Then, with as much drama as any landscape could offer, the Cumberland Plateau would rear up like a giant. It took seven miles of twisty road to travel to the top.

I loved Nashville with its big city bustle, but I would always consider the flat-topped Sewanee Mountain to be my real home. It was an oasis of everything I loved about being a country girl. I'd never have left except there weren't many jobs available on the mountain and, I had to admit, usually not much excitement either. Heading home, though, always made my heart sing, and the tires picked up the tune as the miles flew by.

On the steep ascent, the big trucks slowed to a crawl. They crept so slowly that my car sailed onward and upward ahead of them. I tooted my horn as I shot past a truck driven by an older man hauling for *Piggly Wiggly*. He returned my greeting with a salute of two blasts from his air horn. The next trucker I passed did the same, and soon it sounded like a parade. I slid all the windows down, letting the wind toss my brown locks into tendrils, and waved as I sped along.

As I neared my exit, I saw flashing red lights in the rearview mirror.

"Shoot."

I edged the car to the shoulder and watched a brown and tan sheriff's car park on my bumper. My breath came out in a whoosh of relief when I saw my brother unfold his lean body from behind the wheel. He had been lucky to inherit the height in the family. I'd been left with excess width. I always reasoned that he got to move around with his job while I was tied to a desk. Even worse, my co-workers were constantly using their office-mates as guinea pigs for new recipes.

Gibb sauntered around to the passenger side of my Ford.

"You scared me, silly," I said, leaning over to give him a slap on the arm and a hug as he got in.

"What were you doing? Leading a convoy? No, don't answer." He held his hand palm out as if he were directing traffic. The splash of freckles across his nose and cheeks seemed at odds with the crisp uniform.

I couldn't refrain from patting my chest, although I was trying to break the habit because I thought it made me look older than my thirty-two years. "I thought I was getting another ticket. I got one earlier this summer." I couldn't meet my brother's gaze. I hadn't planned to tell him about the ticket, but, as usual, I'd blurted out my first thought instead of holding my tongue.

"Stella, you were doing eighty just now. You promised me you'd slow down."

"Gibb, this car won't do eighty, and you know that." Lord, I hated these lectures. "And I was going uphill."

He opened his mouth, closed it, and then said, "I can't help out if you get any more points against your record. I don't have any influence with the big city sheriff."

My eyes narrowed, but then my face crumpled as I remembered why I was here, sitting on the shoulder of the highway when I should have been typing away in a stuffy office. "Oh, Gibb, I'm so worried about Mom. What's going on? Is she at home? Is she frightened?"

Gibb shifted on the leather seat and eased his holstered gun forward a bit on the heavy belt he wore. He then examined his hands and picked at a hangnail.

"Gibb, where is Mom?"

"Actually, still in jail." He hunched his shoulders.

"Jail!" My voice rose so that Gibb flinched. "She's a fifty-five-year-old woman. How can she be in jail? Is it even legal to put your own mother in the pokey?"

"Give me a break, Stella. I'm trying. You wouldn't believe how many people have bent my ear on this subject already today. The whole town's in an uproar over this murder. Tom Billings was one of the business leaders of the community. Everyone knew him, and it's been nearly twenty years since we've seen a murder in this town."

"I'm calming down," I said and pulled a few deep breaths in and out while I tugged at my waistband with a thumb. "Okay. Explain why our mother is still in a cell."

"Really, I tried to get her out. I mean after I put her there. I went straight from the lockup to the courthouse to try and set bail. That's where I was headed when I called you. I needed to get Judge Marcum to decide on an amount and sign the paperwork to get Mom released."

"So what happened?"

"Word of mouth got to the judge before I did. His bailiff— Betsy Trotter, remember, two years ahead of you in high school— said he hooted like a drunk when he heard the news. Said the judge grabbed his fishing gear and yelled he was going on vacation but wouldn't say where. I searched all his favorite speckled trout spots."

"When will he be back? Or can't you go to another judge?"

"Betsy assured me he has to be back on Monday 'cause of a full court load, and he is the only one, and no, I can't go out of the county."

"Can't you just kind of let her out for the weekend? What's that thingy called—recognizance or something? You know all the legal stuff." I wiggled my fingers.

"Even if I could, after I told Mom what the judge did, she said she wouldn't leave anyway." He sighed and ran his fingers through his hair, leaving it in disarray. "Said Judge High and Mighty Calvin can just hoist his own petard. That she'd fix his wagon come election time. She's already had someone from *The County Record* over to write an article for next week's issue. Irene took pictures and everything."

"Doesn't Irene do the recipe and church happenings column?" Tears filled my eyes.

"Stella, she's alright," Gibb said, taking my hand in both of his. "Or she will be now that you're here. Mom asked first thing for me to call you."

"She did?" I sniffed and fished a tissue out of my pocket. "She wants me by her side?" I wanted to feel reassured by Gibb that everything was going to be alright, that this just had to be a monstrous mistake and Gibb would set it right.

My brother cleared his throat and mumbled something.

"What?" I had a sinking feeling something wasn't adding up. So often with Cele, short for Celestial, things didn't. Like Mom's name which was really Margaret Hill. Granny told the story that at age eight Mom had decided it needed to be changed to something which would help her spirit soar. She'd done this without any prompting from anyone.

And, refusing to listen to anyone, she'd named me, not Stella—the name I used—but Stellar.

Gibb said, "Mom wants you to run the quilt camp till she gets out of jail."

I watched Gibb lean away as if I'd hit him for relaying our mother's wishes to me.

"You're joking! Mom's accused of murder, and she's more worried about her guests than going to prison?" I flopped back against the car seat. "This is crazy. Why didn't Mom send everyone packing? How come all the guests didn't get out of there as fast as they could run? I mean, I would have, with a murder and all."

Now that I thought about it, it was surely crazy that Mom's guests hadn't run terrified upon finding out a man had been murdered in the house where they were staying. Who would be able to think about patchwork at a time like that?

"First, Mom said she wouldn't even be able to reach some of the attendees. They're on their way here. One woman is flying in from California." Gibb mopped his brow with his sleeve. "It was really weird, Stella. These women were standing around laughing when I got to the house. Not Mom. She was pretty quiet. But the guests were laughing and talking about what they wanted for breakfast."

Only around my mother could life be so strange, I thought. *Well, first things first.*

"I can't run quilt camp, Gibb. How am I going to get out of it?" I appealed to him as if he had some sway over our mother, and then I laughed, hearing an edge of hysteria in the notes.

"You can't get out of it," he said. "You know she always gets her way. And how can you say no to her right now?"

I bit my lip, but I knew in my heart I'd best give in before the fight. It would save me a lot of angst, as Granny used to say. Everyone who knew Mom would think the same.

I had to do it, but how? I'd never been very good at quilting, although Mom had tried to teach me. In my few attempts, my quilt tops had never lain flat, the colors had always clashed, and the seams were all as crooked as a dog's leg. I considered it a real failure for a country girl not to be able to sew.

"Uh, I hate to interrupt your thoughts," Gibb said, "but I'd best get you over to the jail to see her. She wants to give you instructions."

CHAPTER 3

I pulled into the postage-stamp-sized employee parking lot behind the jail a second after Gibb. It was an ugly, squat split-block building depressingly devoid of color. Several signs sprouted from the asphalt, warning people not to park here. These spaces were reserved for law enforcement, making me itch to circle back and escape. Gibb stood by his car, waiting for me to park and then, hand on my back, guided me through the back door after punching a code into the electronic lock. I couldn't help but note the numbers were Gibb's birth date, 032184.

The first thing I noticed was that the air smelled stale as if it too had been incarcerated. I knew Mom would hate that stuffiness. At home, whenever the temperatures rose high enough to be comfortable, she threw open the windows at the cabin. How many times had I seen her stand in front of a raised sash, shoulders pressed back, enjoying the fresh mountain air? She would stand tall, breathing actively as she called it.

Gibb whispered, "Now don't cry when you see her."

Tears already trickled down my cheeks.

We paced down a corridor and passed through another steel door. The door clanged closed behind us, and I jumped a foot as the echo bounced off walls that were painted but barely disguised rough concrete.

I had visited Gibb at work before, but this end of the building looked so different. Coming into the sheriff's office from the street was like entering any business—normal carpeted hallways, ordinary offices, pictures on the walls, water cooler humming. This section was all hard and cold in varying shades of gray. Small windows sat high and hid behind some kind of mesh embedded between doubled panes, barely letting light pass through.

Before us now was another shorter hall with two barred cells side-by-side to our right. The person in one cell couldn't see the other nor could they see us from where we stood.

My feet felt glued to the linoleum floor. Gibb urged me forward with a nudge, but by about my fourth step I realized I had my eyes squeezed closed. I stopped and forced them open, and a sharp gasp escaped my lips at the sight in front of me. A shape bundled in orange sprawled on the floor of the first cell, head beneath the toilet in the corner of the small pen, snoring loudly.

"Mom!" I cried.

"That's William, the town drunk, you ninny," Gibb said under his breath. "You remember him, don't you?"

I nodded, unable to speak. He prodded me with a finger in the ribs.

"Stella? Is that you?" Mom's voice called from nearby. "Stella, come here. You've got to see this, baby."

I side-stepped down the hall, unable to tear my gaze from the sleeping William with his huge beer belly rising and falling, jiggling in rhythm to the rumblings coming from his mouth. I hoped he wouldn't bang his head on the toilet when he awoke and sat up. He really was a nice man when sober.

The image of Mom trapped inside the cold, gray cell took my breath away.

She stood, fists on hips, feet spread, chest and chin thrust forward. As usual, her long hair, dark chestnut brown but generously laced with gray, was pulled away from her face in a thick plait that reached to the small of her back. Around her neck her signature bandanna, this one red, was rolled and knotted loosely. Bright crimson beaded earrings hung chandelier style from her lobes. Both the glass beads and the fabric clashed with the orange one-piece jumpsuit that ballooned on her petite figure. Even bars couldn't contain the energy that vibrated in an aura around my mother.

"Didn't you have a smaller jumper? She looks like a pumpkin," I whispered to Gibb.

"No, and don't start on me about that." He pulled a small, metal box out of his back pocket and pushed it between the bars. "Here's the sewing kit you wanted. Do you forgive me now?"

"Gibb, I wasn't really mad at you. What do I have to be upset about?" She gave him an eye roll and then snapped open the tin to rifle through the contents. "Hope there's enough thread here." She straightened and automatically flipped the braid over her shoulder.

"What are you going to sew?" I asked.

"I've got to tailor this outfit if I'm going to be wearing it for a while. And I'll probably have more photos taken." Cele pulled at the extra fabric on the sides to show the full width. She could have easily fit her whole five-foot-four frame into one pants leg. Years of daily walks and eating organic from her own garden had kept her lean.

"Mom, you can't stay here," I said.

"Oh, I can, and I am. It'll make good PR. I've decided I'm going to run against that Calvin Marcum in next year's election. Old coot is using his position to get back at me."

"Back at you for what?" Gibb asked.

A rare blush tinged Cele's cheeks. "Never mind. Ancient business. Now, Stella, I'm glad you're here. We've got to talk about you running the camp for a few days."

"You said you'd tell me what happened at the cabin once I got Stella here." Exasperation clipped Gibb's words. "We've got to go over every detail, Mom. Let me at least get you a lawyer."

My eyes widened. "You mean you haven't told Gibb what happened? You don't have a lawyer yet? Mom, I've got a feeling you had better take this seriously."

"There's nothing to tell. Me and the gals went out to eat and then to bed. That's all there is to the story," Cele said.

"You might be forgetting something," Gibb said. "We need to talk. I want to hear every detail."

Cele waved her hands in the air. "Didn't do it, and it'll all come clear soon enough. Now, Gibb, leave Stella and me alone for a while. You and I can talk later, but this is important. Get us tea and some paper and a pencil. Oh, and give her my office key seeing as how you wouldn't let me keep any dangerous objects."

Gibb's jaw muscles bunched as if he were trying to chew a mouthful of nails. Without a word, he fished a key out of his pocket and passed it over to me.

I suspected this might have been my brother's most difficult day since taking on the job six months ago. He'd been a deputy for eleven years prior to old Sheriff Linder's demise by heart attack. The town council had immediately, and without reservation, appointed their most experienced and respected deputy to fill the vacant position. But there was a special election to fill the position permanently coming up next month, and Gibb had competition.

My brother jabbed at an intercom mounted on the wall opposite and out of the prisoner's reach from behind the bars. With his first stiff-fingered poke, I thought I heard him mutter the word *blackmail*. The second time I was sure I heard him say *servant*. To his credit his expression was benign when he turned around to face our mother again, but as I watched him, his eyebrows drew together.

"What's that broom doing in your cell?" He pointed to the back corner.

Cele looked around as if she were unaware there was anything out of place in her new home away from home.

"I had to have some way to reach that button and get your deputy back here." Lowering her eyes but not being able to erase a tiny smile from her lips, she said, "Women have needs, you know."

Suddenly the door at the end of the hall swung open, banging against the wall with a thunderous metallic clap. Harold Mullins, Gibb's deputy, burst through. "What now?" When the man caught sight of his boss, he stopped short, sputtering in embarrassment. "Oh, Sheriff, you're back."

He gave a sideways glance at Cele. "Shoulda never given you that broom, but it suits you."

I'd never seen Harold fired up like this before. Normally, the man was so laid back that law enforcement seemed a poor career choice for him. It was impossible to imagine this tubby, middle-aged man chasing after a purse snatcher or bank robber.

"Harold, get two cups of tea for the ladies."

"Sure, boss. Say, could you get your mama to quit calling me Barney Fife?" Harold asked as he spun and stomped out.

"Don't forget milk, Barney," Cele sung.

CHAPTER 4

"I don't understand," I said, yet again, pressing my hands over my eyes. My head pounded so hard that the last hour of Mom's quilting explanations were a complete jumble in my head. I didn't dare tell her either.

Mom had just, for the second time, explained, with the aid of drawings, two different ways to cut squares of fabric into triangles. Somehow, she seemed to think it made a difference which method a quilter used depending on the particular quilt block that was being constructed. The reasoning had something to do with bias, which in turn had something to do with how stretchy a fabric is, but everyone knows cotton cloth doesn't stretch. It's not like spandex. What was so frightening about exposed bias anyway?

Truly, I was too upset to care about quilting with everything that had happened, and I didn't have a clue how Mom could remain so calm, so zen-like. How could she possibly remember all of the cutting instructions for a whole quilt right off the top of her head? Sometimes I could barely remember my own phone number.

"Half-square, quarter-square. Mom, why don't you just call it a triangle? What's the difference?" I jumped to my feet, knocking over the empty plastic cups which littered the floor. This cell had no table since prisoners weren't expected to be teaching classes.

"Now sit down." Cele patted the thin mattress covered in a blue and white striped ticking. "Quilting has changed since you last tried. It's advanced."

Somehow my mother was so dedicated and focused that even working from a jail cell could not break her determination. I'd be totally defeated by these circumstances myself. When I looked at her I saw a woman with an unwavering gaze and green eyes that were unnerving in their intensity. Although a hint of wrinkles, crow's feet and smile lines, suggested her age, Mom glowed with vigor and good health.

"Mom, are you oblivious to all this?" I flung my arms out to indicate the stark furnishings—toilet and sink and the bed chained to the wall. My notes, furiously scribbled over the last two hours, flew through the air, clumsy paper planes of quilt block illustrations.

"Can't you hear that?" Tears stung my cheeks. I'd been listening to William rattle the bars for two hours now, and my nerves were frayed. I felt as if I couldn't draw the stuffy air into my lungs. It was like trying to breathe in soup.

"Stella, it's just a jail cell. I've been in—I mean there's worse in life."

Realizing that I was at the end of my rope, Mom stood to her full height and held her arms out. "It's safe and warm here, and Barney even went out earlier to pick up lunch for me from *JoAnn's Café*, meatloaf with ketchup sauce and peach pie with a lard crust."

I stepped into Mom's hug. It was like being enveloped in an orange sheet hanging from a clothes line. The fabric, rough and stiff, scratched, but her arms made the world seem safe and normal for a moment. I sniffled. "I should be comforting you. Aren't you scared? Upset?"

"You know, I'd be willing to torture JoAnn Fuller to get her to add health food to the menu," she said, her words muffled by my hair.

I jerked back. "You've got to take this seriously. Quit thinking about bean sprouts and your precious quilt camp and talk to Gibb. Now!" I tried to inject some steel into my voice.

As I knew her, Cele Hill was tough and opinionated. I'd always admired her stubborn streak, which was just like Grandpa's. In fact, there were many times I'd wished I could be more like my mother. I wouldn't call myself a doormat, but I usually found it easier to give in to an argument than fight for what I wanted. This was beyond any behavior I could appreciate.

She patted the air with her hands. "Now don't get flustered. Let's just finish up going over this pattern I designed. It's kind of complicated."

"No." I grabbed the broom and jammed the handle between the bars to sound the intercom buzzer. My first and second tries missed, but on the third I held the button down.

In seconds, Gibb burst through the door.

"Let me out, Gibb. I can't take any more of this. My brain will explode if I hear the word quilt again in my life."

As he worked the lock and swung the cell door open, I

scrambled around the floor picking up my notes. I shoved the pages roughly together, dog-earing some and tearing one. I flew out of the claustrophobic space as if a bear were chasing me and said, "Gibb, it's your turn to try and convince Mom to help herself. I'll see you out at the cabin later. You're going to need a drink."

Gibb nodded and hitched his gun belt higher on his hips. The expression on his face told me how much he dreaded the task of interrogating his own mother. I wasn't worried. I doubted he'd come out of the tussle any better than I had.

I paused and pointed to his weapon. "Better leave that gun outside."

As I jogged down the hall, I heard Mom call out: "You numbered those pages, didn't you?"

When I stepped out into the fresh air, I leaned back against the door and gasped, pulling in several deep breaths. It seemed like years since I'd seen the sun and felt the breeze on my skin.

What did it feel like, I wondered, *to be in prison serving a long sentence?*

My thoughts snapped back to Mom in a cell, and I couldn't bear to imagine it lasting for more than a day or two. Could barely stand that thought. That made me think of the task Mom had given me to teach her class. It was impossible, yet she'd expressed complete confidence in my abilities.

Mom, always so supremely cool, made students feel like she knew everything there was to know about the subject of quilting. I'm sure she did know more than most. But what right did I have to stand in front of those women and pretend? Then there was my problem. Crowds, even small ones, caused my tongue to tie itself into knots, and I broke into a cold sweat. I predicted I would last about one minute as the teacher.

I was someone who sat behind a desk juggling numbers and writing words to persuade a corporation or a bureaucrat to give money to a worthy cause. That should be easy, but there were so many causes and so few dollars. I worked hard, but I hadn't made anything with my hands in years. Mom's creative genes had passed me by. My shoulders slumped again.

I realized the pages I held clutched in my hand were limp with sweat. I tried for a second to create order from the jumbled mess. Too bad I hadn't thought to number the pages, but then I hadn't expected I'd scatter them across the jail cell either. Now one page dropped to the ground and the breeze lifted the sheet, scooting it a few feet ahead.

Bent half-double, I followed, grasping futilely, only to see the paper become airborne again. It stayed just ahead of me as I hustled around the building in time to watch the slip float into the middle of the road. One car ran over the page and in its wake flipped it onto the grill of a truck following too closely. I watched as part of Mom's precious mystery quilt pattern instructions headed down Route 41, south toward Georgia.

I slapped the remaining pages against my leg. No use worrying now. What I needed to do was help Gibb get Mom out of jail and clear up this crazy murder charge. She could run her own quilt camp then. Solving a murder had to be easier than making a quilt. Or maybe I could talk the students into leaving. At this point I'd be happy to refund their money out of my own pocket. I had been saving for a new couch, but I would gladly sit on the floor for the next few years if it would save me from trying to teach.

I sighed and glanced around. Sewanee's Main Street, only two lanes, was as peaceful as any town could be. The one traffic light held back only a few cars. It was almost impossible to believe that someone had been murdered here in our sleepy burg.

The sun had angled lower, but the temperature had edged up another degree or two. The mountain was enjoying a period of Indian summer, warm temperatures contrasting with the red and bronze leaves that clung to branches. As usual, high up on the Cumberland Plateau, the air felt lighter without its soggy burden of Tennessee River humidity. The temperature stayed a good ten degrees cooler here on the mountain than in Nashville's asphalt jungle.

But the biggest difference from the city, which I noticed with each return visit, was the sound of nature. I heard birds singing and the breeze in the leaves instead of the constant roar of traffic. Outside of my apartment there grew—not well—a row of spindly Bradford pear trees, but they were just saplings so not enough leaves were available to rustle in the breeze.

Under the fall sunshine, the chill of being in the drab building passed, evaporating from my skin and lifting my spirits. I peeled my sweater off and pushed my shirt sleeves up past my elbows.

I checked the time on my cell phone. It was five-thirty now. I needed to get over to Mom's house and make sure all her guests were okay. Supper needed to be on the table by six, but, fortunately for me, Mom said she had a woman coming in to cook, so I could concentrate on preparations for the workshop. Mom already had a regular cleaning lady since she was pretty busy with her business, but Mrs. Cabel refused to take on the extra cooking duties. The temporary cook often made meals in her own home and ferried dishes to the cabin. That left Mom free to work on the quilt lessons and to make sure the students were happy and occupied.

For the last twenty years Cele had been holding Quilt Camp at her mountaintop home. From the very beginning it had been successful, but after a favorable write-up in a popular quilter's magazine eight years ago there was a perpetual waiting list. All Mom did was run ads to announce the upcoming planned project. Lately, she'd become quite famous for her mystery quilts. She'd even had a few appear in quilting magazines.

With these mystery patterns, students didn't know what their quilt was going to look like until the smaller units were pieced and the design emerged. Mom had clues planned that guided her students through the entire project from fabric selection to the final border. By the end of the retreat, every student would go home with a completed quilt top, ready to finish off their masterpiece with the standard instructions to quilt as desired.

I couldn't quite fathom the fun of making a quilt when you didn't know what the result was going to look like. Of course, none of my attempts in the past had ever turned out like they were supposed to when I'd had directions to follow and pictures of the finished project to guide me. After the first few failures, I hadn't thought any of the quilting forms—crazy, pieced, or appliqué—were fun. That was about as much as I remembered of the subject. I supposed if, as a young girl, my initial attempts at sewing had been more successful, I might enjoy it today as much as Mom did.

Suddenly, I realized that I'd learned more today, in the

last two hours, about Mom's business than I had over the last decade. Well, I was about to find out more than I ever wanted to know.

My first official job as the creative Cele's replacement was to escort the students to *Mimi's Quilt Castle* in the morning to buy fabric. She'd said this was just a break for the women who'd attended the meeting and were staying over for class. There would be a second shopping trip on Saturday once all the students had arrived. That outing to Nashville included stops at not one, but two fabric stores, and then on to a quilt show.

I had asked Mom if that wasn't overkill on the fabric spree, but she'd just looked at me as if she wondered if I were really her own flesh and blood.

The class would have twelve students total. Five had already come for the meeting, which had something to do with a national program to make quilts for sick children. Mom told me that five others, who had been at the meeting but were not attending the retreat, should have already departed. Two students were arriving tonight and four more sometime tomorrow. The last one couldn't make it until Sunday and was bringing her fabric with her. The woman knew she was missing the beginning of the class but still felt it was worth attending. Mom had told me she'd already mailed her the fabric requirements and cutting clues. Mom didn't think email was reliable and still used snail mail.

Arrangements had already been made for a van to arrive in the morning at nine. *Sharp*, Mom had emphasized. We would take a driving tour of the University of the South with its beautiful campus before heading to downtown Sewanee.

I leafed through my notes for the part about what the students should be buying.

Here it was.

They were to choose one and a half yards of a warm-colored fabric as well as two yards of a cool fabric that would have high contrast with the first choice. She'd clarified that the fabrics did not have to be solids but had to read as a solid. I didn't ask her to explain the reading part. At this point in the conversation I remembered Mom had gotten very excited. She'd said that the hues should be pure and not muddy. What did she mean by that? Did Mimi sell dirty fabric? For that matter, since when could you take the temperature of a color?

I had to tell myself two or three times not to panic as I looked over the instructions. I would ask Mimi to interpret everything for me.

Mom had discussed the merits of a second option. The students could go with a simpler four-color scheme or, if they were adventurous, they could make the quilt a scrappy one. Mom had been very emphatic, jabbing her finger with each word as she spoke, that the fabrics had to stand firmly in one or the other camps, warm or cool. No middle ground choices allowed, she'd said.

That was my mom. She held strong opinions and always took the road less travelled. To her, life was all about creativity and adventure. I guessed she also had a reputation to uphold. The name Cele Hill was synonymous with bold color combinations.

I dropped my gaze back to the notes, squinting at my own squiggly writing. What was the next word? The ink was smeared. I couldn't quite make out if it was *one yard or seven*. It probably wouldn't matter but seven yards? Now that seemed like a lot. I held the crumpled page closer to my face.

Better go with the larger amount.

Now what had Mom meant when she said her preferred color scheme was—I sorted the notes to inspect a different page—a split complementary? That sounded much too scientific for my brain. I would just ignore that part even though she had made me promise to scrutinize every student's fabric choices before they reached the cash register.

What was a fat quarter? It seemed downright mean to call it fat.

I huffed and shoved the pages together, folded the stack in half, and worked the bundle in among the jumbled contents of my tote bag. I had a lot of work to do tonight.

Mom thought I should go through everything in her office from the student handouts to her teaching aids of quilt block samples, all to familiarize myself with the project. I hoped Gibb would take me up on the offer to come by for the drink I'd offered him. I don't drink—though I was starting to see the appeal. I'd just figured Gibb wouldn't want me rummaging the crime scene without his supervision. I shivered at the thought of being in the room where someone had been murdered, and having my brother with me would make it less scary.

Earlier, Gibb had told me that he and his two deputies had searched the office, in fact the whole log cabin, and found no clues. At least none that pointed to the real killer and not to our mother. So far Gibb didn't have a theory about how Tom and his murderer could have entered Mom's locked office or how the murderer could have exited, leaving Mom looking guilty. Mom swore she had the only existing key, the guests backed up her oath that the door was locked at all times, the lock didn't appear to have been tampered with, and no one in the house had heard or seen a thing.

Now Gibb had turned Mom's key over to me for safe keeping. I shoved my hand into my left pocket to retrieve it. Two Chiclets. I checked the other pocket. Nothing. Where was it? A quick rummage through the contents of my bag didn't turn up the precious object either, and I felt a tickle of panic in my stomach. I swear I could lose things, especially keys, faster than a three-year-old.

I crossed the parking lot, intending to dump the contents of my purse onto the car seat for a good look-see, but when I tugged my car keys out of a compartment in my bag, I saw I'd absentmindedly slipped Mom's in there, too. I gave myself an imaginary pat on the back.

The key was threaded onto a stretchy green plastic band meant to be worn around the wrist. Rolling it on over my hand I thought I'd best leave it on at all times, even to shower. I gave the cord a tug, and it snapped back sharply against my skin.

"Ouch." I rubbed my wrist and then slipped behind the wheel. No time for self-pity today. The car surged down the two-lane out of Sewanee.

The police station sat on the edge of town near where Mom had grown up in a log cabin in the woods. That's where she'd raised Gibb and me. Her father and mother had built the home from the ground up with their own hands. Although our family's cabin sat in the middle of a forest, it was actually a subdivision called Mountaintops with each of the several acre lots left wooded. A carved wooden sign stood at the entrance to the community. It displayed its name in bold gold lettering and beneath that, in smaller print, the words *a private community*.

I encountered the sign more quickly than I'd expected, and I decided it was too easy to speed when there wasn't as much traffic as I was used to in the city. I made the right turn and braked at a guard house which was barely bigger than a phone booth. I knew the guard's presence was more for handing out maps and making the homeowners feel special than for security. Susan Bailey, the gate attendant, peered out with eyes magnified behind round, purple glasses.

Being too nearsighted to recognize me, she scooted out of the building, flapping her hands.

"Dang kids. Git! Git out of here right now! Oh, is that you, Stella?" The stout woman, girdled in an official-looking uniform, leaned forward so that her head was almost in the car. She lifted her bifocals and then let them fall back on a petite, shiny nose.

"It's me," I said. "Sorry. I've got Mom's gate card, but I wanted to let you know who I was and what I'm driving." I waved the credit-card-sized piece of plastic that, when inserted into the reader, raised the gate.

"Thanks, doll, but don't nobody else drive like you." Susan hee-hawed a laugh and slapped her thigh. "I'd heard you was coming. Shoulda known immediately that was you braking like a cat spying a dog."

I tried to laugh like I truly thought her little joke was funny. I swear, one accident when I was in high school, and I was forever labeled a bad driver. Surely thousands of people have driven cars into lakes. At least hundreds.

"How's your mama?"

I twisted my grimace into a smile, knowing that I'd have to field the question probably a dozen times a day until this was over. "She's doing fine. I'll tell Mom you were asking after her. Talk to you later, Susan. I've got to check on supper," I said, accelerating.

CHAPTER 5

"Lam? Good gosh. What are you doing here? I haven't seen you in ages." The wooden screen door to Mom's kitchen banged against my butt when I stopped suddenly on the threshold. "I mean, it's obvious you're cooking, but why are you making biscuits at Mom's house? Wearing her apron."

My old childhood friend, Lam Wythe, turned to face me and gave me his signature slow grin. He hadn't changed one bit since I'd moved away. Through the years, every girl in Sewanee had been openly in love with Lam, short for Lamont. He and Gibb had always been best buddies, and that fact had made me pretty popular. Lam was a cross between Jon Bon Jovi and Brad Pitt with a little of Cele's bad-boy favorite Mick Jagger thrown in for good measure. It hadn't hurt one bit that he was as nice as a slice of chocolate pie.

"Stella, darlin'. Why, aren't you beautiful! I see you're still wearing big hair, and on you it looks lovely."

Now, coming from anyone else, that would have sounded snide, but Lam, affecting an accent so thick it fell south to Mississippi, was always giving compliments and making women feel as if he loved everything about them. Listening to the man was like rubbing a delicate floral-scented lotion or Tennessee barbecue sauce all over your body.

"How long has it been? Six months? Eight?" he asked. "And you look so sophisticated. You make me feel like nothing, but a country rube."

"Shue, you ol' flirt." My hand went up automatically to pat my hair styled like Loretta Lynn. "What are you doing here?"

"I'm Cele's cook." He pinched off a chunk of the dough that he'd been kneading and dropped it into a large stock pot on the stove. The aroma made my tummy rumble.

"Oh, you're making chicken and dumplins," I said, as if that answered the question better than his own reply. "But Mom said there was a woman coming to help out." I forced my mouth closed. Somehow the man's amused grin and smooth good looks churned my senses, and they'd already been shaken up enough today.

"Gibb called me and asked if I could come hold down the fort. He said he wanted a man around since these quilting ladies were sticking fast." Lam flashed a body-builder pose and then laughed. "This has been the most unbelievable day, Stella. When Gibb told me he'd arrested his own mother, well, of course I thought it was some kind of bad joke. Cele doesn't even know that old Mrs. Curtis—she's the one Cele hired to cook—well, she came to the back door right after I got here and quit straight out. Wouldn't put her dainty foot inside the house even. I called Gibb with the news, but I don't think he had the nerve to tell your mama."

"So you're doing the cooking all by yourself?"

"Well, someone's got to do it, and I'm a darned good cook."

"I didn't mean you weren't, just that it's a lot to ask of you. I'll help."

Lam's shoulders stiffened as he dropped the last of the dough into the pot.

"Hey, I can cook." I tugged one of the kitchen chairs away from the table and tossed my overnight bag and tote onto the seat.

"Last I remember you weren't too, uh, domestic, and I don't mind helping Cele out."

I knew that Lam loved my mother as much as me or Gibb. He'd spent many a mealtime at our table and nights sleeping over too. His dad had been through three wives by the time Lam had become a teenager, and not all of them had been stepmother material. If not for Gibb's friendship and willingness to share his own mama, who knew what direction Lam's life would have taken.

As it was, he'd turned out mighty fine. The man, still the most handsome in half the state, had his own big truck repair shop and favored donating money over drinking.

Lam dusted flour off his hands with a dishtowel tucked into the ties of a red-checkered apron. "Now that I won't get dough all over you, let me have a hug, sweet Stella."

Lam wrapped strong arms around me, squeezing me tight and even lifting me so that my toes were all that touched the floor. I swear it was the best thing I'd experienced for six months or more. Okay, definitely more.

When he finally let me down, he said, "Can you believe that Cele's students have refused to leave?" Lam shook his head. "Gibb tried to shoo the ladies away."

"It is crazy."

I knew there would be a jug of sun tea in the refrigerator, and I wasn't disappointed. I slid the pitcher onto the counter and took a glass from the old metal cupboard over the sink. The syrupy cold drink was a balm to my throat and helped cool the heat from a hectic day. It also gave me a chance to calm myself after the warm embrace.

For the first time all day, I felt my nerves quiet and my breathing slow. I knew it was the presence of the old log cabin, my birthplace, wrapping its protective walls around me. Every time I came home it was the same. The first glimpse of the big logs through the trees made my heart warm with anticipation of the comfort it offered. This is what I meant when I told Nashville friends that I was just a country girl. They never quite understood.

It wasn't that the house was huge or that impressive even though Mom had a dorm-like room added onto the back for the students. It slept fourteen in bunk beds and had enough showers to keep the ladies happy, but the addition wasn't visible when you drove up the gravel driveway. What caught the eye was a cabin so fitting and settled into the Tennessee hardwoods that a person might imagine it growing there like the trees. The chimneys were made of field stone gathered right from the property, and the roof was dressed with split oak shingles. The materials were the essence of the mountain and imparted the spirit to those who lived here.

The sizeable kitchen, the heart of the cabin, was pure country. In this room, two of the walls were the outer log ones of the structure while the other walls wore rough plaster coats. The flooring was wide pine planks. The effect might have been dark except the sharp autumn sunlight glowed against the golden wood tones, making the room warm and inviting. Even with less light in the winter, it still looked good. Braided rugs, made by a local family, added touches of bright color and wool warmth.

The old kitchen table, painted white, sat in a small breakfast nook, and the appliances ringed a well-used free-standing butcher block. With my finger, I traced my initials where Gibb had carved them into the top of the cutting block alongside his own. He'd done that when he was eleven with the knife he'd gotten from Grandpa for his birthday.

Looking at the window over the sink, I smiled. Every year there were new curtains, and this was the first time I'd seen these. Cele had cut fabric in the shape of leaves, painted them fall colors, and scattered them randomly, stitching them together with open spaces left between the pieces. It was as if the wind had picked up the last vestiges of the season and blown them into the kitchen.

The swinging door from the dining room opened, and a bottle-bright redhead appeared.

"Oh. Sorry to interrupt." Heavily made-up eyes narrowed when she found the cook was no longer alone. The woman, who appeared to be in her mid-fifties, didn't seem at all as if she were sorry.

"I just wanted to see if you needed any help, sugar," she said, directing considerable attention at Lam.

"Now, darlin'," Lam said, accent revived, "aren't you an angel. You let Lam serve you. Tell the other ladies I'll be in with the salad course shortly." His smile could have melted asphalt.

"I hope she's not diabetic," I said after the door banged closed.

Lam wiped imaginary sweat from his brow, sweeping overly long straw-colored hair back from blue eyes. "You know it is hard work keeping women happy. By the way, that one is called Sherri Bane. But seriously, Cele was pretty flustered this morning. Never seen her like that before, and it made me mighty sad. She said she was going to ask you to fill in for her teaching, Stella. You're a good daughter."

He took a large salad bowl from the refrigerator, placed it on the table, and stripped off the cling wrap. There were colorful vegetables blended with torn lettuce. I knew that every morsel had come from Mom's garden. Every plant had been lovingly tended, even sung to.

"We'll see if Mom still thinks so after I've muddled the job." I placed a hand on Lam's arm and then collapsed against him into another hug. "You'll stay, won't you? You won't take off now that I'm here, will you?" I knew my voice sounded desperate, but I didn't care.

"No way. I'm here all the way for Cele and you and Gibb."

"But what about your shop? You can't close for too long."

"Darlin', I got two guys working for me now. Didn't you know? I'm moving up in the world."

I pushed back from his warm embrace and grabbed plates for the salads. "Let me take this in. I need to introduce myself and see if I can talk these women into leaving." I loaded everything onto a tray that Lam already had out on the counter.

Lam stopped me with a hand on my shoulder. "Be careful. Mrs. Billings is in there."

The dishes rattled in my shaking hands. "Tom's wife? You mean Thomas Billings who was killed in this house? His wife is in the dining room right now? What does she want?"

Was the woman here waiting on Mom to be released from jail? Had she come to confront Mom? Shouldn't the new widow be home grieving? Mother in jail, guests who refused to be scared off, and the widow here. What next?

Lam said, "She's enrolled in the workshop."

"She still wants to be here after what happened?"

"Yup. Said she needed something to occupy her mind. A couple of women left this morning, but they didn't seem scared. They were here for the meeting and hadn't planned to stay for class anyway. Stella, I know I already said this, but it is the strangest thing that a murder didn't scare these people away." Lam rubbed a thumb and forefinger down either side of his mustache to the goatee. He looked like a pirate or a rather handsome, good-natured actor playing the role of one.

I just shook my head and shoved the door open with my shoulder to turn into the dining room. Silence fell with my entrance.

Mom kept a long pine trestle table set up in the big room with its low ceiling ribbed by ax-hewn beams and a fireplace along one wall. At the table there were fourteen seats, a few empty.

I introduced myself as I scanned the faces of the women, most smiling and eager. Even in this casual setting, I could feel a major case of nerves building. Plus, I didn't see Christine Billings.

"So you're Cele's daughter. Just think, two quilting and design experts in one family. I'm impressed."

This comment came from the woman I'd seen earlier in the kitchen. Her words made my thoughts spin. Mom hadn't done that to me, had she? She abhorred lying, but it sounded as if she'd misled her students making them believe they had a competent substitute teacher.

Another lady, this one with an open, friendly face asked, "Cele said you've won several awards, dear. What contests were they? Paducah? Houston?"

My smile stiffened. Yes, I had won a few contests in elementary and high school. Which had Mom been thinking of? The spelling bee or baton twirling?

"Uh—" I started forward with the tray and hooked the toe of my sandal on the edge of the braided rug.

A young woman, sitting closest to me, lunged faster than I'd ever seen anyone move. She leapt from her chair and caught the tray as I lurched forward.

After settling the tray on the table, she said, "I'm Julie, and this is my friend Leann." She pointed at the friendly woman as she grasped my hand and started to shake it up and down. "We're up from Florida. Sorry we're here a day early, but the tickets were 'bout half the price. I mean, sorry about not waiting for the weekend, not sorry that we're here. I couldn't wait. This is just the most thrilling thing I've ever done. Oh, that makes me sound like a dull person, though, doesn't it?"

All of us watched in amazement as Julie kept talking. She couldn't seem to stop and I wondered if she was always like this. It did give me a moment though to catch my breath and slow my racing thoughts.

"No problem," I finally interrupted, deciding there was no other way to talk to Julie.

I felt like I should look under the table for Mrs. Billings. The older woman simply wasn't in this room, but Lam couldn't have gotten something like that wrong. Had Christine Billings excused herself before I came in?

I examined each face carefully as I passed salad and bread plates around.

"Be right back. Go ahead and dig in," I said, tugging my shoe back on while tripping my way into the kitchen.

Lam had his back to me, balanced on a one-step stool to reach into a high cupboard.

"Lam, where is—"

Just as I came up behind him, Lam stepped down and caught me in the cheekbone with his elbow.

CHAPTER 6

I let my head drop forward onto Mom's desk, my forehead clunking against the oak harder than I'd intended.

"Ouch."

"It couldn't have been that bad," Gibb said. He straddled the straight chair beside me, crossing his tanned forearms on the seatback. Having traded the crisp tan uniform for a plaid shirt with a frayed collar, he looked more relaxed and seemed younger than his thirty years.

"Oh yeah? Wanna bet?" I asked.

I'd been telling him about supper and the grilling I'd endured from Mom's students.

"It was worse than any job interview in history," I said. "I spent a good hour trying to talk them into leaving, and they just laughed at me and kept bringing the subject back to quilting. I finally had to let go with tears over Tom's death and Mom's arrest to get away from the vultures—I mean, ladies."

"So they jumped you like a June bug," Gibb snickered.

For the first time in my life, I won the eye-wrestling contest with my little brother, and Gibb mumbled an apology.

"It's not funny." I sniffed as I rubbed my forehead and then the tenderness on my cheekbone where Lam had accidentally hit me. I felt I definitely deserved a reward for all I'd endured today. I snapped my fingers and rummaged through the desk drawers. "I know there's one here somewhere."

"What are you looking for?"

I shook my head and continued the search. All six drawers were empty. Well, not empty, but they didn't contain the object of my desire. Darkness filled each of the cubbyholes stacked behind the writing surface of the antique roll top. I jammed my hand into one after the other and got lucky on the third try as my fingers found a round cake wrapped in cellophane. A moon pie.

"Ah, the best thing to ever come out of Chattanooga." The fresh marshmallow layer was like sticky gum as I bit into the sweet. "Mom's one junk food weakness," I said, waving the pie with a quarter moon-shaped bite missing. "Want some?"

"No, but that reminds me that I'd better buy a box to keep at the jail for Mom. Otherwise, she might go into withdrawal."

"How is she? Did she talk to you after I left? Did you get her to quit treating this like it's a joke?"

"Yes, and I think she is taking it seriously. You know Mom's pretty sharp."

"What are you getting at?"

"She didn't come out and explain, but I think she wants to stay in jail to protect me."

"Oh, the election. She doesn't want it to seem like you're giving her special treatment."

Gibb nodded. "I always said you were quick. For an older sister."

"We'll have to respect her wishes then, but seeing her in that cell really makes me sad."

"Me too. I'll respect her wishes until Monday morning. Then I'm getting her out of there." Gibb's eyes darkened, and the muscles in his jaw bunched.

"Has anyone seen the judge yet?" I asked, swallowing the last bite of the Moonpie and already wanting another.

"Not hide nor hair."

My watch read nine. I was tired and chilly. One of Mom's sweaters hung over the back of my chair, and I pulled it on, hugging the warmth and the scent of my mother to me for a moment. It brought back a flood of good memories like sitting around a campfire or putting up the biggest Christmas tree we could find. We'd always decorated with handmade ornaments and strings of popcorn. Mom had always been there for us.

"What we need to do is solve this murder."

Gibb reared back. "Wait. Me." He tapped his chest with his thumb. "I'm the sheriff. There is no we."

"Come on, Gibb. You're going to need all the help you can get. You've got Lam helping. Plus, you said yourself that you didn't find a single clue here." I flung my arm out to indicate the room and, in doing so, knocked over several boxes stacked beside the desk. The top carton, the smallest one, landed with a solid thud while light-weight bundles of quilt batting tumbled out of the two larger containers without making a sound.

My brother started to get up to help me, but I waved him back to his chair. He looked exhausted and gave me a grateful look as he tossed back the last of his small glass of whiskey.

"Where is Lam?" he asked.

"He went back to his place to pack some things, one of which is his cast-iron frying pan, which he considers essential." I snorted.

"Hey, just because you can't cook, don't make fun of someone else who can. We double dated last year, and he insisted on making supper. After that my date left me for him. But you know Lam. That lasted about a month."

"Where's he living? Still in those rental townhouses? Is he between girlfriends?" I asked, wondering why the answer seemed important to me now. Something in the hug earlier had just felt so right. If I guessed correctly, my friend had probably recently dumped his latest girl and was just bored.

"Yep. Still lives there, but he hasn't been dating recently. He actually—" Gibb laughed. "He said he thinks he's tired of all those cookie cutter dates. He wants to find somebody to be serious with. Can you imagine Lam married?"

Suddenly I wanted nothing better than to change the topic.

"So you don't mind me going through everything in here?" I asked. I tried to push the small box I'd dropped aside with my foot, but it was too heavy to budge. I picked it up with a grunt and shoved it back out of my way, noticing that the carton was still sealed shut.

"No. There's no evidence to find. The tech guy from the state boys came in and gave us a hand, but the weapon, the scissors were wiped clean. I've already released the room..."

His tired voice trailed off.

"I'll let you know if anything weird turns up," I said. "Do you have any suspects?" My arms were now full of the batting, and I noticed the label said it was wool. I hadn't known that wool was one of the options available.

"No. First, I've got to figure out how someone got into this room." Gibb rolled his empty glass between his palms.

"I was thinking about that," I said. "It has to be the window. Is there a nail, a stout nail, holding the window sash closed?" I dumped the rolls back into the boxes and went to examine the window frame. I stood on tiptoe, squinting, and then bent at the waist as I let my gaze move down over every inch of the wood.

My brother laughed. "Stella. This isn't an Edgar Allan Poe story. There's no orangutan roaming the mountains."

"No chimpanzees either?" I asked, giving Gibb a grin to let him know I didn't mind him shooting down my literary theory. Maybe this sheriff business would be harder than I'd anticipated.

"No. Well, someone got in here. In fact, Tom Billings himself got through that locked door without Mom or any of her students seeing him."

I thumbed the lock on the window and found that the sash lifted easily. Pushing it closed, I made sure the window again latched securely.

"You said this was locked when you got here this morning?"

He nodded. "And there were plenty of ladies around once the body was found. The woman who was with Mom, a Sherri Bane, said that when they found Tom, Mom immediately told her to get out of the room. They were all of them milling around in the hall right in front of the door when I arrived. Every one of them told me Cele was never out of their sight once the body was found."

"Do you know when Tom was murdered?"

"Doc says probably between eight and midnight the previous evening."

"Seems like Mom would have found him earlier."

Gibb rose and started pacing. "Everyone went out to dinner last night up in Manchester and returned at eleven-thirty. I talked to the waiters at the restaurant, and they say the group left about ten minutes after eleven. They remember because they close at eleven. They said the group was having a great time, but they finally had to ask them to leave."

"And after they got home?" I asked. "What happened then?"

"Mom says she went straight to bed when they got back. Some of the ladies stayed up for a while, but they said they didn't hear anything. Of course, their beds are as far from this office as you can get and not be out in the yard."

"But Mom can't prove she didn't come back downstairs," I said. Mom's bedroom, as well as the other two, were on the second floor. "Were there fingerprints in the room?"

"Sure. Hundreds. That's no help. Here's the thing, if you start with the assumption that Mom could be the murderer—"

"Gibb, you don't suspect Mom."

He held up his hand to stop my protest. "Of course not. Let me finish. If the sheriff of Sewanee weren't Cele's son, she would be the prime suspect in the investigation. It would be plenty easy to believe she did it because Mom swears the window and door were locked."

I gave him a questioning look.

"But I am the sheriff and Cele Hill's son, and I know Mother didn't commit the crime. That means I have to prove someone else, plus the victim, got into a locked room."

"Knowing Mom, if she says the room was locked up tight, then it was." I sighed.

Gibb poured another finger of liquor into his glass, his mouth set in a tight, grim line.

Another thought came to my mind. "It seems like Mom would insist on canceling the class."

"You know our mother. Look up obstinate in the dictionary and you'll find her picture." He glanced down at the floor. "Actually, she did suggest to the students that they should all leave. She offered a full refund and to pay for any charges for changing their plane tickets or for gas."

With that last sentence, his voice had grown so soft I wasn't even sure I'd heard the words. I reached out and patted his arm. I guessed this was tearing Gibb up inside, but I also knew he was a good cop and he'd get this straightened out.

"Do you have any theories yet?"

Gibb flopped back to the chair, looking spent, and shook his head no. "She told me this morning that she hadn't seen Tom Billings since he was out here a week ago ranting and raving."

My head jerked up. "Why was he ranting? What are you talking about?"

"Mom didn't want to worry you, Stella. I've asked her several times to talk to you about this."

"What was going on between her and Tom Billings?" I could feel the bile rise in my throat from the serious expression on Gibb's face. "You're talking about motive here aren't you?"

He nodded. "It started about six months ago. Started kinda slow. Somehow Tom has, er, had it in his head that Mom can't have a business here."

"Isn't that the end of it then? Someone can't make you close your business." I could feel my anger rising and reminded myself that the man was dead. Dying in this very room. I looked at the freshly scrubbed floorboards. They'd been cleaned so well that some of the wood's stain had been removed. The oval braided rug that usually decorated the floor was missing, and I didn't ever want to know what had happened to it.

"It's a little more complicated than that, Stella. Technically, this house and the property are all within the boundaries of a private, gated subdivision."

"I know that, brother, but Grandpa created Mountaintops."

Originally, Mom's parents had owned over two thousand acres of the plateau. For years their lumber trucking business had been successful, but increasing fuel costs and a growing family had forced the sale of most of their land. Instead of letting the land go piecemeal, Grandpa had the idea to turn it into something akin to a resort. The area was certainly beautiful enough to rival any state park. Besides the beautiful forest, cliffs along the edge of the plateau dropped dramatically to the valley floor almost a thousand feet below, and there were several waterfalls. It was all postcard pretty.

The cities of Nashville and Chattanooga, each a short drive away, had plenty of families with old money who could afford weekend cabins in the cooler, higher elevations. They'd snapped up the ten-acre lots. Grandpa had stopped selling and kept the final, and prime, five hundred acres. He and Grandma had retired with the profits.

"I know Mountaintops has a homeowners' association and everything," I said, "but Mom's property is exempt from all that. She's grandfathered. That's the legal term."

"Gramps was pretty clever when he had the lawyer draw up the paperwork, but he left one loophole that's been causing Mom problems. The original wording called this piece of property," Gibb gestured at the floor, "a home site. And all the other lots they sold were listed as home sites. Land for homes. See what I'm getting at? She operates a business here."

"But it's quilt camp." I frowned. "Oh, that is a business, I guess. And I suppose Mom has dug her heels in and refused to move the camp out of Mountaintops. Right?"

Gibb nodded. "I suggested she rent a place in town for the teaching. With the bad economy, she could have her pick of several places for next to nothing. The students could still sleep over and eat here. Nobody could stop that as long as the actual teaching was done elsewhere."

I lifted my feet and boosted the desk chair so that I spun around. As it whirled on the seat, I noticed the framed map of the Mountaintops property hanging on the wall where Grandpa had placed it years ago when this was his office. Even though the paper was yellowing, Cele left it in place. The hand-penned lines showed the layout of the subdivision. All the ten-acre lots were in neat rows. These five-hundred acres looked huge in comparison. Whoever had drawn the map had sketched the log cabin in its place on the eastern edge of the development.

"So, is this over now that Tom's dead?" I asked, not able to keep the dread from my voice.

"No, I'm afraid not. Several others in the homeowners' association liked the idea of getting rid of Mom. They mostly don't like her guests having to go through the security gate the association set up five years ago."

"That seems petty."

"Sure, but as sheriff I get complaint calls all the time. Her students are mostly middle-age and older ladies, not rowdy teenagers or your typical robbers. When they come through the gate, the guard gives them a map and instructions to head straight to the camp, but they get lost on the twisty roads through the woods or decide to sightsee around the lake or on Top o' the Cliffs Road. A few have even pulled up to residents' houses and asked for directions after they get all turned around. That's when the calls come in."

"And Mom just has that effect on some people." I pushed back into the leather cushions of the desk chair, thinking about my mother's many rocky relationships in Mountaintops and Sewanee.

Gibb and I both knew Mom had made her share of enemies on the mountain. She had the type of personality that no one could be neutral about, like when she protested logging on the mountain. How many times growing up had someone said, "Oh, you're Cele's girl" or even worse, "You're that Celestial's daughter?" Maybe that's why I'd fought so hard to be different from her. I'd longed to blend in with the neighbors. Whatever the current fashion had been, I'd worn it. Knowing the locals mostly liked country music, not Cele's rock, I learned the lyrics by heart. Baptist was the religion of choice. I'd joined the choir.

Celestial was just one of those people who burst through life. She was a cannonball—and I didn't choose that analogy loosely. Mom always had an opinion and never failed to express it. She championed causes. She fought for the underdogs. Really, for dogs and cats.

I looked down at the floor where two dogs sprawled, sleeping. One was about fifty pounds and covered with a wiry grey coat that stuck out every which way in the worst case of bed hair ever seen. He was named Doodle Dog. The smaller, Carly, was twenty pounds of sweet kisses and snuggles. A black cat Cele called Baby had jumped onto Gibb's lap earlier and settled down. All strays. Then there was a calico known as Sleepy curled on the mantle over the fireplace.

Fireplace.

"Hey, Gibb," I said, jerking to attention, "I bet the killer came down the chimney."

"Not unless he or she weighed in at about seventy pounds. And Tom was six-four and easily two hundred and forty pounds."

Although it had been a while since I'd run into Tom Billings, I remembered him as a solid mountain man who had liked his chicken fried, ham smoked, and moonshine local. Too boot, he played the fiddle. Gruff, but an upstanding businessman in the community. He may not have been the most well-liked man around, but he'd been respected by most and needed by all since he owned the only hardware and feed store for miles. I supposed he must have been in his late sixties by now, maybe even seventy. That made him ten to fifteen years older than Mom.

"Oh, that reminds me," I said. "I didn't know Tom had divorced and remarried." My feelings were hurt that no one had shared the gossip with me. Earlier I'd finally had the chance to ask Lam where Mrs. Christine Billings was since I hadn't seen her in the dining room. Turns out I'd been look-ing for the wrong face. A young woman—Mrs. Billings number two—had introduced herself simply as Lori, and I had been none the wiser.

Gibb grimaced. "Sorry. Don't see how you missed that bit of news. Tom dumped Christine for the newer model about eight months ago." He stroked the cat as he talked. "Figured Mom would have told you."

"Lam thought I knew. When he told me Mrs. Billings was in the dining room, I was looking for a grey head. How old is Lori anyway?"

"Twenty-eight. Forty years younger than Tom was."

"Do you think Christine could have killed him?"

"Naw. She still lives in Sewanee, but she was visiting someone else here who's vouched for her."

"Well, who was it?" I asked, irritated to have to drag every bit of information from Gibb.

"Stella, I shouldn't be talking about this."

"And our mother shouldn't be in jail."

My brother's face glowed red. "No, and I guess you could find everything out by asking just about anybody in Sewanee. Christine was with Lori."

I leaned back in my chair surprised at the answer.

"Did they all get along? Was it a friendly divorce?"

"Hardly. Tom was cheating on Christine with Lori for a few months before they separated. Let's just say she didn't take the news well. People were betting on which one would kill the other first. It settled down finally."

"Did it divide the community?"

"Sure, but I probably didn't hear all the gossip," he said.

"At least Lori's not a gold-digger," I said.

"Why would you say that? Tom was worth a bundle. One

of the richest men on the mountain."

"You're kidding me? How? Is there that much money in chicken feed?"

"He owned half of the construction equipment in the county. Rented it out. You and a lot of people were fooled by his simple lifestyle, but I'm sure Lori knew."

Something in my brother's voice, a tinge of bitterness, sparked my curiosity. "Do you know Lori well?"

Gibb shooed the cat off his lap and stood. "We were dating when she started fooling around with Tom."

CHAPTER 7

Gibb had gone home hours ago, and I was still working in Mom's office, having pulled the shade over the window to prevent any prying eyes from seeing what I was doing. Hopefully, all the students who were here now were tucked safely in their beds. Surely no one would be crazy enough to stroll the lawn after dark less than twenty-four hours after a man had been murdered here. But the ladies didn't seem frightened by the murder so, earlier in the evening, I'd claimed that there had recently been a few bear sightings in the area. Surely they'd believe in the danger of becoming a midnight snack.

Right now I needed time alone to try to get myself up to speed on this mystery quilt. Heck, on basic quilting after so many years. With my mind spinning I doubted I'd be able to sleep anyway. I already realized that this was futile, but Mom had never heard the word *no* in her life.

Mom had quilted for most of her life, and I'd always taken it for granted, just like the soap-making, spinning, weaving, and knitting that she did. There was one quilt in particular that I'd grown up with and loved to death, cuddled pets with, and wrapped sick dolls in. The fabric had been, in the beginning, bright yellow with purple accents. For my mother, the brighter the better. She had told me she made it during the long months of her first pregnancy and by the time it had been thrown out, it was almost white.

My mind drifted to when I'd first decided to try quilting. At thirteen I'd won a church raffle, and the prize of a hand-pieced, hand-quilted Grandma's Flower Garden quilt delighted me. Mom hardly gave its pastel glory a second look, but she did allow me free reign with her fabric and sewing supplies when I told her I wanted to give quilting a try! I'd checked a book on historical quilts out of the library and chosen a Double Wedding Ring pattern to try as my first quilt. I'd had no idea that it was one of the more difficult patterns, and it doomed me to failure. Of course, all I would have had to do was ask Mom for help, but like most kids I'd wanted to do it by myself.

I'd thrown that attempt in the trash, but I did finish a few more quilts before heading off to college. Simple ones. Yet here I was, back at it after a break of more than a decade.

What genius woman, I wondered, *had grabbed the pizza cutter from the kitchen and first used it to cut fabric?* It was so much better than scissors. I remembered making my templates out of cereal boxes, tracing around them with a pencil onto the fabric, and then cutting the shapes out, sometimes with rather ragged results. Of course, to sell the cutting device, the name had been changed. It was now a rotary cutter. Mom was right: quilting had advanced.

I held it up, admiring the ingenuity for a moment, and then pressed the button to expose the disk-shaped blade. I touched the honed edge to test its sharpness. Ouch. Scalpel-sharp. I sucked my nicked finger, wrapped a tissue around it, and held it in place with a strip of scotch tape.

I rewound the VCR and started the tape again. There was no computer in the house, and of course no Wi-Fi, and I doubted Mom knew what a DVD looked like. She owned dozens of instructional videos, though, on the basics of quilt making, had even filmed some herself. She wanted me to go through as many as possible tonight or at least stay a day ahead of the ladies. I turned the volume up.

My fabric lay smoothed on the cutting mat—another great invention—with the folded edge of a chartreuse print lined up against the one-inch mark. I had chosen the ugliest piece of cloth I could find on the shelves that held all Mom's fabric since I knew it was going to be thrown away. I watched as the video showed a brisk cutting action. No blood there.

It was beginning to sink in that both my mother and my little brother had motive for murder. In my opinion, not enough, but I worried others might think so. Earlier this evening Gibb had dropped that other shoe about dating Lori. Then afterward, he'd refused to discuss the subject with me, saying it was personal. I'd wanted to pull his hair like I used to when we were kids. Gibb was worse than Mom about withholding information. How close had he been to Lori Billings? Had they dated for long? Did the whole world know she'd dumped Gibb for an older, richer man? What I needed was to talk with someone who didn't mind gossiping.

I planned to stay until my mom was in the clear. After

that, I wasn't sure what I would do. Mrs. Howard had been quite unhappy this morning and had refused to let me take time off without knowing when I might return. I'd had no choice but to quit my job. Well, that would be my problem to worry about another day. Between the murder and quilting, it felt like my brain was on a tilt-a-whirl. I could only handle one problem at a time.

Just then both cats, curled on the desk amid my clutter, lifted their heads and stared at the door. I held my breath. Doodle Dog raised his head and growled low in his throat. Did the doorknob turn a bit?

I couldn't be sure, but as quickly as the animals had alerted to the noise they settled back to sleep. I dropped my gaze back to the work table but heard the doorknob turning. The hairs rose on the back of my neck as the door squeaked open a couple of inches.

I saw straw-blond hair that could only belong to one person.

"Lam, you scared me. I didn't hear you come back. Did you get everything you needed?" I knew I was rattling on again, but every time Lam so much as looked at me, I felt dizzy.

"Sorry. I didn't mean to frighten you. I've been back for a while, but I was being quiet so I didn't disturb the students. I think they're all asleep now. It's been a big day for us all." He stepped into the room and closed the panel behind himself. "What are you doing? Shouldn't you be in bed?"

I bent my head to my work to hide a blush and rolled the blade down a length of folded fabric, guiding the rotary cutter's path with a long plastic ruler. I unfolded the two inch wide strip. It looked like a gull's wings or a shallow V shape, not straight. I pushed one side of the fabric while pulling with my other hand. Shoot. I dumped it into the trash can beside the cutting table to join the eight previous attempts. There might be new tools and methods, but it was still more difficult than it looked.

"What am I doing?" I cried, echoing his question. "I don't have the foggiest idea."

"You know you're supposed to keep those pieces. Stella, darlin', you really don't know how to quilt, do you?"

He now stood close.

"Mom knows I can't. This is hopeless." I punched the stop button on the remote to cut off the droning voice going on and on about fabric preparation and cutting. I promised myself I'd work on the lesson again tomorrow. I clicked the blade closed.

For some reason, I felt the need to put more space between Lam and myself. He was certainly an old friend, but tonight I felt vulnerable and lonely. I turned back to Mom's desk and, for the first time this evening, looked at the stack of Mom's block samples and handouts for the class. After supper, I'd found everything in a hutch tucked in the corner, just where Mom had promised it would be. She was always neat and organized.

I picked up the sewn blocks. Lam stepped near again and reached around my shoulder to take them from me. He flipped the first over to reveal swirling, brilliant colors, but the heat of his body so close was distracting. I found myself staring at his hands and not Mom's handiwork. My face probably matched the hot orange colors of the fabric that were just a blur in my vision.

"Cele does all her own original designs now. You knew that, right?"

"Mom certainly prefers bright." For myself, I liked antique quilts in soft, faded hues.

Lam turned the block over to the back again and pointed out a label. The words Twisting Stars were written in red ink in Mom's handwriting along with other information like the year.

I sighed. Everything I'd seen and heard today seemed too much. I went to take a step back and found Lam standing even closer than I'd realized.

He leaned into me. With the light touch of one finger, he turned my face toward him and rubbed a thumb over the bruise on my cheek, the one he'd given me with his elbow. I thought he was going to kiss me—mouth or cheek, I wasn't sure—and I took a step away from him until I was hemmed in by the desk. I said, "I'm happily dating someone." I wasn't. Not for months, but I didn't want any complications with my old friend.

"Are you sure?"

"What's that supposed to mean?"

"It means ol' Lam is an expert, and you have a certain look. You know earlier in the kitchen. Like a little girl staring at candy."

"No, keep your distance," I said. I tried for a light tone, not wanting Lam to know how much he'd unsettled me. When we were kids, being a couple of years older had meant I'd never been one of the girls with a crush on him, but with this trip that age difference seemed to have melted away.

"I've always liked you, darlin'."

"Like a friend," I said, but a question mark I hadn't intended clung to the end of my words.

"Well, that too." He stepped around me and strode to the

door, giving a final look over his shoulder. "Let me know if I can help you. In any way. I'll see you tomorrow," he said, laughing softly as he pulled the wooden door closed.

I decided to play Scarlett O'Hara. I wouldn't think about Lam right now. I had no idea how a life-long friendship had flared so suddenly into something else, or even if it had. Was Lam just bored babysitting Mom's students, or had the spark always been there and been flamed by the madness of this day?

Now I found that fatigue had killed my appetite for work. *Bad choice of words,* I thought, making a snap decision that I would take all these samples and handouts with me to the fabric store tomorrow. The students were scheduled to shop for two hours and then have lunch next door at *JoAnn's Café.* Maybe if I skipped the food, Mimi would take time and help me understand Mom's pattern while the students were happily enjoying old-time cooking and homemade pie. I thought she made great desserts, and I didn't care that the cook favored lard.

I surveyed the office, looking for an empty box. Mom, being a neatnik, probably stored extra cartons somewhere like the basement. I wasn't going down there tonight.

The boxes holding the quilt batting were too large. The other cardboard container I'd knocked over earlier was the right size though. I lifted it to the desktop, surprised again at the weight. The flaps were sealed with reinforced tape. I flicked open the blade on the rotary cutter and sliced the box top.

The carton was filled with books but not on the subject of quilting. In fact, these were library books complete with the plastic covers stamped "library binding." I ran my finger over the spine of *The Years of the Russian Revolution* and wondered what was going on. Finally, I glanced at the shipping tag and saw that this box had been intended for the Sewanee Library. I would need to return them to Mrs. Fleck, the librarian. The UPS delivery man must have made a mistake.

Well, I needed the box. Dumping two armfuls of history volumes onto the desktop, I refilled the carton with everything I'd found in the office that pertained to class. There were a dozen copies each of about ten handouts, but I didn't take time to separate anything or even to admire the blocks. I stuffed it all in. I'd take the whole lot to Mimi and get things organized tomorrow.

I interlocked the flaps, deciding I'd earned a night's sleep or at least the few hours left of it.

I hurried into the kitchen to retrieve my overnight bag and tote. Before switching off the lights, I turned the dogs out and snacked on cookies in the dark until they wandered sleepily back to settle on their beds in the corner of the kitchen. One, two, three cookies. Well, one more wasn't going to hurt my diet at this point. Plus, I'd hardly touched the chicken and dumplings at supper because I'd been so nervous talking to the students. Six cookies later, I dusted crumbs off my mouth with my fingers.

Slipping across the foyer and down the hallway, carrying my shoes and bags, I stopped in front of the door to the dorm room on the first floor. Not a peep. No light shining under the door.

Many of the women who took the class were old friends of Mom's. They'd come back several times and always stayed here so that there was the feeling of a reunion during the five days. She told me how the gals, as she called them, would sometimes stay up half the night talking and eating as if they were at a slumber party. It would certainly be different this year without Mom.

When the image of her in the jail cell started to form in my mind, I stamped it down.

Now I tiptoed up the stairs, careful to avoid the third step because it screamed like a cat with its tail under a rocker. Once on the second floor, I paused near Gibb's old room. I could hear Lam's soft breathing because he'd left the door partly open.

I crossed the hallway and slipped into my room. Before heading home, Gibb had made me promise to lock the door to my bedroom when I finally went to bed. This trip was going to stretch into who knew how long, and I at least wanted a decent night's sleep. I turned the lock, but my thoughts were on Lam and not a murderer.

CHAPTER 8

"Oh. Oh. Please stop." I realized I'd spoken aloud and pried one eye open with a finger. The bright morning sunlight made my head pound even harder with a didn't-get-enough-sleep headache. To my surprise, when I swung my legs over the edge of the bed, I found myself fully clothed. I'd been that tired last night. Actually, I'd just meant to sit on the edge of my bed for a moment and, at some point, I'd curled up and sunk into a deep but dream-disturbed sleep.

I realized the chirping noise that had awoken me was coming from my cell phone on the dressing table where I had dropped my tote. The distance was all of five feet from the twin bed, but to my bleary eyes it looked like miles. I've never been a morning person, and I lurched for the phone with my eyes squeezed closed. It took me two tries to turn the phone on.

"Help," I said.

"I knew it!" Gibb's voice was like a knife slicing across the airwaves. "I thought I'd better call and get you up. It's after eight."

He disconnected. I was going to have a little talk with my younger brother about his rude habit of hanging up on me before I'd had time to respond.

Wait. Had he said it was after eight o'clock? I hurried through a shower, barely brushed my teeth, and raced downstairs with my wet hair frizzing as I ran. I slowed to catch my breath as I approached the dining room but found it empty. My stomach growled and I tried not to fret that I'd missed breakfast. Through the window I saw that the students were gathered on the back porch.

I stopped on the threshold of the back door to listen.

"I'm sure that was just ketchup." Claire Benton nodded her head with each word to give them added emphasis. She sat in one of the rockers. "The man wasn't even a very good actor. When they carried him out of the office on the stretcher, I saw him breathing," she hissed in a pseudo whisper that everyone could hear. A twitter ran through the group.

"Did Cele tell any of you about this murder mystery? I wonder if there is a prize for solving it," Julie asked. "Do you think these are part of the clues for the quilt mystery, or is it an extra game? You know, like dinner theater. I could hardly sleep last night, tossing and turning, trying to figure it all out. What—"

"I bet it's part of the mystery quilt," Leann interrupted the talkative young woman. "You know, clues. I worked on it last night."

"What did you come up with?" asked Julie.

Leann huffed as she crossed her arms over her chest.

"Dear, work the clues for yourself. It's really quite an easy puzzle."

I held my breath, listening. The students had not yet seen me. Did everyone believe the murder was a game? Was that why they hadn't fled in fear? I guessed it was easier to believe this was part of Mom's class, her showmanship, than a real tragedy.

Finally, Sherri saw me and shouted, "Good morning, teacher." The nine students already present for class were lined up on the rockers and the porch steps, waiting for the bus to take us to *Mimi's Quilt Castle* for our fabric shopping spree. They all appeared well rested and happy, unlike me. I cradled the box containing Mom's teaching materials in my arms. It was heavy and not helping my headache one bit.

"Leann, a man really was murdered here yesterday," I said. "My mother is in jail."

"My, dear," she said, "sweet little Gibb would never arrest his own mother!" She searched her large purse and finally retrieved a roll of mints. "Anyone want one? Spearmint. This is my fifth year coming here, and Gibb is just a treasure. He's always over helping his mama, and imagine Cele a murderess." Leann tossed a candy into her mouth catching it with a crunch between her teeth.

Claire reached behind her friend and patted me on the arm while winking. "We know you need to keep up the ruse, and it is wonderful fun. I swear Cele has more good ideas than any ten people I know."

Everyone chimed in their agreement, and the old-timers, those who had attended more than once, started to reminisce about previous fun events.

I rolled my eyes in disbelief. How could these women actually think that Mom would fake a murder, that this was all part of the mystery retreat, maybe clues for the quilt pattern? But as I listened to their stories, I began to understand. I'd forgotten how things had gone awry five years ago on a scavenger hunt. One student had been picked up by the State Police, not officially arrested but embarrassed, and another got married a year later as a direct result. Then, oh lord, there was the protest. I groaned.

Julie asked, "Do you think Lam has any more of those delicious biscuits?" She peered over her shoulder through the screen door into the kitchen.

"His ham biscuits sure are luscious," Sherri said. Leann and Claire laughed at the double entendre while Julie blushed.

"I'll check," I said. "I mean if there are any ham biscuits left." My rumbling stomach would sure appreciate one.

I stooped and set the box of Twisting Stars patterns, clue sheets, and samples on the porch. I wasn't worried about the ladies peeking as they didn't even know what was in the carton. I was playing it smart and keeping mum. Plus, I could see everything from the kitchen while I talked to Lam.

I stepped forward and reached for the handle of the screened door just as Lam started out with a large trash bag in each hand. He was turned to push the door open with his hip and couldn't see me. I tried to step backward, but I wasn't quick enough. The screen door banged me in the nose.

My hand flew to cover my face. "I think it's broken." When I felt wetness, I brought my hand down and saw a few drops of blood. Then, I slapped my palm back over my face as the world began spinning in front of my eyes. I've never been good with the sight of blood.

The students clustered around me, and at that moment the van, which was painted white with a bright rainbow sweeping the side, rumbled up the gravel drive followed by puffs of exhaust as if it had just rolled out of a cartoon.

Leann pried my hand off my nose while Claire riffled her purse for tissue. She pulled out a travel pack and passed it to her friend.

"It's already stopped bleeding. Just a little swollen."

"And red," Julie added.

"Stella, I'm so sorry, darlin,'" Lam said. "Do you need to stay home?"

"Nonsense," Claire huffed. "She's fine."

"Let me at least get a cold pack for her." Lam called as the students herded me into the van. I had a woman on each side grasping my elbows and someone pushing from behind.
Lam dumped the plastic bags onto the porch, ran into the kitchen, and returned with a few ice cubes wrapped in a dish towel.

I gratefully held the cold cloth to my nose and sank onto a seat at the front of the van with Claire squeezed beside me.

This is just what I needed, I thought. My headache intensified ten-fold and, although the spinning had settled down, spots danced in front of my eyes.

Someone at the back of the bus sang out, "Does anyone have a bottle of water?"

There were sounds of chatter, but I didn't look around, didn't even open my eyes. I sat with the dishtowel covering my face until someone patted my shoulder.

"Here, honey, my sister gave these to me. It'll fix you right up." She tugged my hand away from my nose, pressed something into my palm, and pronounced that the injury wasn't even all that bad.

I peered at the tiny green tablet lying innocently on my palm. I didn't normally take medication, being generally healthy as a horse, but how much damage could such a small pill do?

CHAPTER 9

"I'm blind. Oh, Lord, I've gone blind." I knew my eyes were open, but the only thing I could see was gray. Fuzzy gray.

"Stella, what are you screeching about?"

Mom's voice floated around me from several locations then seemed to settle at my right. At the same time, that gray fog swimming above me focused into a ceiling painted jailhouse dreary.

"Have I been arrested, too?" I asked, as my vision cleared somewhat and I raised my head.

Mom sat in the middle of the jail cell on the concrete floor in a yoga pose. Her legs were crossed while her wrists rested loosely against the knees, thumb and middle finger touching in a perfectly formed circle of completion. Her straight back completed the pose.

"Of course not. Stella, if I didn't know you so well, I'd think you'd dropped acid." Cele stretched her legs straight out in front of her and leaned forward to grasp her toes. Lying with her forehead resting on her knees, she said to the general vicinity of her kneecaps, "Stella, you said you needed a nap. I thought it was strange."

I sat up on the narrow bed, leaning my back against the rough wall for much-needed support. "What am I doing here?" I said, clinging to the edge of the metal cot as if it might, at any moment, decide to buck me off.

"You said you wanted to visit. That you had a few questions for me." Cele spiraled up from the floor like a time-lapse film of a flower growing. She reached her fingers toward heaven and then rotated, bending at the waist, until her palms were flat on the floor. She made the position look comfortable.

"I took the liberty of borrowing your cell phone," Cele said, pointing, with a slight lift of her head, at my tote bag lying against the bars. "I spoke with several of the students. They said you were a dynamo at Mimi's. Said your color choices were stunning."

She rose slowly, stared at me, and then her brows drew together. "You haven't been using drugs have you?"

Some of the morning's events were returning like the remnants of a bad dream. A nightmare to be specific.

"Yes." I groaned. "But it was just a tiny pill. Such a pretty spring green." I rested my head, pressing my chin to my chest. "So I've already been to the fabric store?"

"Yes. You're telling me you don't even remember?"

"It's been a rough twenty-four hours, Mom. Where are the students now?"

"They're back at camp. Today's schedule was all about fabric. Buying in the morning and washing and ironing this afternoon. As you probably know by now, there are two theories on fabric preparation, to prewash or not—"

I put my fingers in my ears, but the droning was still audible. "No. No more. I've always been a good daughter, haven't I?

"Of course. What's that got to do with anything?"

"Mom, I'm not talented like you are."

My words unleashed a thunderstorm in my mother.

"Don't you ever say anything like that again!" She pointed her finger at me like a gun. "You're beautiful, smart, and talented." Her voice trailed off and when she spoke again she was calm. "You just don't know it yet. Maybe yoga or meditation would help you find yourself."

She sat next to me on the bed, rubbing my back like she had when I was little and I was sick or upset.

I frowned. How could she be recommending yoga in response to a crisis like the one we faced? But it wasn't just Mom's comment bothering me. Something, some disaster, was tickling at the fringe of my mind.

"Promise me, Stella, that you'll feed your soul daily from now on."

"Okay." I had no idea what my soul was hungry for other than extra sleep. Maybe Lam.

Cele said, "Now, tomorrow the students are going to Nashville to the quilt show at the Opry Hotel and then to the big fabric store and the batik specialty store. You'll have plenty of time to review the cutting layout for the blocks while the house is empty."

"Not as much time as you think, Stella." Gibb's voice

from the doorway caused Mom and me to both jump.

"Why not?" I asked. From the look on Mom's face, I'd bet my cotton bloomers she already knew the answer.

"Because we, just you and I, are going to the Mountaintops Homeowners' Association meeting," he said.

"Oh goodie. Sounds as much fun as cutting up fabric into little triangles and squares," I said. "Wait." I held my hands palm out to quiet Mom before she could argue with my brother. She had that look brewing on her face.

The fragment of memory from earlier sharpened. Disaster bobbed to the surface. Squares. Blocks.

"Oh no." I jumped up and grasped the bars as if to rattle them, but I knew they were too solid. "Let me out, Gibb."

"Sure, Sis." He pulled the door open. It hadn't even been locked.

I ran down the hallway then came to a stop so quickly the soles of my sandals squealed. "How did I get here? I didn't drive, did I?"

"The rainbow bus dropped you off out front," Gibb said. Cele in the doorway of the cell and Gibb in the hall were both staring.

"Give me a ride home, Gibb."

He thankfully ignored Mom's protests about me leaving. As the door slammed behind us, I could hear her shouting details about the weekend schedule. Something about a party. Why in the world did she want to have a party in her jail cell?

My brother fished car keys out and guided me toward a brown SUV with the sheriff's seal on the door.

"It's got to be there. Please, please let it be there," I moaned.

"Stella, what are you jabbering about?"

"The box, Gibb. The box with everything in it."

"Slow down. Everything what?"

"The whole Twisting Stars class."

It took only ten minutes to drive home, but it felt like hours of worry. Lam told us right away that it was too late.

"The dump." My knees gave way, and I slumped slowly to sit on the porch step.

Lam and Gibb both stood staring, worried expressions on their faces.

"Sis, how could you leave it with the garbage?"

"I didn't." The pitch of my voice rose with each word, a siren of guilt and irritation.

Lam said, "She didn't. It's my fault. I dropped the trash bags right there." He gestured at the porch flooring. "They must have covered up your box. Billy came by about fifteen minutes later. He would have thought he was supposed to pick it up."

"When did Mom start paying for trash pick-up?"

"Last month when I got too busy to always cart her bags off for her. And how could you forget something so supposedly important?" Gibb asked, scowling.

"Well, maybe it had something to do with being walloped in the nose by Lam." I rubbed the tip of my still somewhat swollen nose. I immediately felt sorry for my harsh words.

"Hey, I didn't hit you intentionally. Either time." Lam's blue eyes expressed sincere embarrassment.

Gibb glared back and forth between the two of us. "I don't think I want to hear about this."

"Go easy on her, Gibb," Lam said. "She's trying hard and has had a really rough day. Believe me, keeping up with those ladies is no easy task. I know I've never seen women eat so much. They have me chained to the stove."

"They'd like to chain you, alright," I mumbled.

"What?" Lam asked.

"Never mind." I said, and then turned to my brother. "Just help me, Gibb. Let's ride out to the dump. Maybe it's not too late."

"Stella, the dump isn't really a dump now that Billy Taylor has the state contract for the county. It's a modern incinerator, and that man doesn't waste a moment. Why don't you just tell Mom? This might be a good way to get these ladies to leave. I don't feel comfortable with them here after a murder. Even with Lam here to help and watch out."

"Agreed," Lam said. "Then you won't have to worry about the class, Stella."

"I'm a failure. I can't do anything right." I dropped my head to my knees and gave a fake sob, letting my shoulders rise and fall. I used to pull this on Gibb all the time when we were kids.

"All right. Come on. I'll take you to the dump." He extended his hand to help me up. "I know you're jerking me around. You've pulled that fake crying gig too many times."

"Give me just a minute. We'll be going right past the library. On the way back, I want to drop some books off for Mom."

CHAPTER 10

Like most drives around Sewanee, the trip to the dump had been a short one even though it was located close to the county line. In all, our mission took less than two minutes because it was easy to see that Billy had already burned all the garbage picked up that day. The man was practically ready to lock the gate and head home although he'd been glad to see company.

Even I admitted defeat and allowed Gibb to steer me back to the car. Now my brother parked close to the door of the library and came around to help me out of the car since I had a lap full of books. He lifted them all and then gave me half the stack back once I was on my feet.

"Hurry up," he called over his shoulder as I shuffled up the walk to where he held the door open. For a second we stood still as cemetery statues in the open doorway.

"Shhhh!" Mrs. Fleck's hiss carried throughout the entirety

of the one-room library. The noise was the mental equivalent of having your fingernails tugged out by an old lady who was as evil as she was sweet-looking.

"Isn't that woman ever going to die—I mean retire?" I leaned as close to Gibb's ear as I could, given that he was six-foot-two to my five-foot-six.

"The theory is she's too mean to kick the bucket."

Gibb flinched as his voice roused another hiss from the librarian.

The tiny old woman stood behind the circulation desk, and I knew she was standing on a wooden orange crate to enable her to see over the counter. Her stare rotated like a radar beam, seeking the perpetrator who dared break her rule of absolute silence. I half expected her head to turn a full three hundred and sixty degrees.

The dark eyes met mine, and her hand rose. Mrs. Alma Fleck pointed an arthritic finger to where we stood in the doorway. It looked a lot like the skeletal hand of death.

"You. And you." Her gaze swung to Gibb. "You're that Margaret Hill's children. Ha. Get over here." Mrs. Fleck never left the safety of her orange crate. She relied on her assistant, Patty, to shelve books, straighten, and clean. Alma Fleck ruled her domain from her own fruity version of a bully pulpit.

I shifted the stack of books I carried from one arm to the other and fell in behind Gibb. It wasn't that I was really afraid of one teeny-weeny, old woman. Okay, I was terrified of her, but so were half the adults and every child in the county. Children in Sewanee had been terrorized and traumatized at the local library for fifty-odd years. I'd just never outgrown my fear. Rumors used to circulate around the shelves of picture books that Mrs. Fleck cooked bad boys and girls for her Sunday dinners.

Gibb looked over his shoulder at me. "Chicken."

"Only for Sunday dinner."

Gibb gave me a dirty look before putting the books he carried for me on the counter and stepping back to show that this was my business.

"So your mother's in jail," Mrs. Fleck said in a voice that crackled with glee.

I stood for a second with my mouth hanging open. I should have remembered that the woman always liked to get in the first word.

"Uh. I found these at Mom's house. I mean a box intended for the library was delivered to Cele's."

"Are you sure that hippie didn't steal them?"

"Mrs. Fleck, I'm just trying to be nice and return these."

"Wait a minute," Gibb interrupted. "I thought we were returning overdue books of Mom's. What do you mean they were delivered to the house instead of here?"

I explained to him about finding the unopened box in the office.

"And the box they were in is the one that went to the dump? The one that was destroyed?"

I nodded.

"Son of—"

"Young man," Mrs. Fleck snapped, "I won't have that kind of talk in my library. Do you hear me, Aries Gibson Hill?" She rapped a pencil on the wooden countertop in time with each syllable.

At her use of my brother's full name, I cringed and glanced around to see if anyone else might have overheard.

Gibb hated the name with a passion, and everybody else in town was kind enough never to use it—afraid maybe of a black eye—except, of course, Mrs. Fleck.

He ignored the old woman and said to me, "I wish I knew when they were delivered. I'll have to ask Mom. I'd like to know if whoever brought it to the house carried the box into the office themselves. Quite often Mom gets several boxes of supplies at a time, and they use the dolly so it's only one trip."

"You think the UPS guy could have seen something?" I lowered my voice. "Or done something?"

It seemed Mrs. Fleck didn't appreciate us talking as if she weren't present. "I got Ed Goody fired." She crossed matchstick arms across a flat chest.

It was my brother's turn to stare.

"Who's Ed Goody?" I asked.

Gibb tore his gaze away from the stare-down he was having with Mrs. Fleck.

"You probably don't know him. He's—was—the UPS guy for this route. Comes up the mountain from Manchester." Gibb squared his shoulders and looked as if he wished he could draw his gun. "Now, Mrs. Fleck, I didn't hear a thing about that."

"You think you know everything that goes on in this town, Sheriff?"

I edged back a step. This was eerie, like being caught in an old TV western with Mrs. Fleck in the role of gunslinger. All she needed was a black cowboy hat.

"Why did Ed need to be fired?" Gibb tried again.

"Being a librarian is akin to being a doctor. We are privy to all manner of rumor. I consider it my duty to protect the confidentiality of the patrons of the library." Her chest puffed out farther with each word.

Gibb tapped the badge pinned to his shirt front. When Mrs. Fleck didn't waver, he fiddled with the handcuffs hanging from his belt.

"Come into my office." She took a careful step backwards off of the orange crate and disappeared through a door behind the counter.

Gibb and I followed. It was then, for the first time in my life, that I noticed the woman walked with a severe limp. It made me feel sorry for all the times I'd thought of her as horrible and evil.

With her shuffling gate, Mrs. Fleck led us to a small room that was part office and part storage room. Shelves of books lined every wall. Reading material crowded every surface. She sat behind a folding table on a metal chair and indicated we should also. Evidently county funding didn't extend to real office furniture.

"You know Patty Hartman? My assistant?" she asked. "Caught her in the back room with Ed." She hooked a thumb over her shoulder toward a closed door. "Doing the deed." Her eyes narrowed. "Fired her, too."

"But Patty's married. She has kids," I said.

Both Gibb and Mrs. Fleck gave me withering looks.

"Was this yesterday?" Gibb asked.

"Day before."

"That would be the day before Tom was killed," I said.

Gibb pounded his thigh with his fist. "I need to talk to Ed and Patty." He started to rise, then looked back to the librarian. "Is there anything else I should know?"

"Harold Mullins owes almost eleven dollars in overdue fines."

A muscle in Gibb's jaw tightened. "About the incident, Mrs. Fleck."

She sniffed. "Perhaps Patty would be a better suspect for your interrogation."

I rose when Gibb did and decided to practice the Golden Rule. Her limp had made me see her as human, something I'd never considered before. I said, "It was very nice seeing you again, Mrs. Fleck."

Her eyes narrowed until the irises were almost hidden. She wagged one crooked finger. "I know it was you who tore the cover off of *The Secret of the Old Clock*."

I'd forgotten she liked to have the last word too.

CHAPTER 11

Gibb turned the SUV out of the library's gravel parking lot onto the hardtop, the wheels kicking up dust in our wake. I could feel his excitement at the possibility of a lead in the case.

"You want me to go with you?" I asked.

"No."

"But you are going to talk to Patty and this Ed?"

"Of course."

"And you need to ask Mom about the delivery."

If it weren't for worrying about Mom, I might enjoy this detective work, I thought.

"I bet this UPS guy hid in Mom's office and killed Tom. Now we just have to figure out how he got Tom Billings over there. Oh, and why he wanted him dead. Oh, and where he hid. Um. Maybe in the hutch."

My little brother said, "You are not going to play Jessica

Fletcher on me. Not on my watch. I'm taking you back to the cabin."

Gibb stared straight ahead out the windshield, fists tight on the steering wheel. I realized I was telling the man how to do his job.

"Sorry, Gibb, I'm playing big sister. Say, can we turn on the siren and speed home?"

He cracked a smile, and I relaxed a bit. To change the subject I said, "I can't believe Patty was having an affair. She's been married to Dean for over ten years. They have three kids."

"Stella, you always were a bit innocent. Lots of people—even ones you wouldn't suspect—cheat on their spouses. As a deputy, and now sheriff, I see the dirty side of people all the time."

"That's a shame." As I said the words, I wondered if I was really so naïve. Then I realized Gibb had said something I'd missed. "What?"

"I'll pick you up at eight-thirty in the morning. The meeting. Did you forget already?"

I groaned. "Why so early? Why can't they have the association meeting in the afternoon? Then I could be awake for it."

"You have to be up early anyway to get your students on the van to Nashville. I think I heard Mom say seven."

"Why are we even going to the meeting?" The whine in my voice made me feel guilty. Gibb and I needed to do everything possible to save Mom from this threat of losing her business, not to mention the nightmare possibility of going to prison. I just wasn't sure where this would take us. Somehow the meeting didn't relate to the murder in my mind.

"Mountaintops was Tom's home for thirty-plus years. These people are his friends, and maybe, in some cases, enemies. I want to ask questions and watch people's reactions, and Mom may need us there to protect her interests."

I mulled his words over and quickly realized he was right. Tom wasn't in Mom's house by accident when he was killed. The only tie between Mom and Tom was the homeowner's association. It seemed Gibb knew his business. Mom trusted that he did so I would too.

Then, another thought crept into my mind. The other connection between everyone was Lori Billings, at least in the sense that the woman had been dating Gibb before her recent marriage to the victim. She was enrolled in the quilting camp, but since she lived close by, Lori wasn't staying at the cabin at night with the other ladies.

She hadn't even been at the cabin when her husband's body was discovered; she'd been home. Or so Christine, Tom's first wife, said. Gibb had told me all of this. When Gibb had asked Lori where she thought Tom was the night he didn't come home, she'd answered that her husband had probably been with another woman. Seems the mismatched pair hadn't had much of a marriage.

Gibb slowed to a stop by the back door of the house but left the engine running, anxious to make progress on his investigation.

I bent down to tug my shoes back on and then slid off the seat, pulling my tote bag after me. Before closing the door, I asked, "Will you at least let me know what you find out from Patty and Ed?"

"I shouldn't, but I will."

I gave him a smile as I slammed the door and watched

KAY VELARDE

him wheel away. Standing there, I gently touched my cheek, which I knew was blue, and the tip of my nose, which completed the patriotic theme by glowing red against my always-pale skin.

In the kitchen I found Lam slaving away, preparing a tray of refreshments. The students usually sat around together in the evenings, talking and enjoying the company of other quilters, and they expected something to munch on.

"What's up?" I asked.

"Party. Haven't you read the schedule?"

"Schedule?"

Lam pointed with a dripping hand to a piece of paper attached to the refrigerator with magnets.

"Oh, that schedule." I washed my hands and started hulling the strawberries that were draining in a colander. I'd yet to have time to give that schedule more than a passing glance. Or maybe I couldn't bear to be reminded of what was ahead in the next days.

"I'm sorry you're having to do so much work, Lam. It's really good of you. When you agreed to help Gibb, you probably expected to just sit on the porch with a shotgun to scare the murderer away."

"Well, can't say that I own a long gun, but you know I'd do anything to help Cele."

"I know. She's lucky to have you."

"Hey, I could put some mash whiskey in the tea before I put it out. That way you wouldn't have any problems with the ladies," Lam said as he sliced another lemon. He dropped the wedges into a bowl which he set on the tray next to a pitcher of sweet tea and plates loaded with cookies.

"Maybe I should borrow another one of those little pills.

I could sail right through this ordeal."

Lam threw his head back and laughed.

"Stop that. Stop laughing at me all the time." I dropped the knife and swatted his hand.

"But you're so sweet, darlin' Stella. I really wish I could have seen you dancing around the fabric shop."

He stopped talking for a moment as he worked the knife expertly around and around a whole lemon and then fanned the result into a beautiful decoration. Lam cradled it carefully onto the top of the dipping sauce. The fragrant juice was running over his hands, and as he wiped them on the dishtowel he said, "Sherri told me you were particularly fond of bright colors like lime green, hot pinks, tropical blues, and something she called batiks. What kind of color is that?"

"I have no earthly idea." I dabbed my forehead with a paper towel. "And I like pastels."

"Didn't you know you had such a passionate soul, Stella?"

"I've already had my soul examined today, thank you."

"Well, I'll be honest and say I was dreaming more about the passion and not so much the soul, darlin'. Seeing you again has stirred up some memories, thoughts like I used to have about you when I was a teenager."

That comment sent my mind spinning. To change the topic, I asked, "How'd you learn to cook?"

"From hanging around women all the time."

That comment was so like the man. I watched him move around the kitchen, lithe and powerful but, oh boy, when that lock of hair fell over his eye, it made my mouth go dry.

"Hey, you daydreaming? By the way, you've got cookie crumbs on your, uh, shirt front."

I'd been sampling cookies as I worked on the strawberries.

Lam's hand moved toward my ample bust to dust my blouse. I leaned away from him but didn't step back.

"Relax, Stella," he said, flipping the dishtowel lightly back and forth across my chest causing the muscles in his arm to ripple with the movement. Then he leaned in with a surprise attack and brushed his lips across my cheek, his soft lips lingering on my earlobe. The tingling of my skin silenced me.

"Now get in there and wow them with the clues." Lam grasped me by the shoulders and turned me toward the door. I managed to gasp, "What are you talking about? What clues?"

"Darlin', that's what this party is all about."

"I forgot all about those silly clues."

His strong arms continued to push me past the dining table and into the family room where he abandoned me. The women were scattered around the large area on the various sofas and chairs. One couch was placed in front of a huge stone fireplace. A rustic hand-carved bear, four feet tall, stood near holding the grate tools in wooden paws. Julie sat on the low hearth, reading a paperback by the extra light from the fire. Four of the women were at the game table in the corner playing Scrabble, and Sheri lounged on the love seat.

In sharp contrast to the wooden walls, bright, modern quilts were hung around the room. I noticed one in particular that caught the natural light from the fire. The fabrics ranged from red to orange with touches of yellow. Suddenly, I understood what Mom had meant by warm, or even hot, colors. These danced right off the flat surface as if the flames licking the logs had caught on the fabric, too. I saw there were small touches of blues and greens scattered over the quilt canvas. They definitely cooled down the heat as they melted into the background, giving the eye a break. Maybe the quilt would have been too hot without Mom's skilled addition of the soothing hues.

Everyone looked up at me.

"The food is so much better this year," Leann said, nibbling a cookie.

"Lam is good in the kitchen." Julie's cheeks flamed just mentioning the man's name.

Claire looked up at me. "Stella, no offense about Cele's cooking, but that health food she's always serving. . . ." She made a face and let it finish her thought for her. "Last year several of us finally had to make an emergency run to Nashville for some Dunkin Donuts. So I brought a suitcase full of goodies this time." Claire smiled as the others expressed their appreciation.

I murmured my agreement with the sentiment. Gibb and I had been lucky, growing up, that our grandparents had refused to go along with their daughter's passion for a vegetarian diet. They had allowed us to have whatever we wanted when Mom was busy and out of sight. It was my grandmother who had taught me to make a killer pan of brownies.

I thought I'd better say something that sounded like a teacher. Now what had Mom said this afternoon about two schools of thought?

"Did everyone get their fabric washed and ironed?"

"Obviously you prefer prewashing," Sherri said, "but don't you think there is something to be said for the antique appearance of the post-wash puckering."

Oh, Lord, what had she just asked me? Thankfully Lam entered the room at that moment with another tray of drinks, drawing Sherri's full attention.

"Does anyone think they'll be needing anything else? I've got to go out for a few hours."

"Hot date, honey?" Sherri asked. Her lipstick was glossy where she licked her lips.

"Sort of, darlin'." He passed the glasses around the room.

I watched as he handed one to Sherri. His hands lingered on hers while he stared into her eyes for a second too long. Lam gave me a slow wink as he walked past. What was that show about? Was he trying to prove to me or himself that he was a playboy? I already knew that he was. Lam was the most notorious couldn't-be-caught bachelor on the mountain. It would be best for me to remember that he was a ladies man through and through.

After watching Lam saunter out of the room, I turned back to the students. I'd worry about him later. "Hey, I've got a great idea." I knew I was babbling, panic right there at the edge of my mind, but I couldn't stop myself. "Let's play charades."

Now where had that come from? I hadn't played that game since sleepovers in my early teens.

"But what about the clues?" One woman waved a spiral notebook in the air.

My gaze darted around the room until I noticed the elaborate quilted vest Julie wore. It was the very recognizable Log Cabin pattern. "We'll be using names of traditional quilt patterns." A few of the students looked as if they were starting to get interested, but the others, I could tell, were skeptical. "The one who wins the most times gets to dip into Mom's fabric stash. Five, uh, fat quarters."

I'd only learned earlier today that quilters called the

fabric they owned a stash and I'd discovered that the disparaging name for a quarter of a yard merely referred to the shape of the cut. Now I was proud of myself for using the terms in conversation.

"I'm first," Julie shouted, jumping to her feet. "I'm sure I'm first."

When the young woman started pacing back and forth in front of the window, stooped and pretending to use a cane, I dashed out of the room and down the hall to the office. I landed so hard on the office chair that it rolled halfway across the room. I peddled back to the desk and grabbed the notes I'd made in the jail cell yesterday. I'd forgotten all about them after removing the bundle from my pocketbook and tucking the pages into the center drawer last night. They were all I had left of the Twisting Stars pattern now that the box had been incinerated.

I wasn't going to tell Mom I'd lost her stuff if I could help it.

I scanned the words and drawings and then forced myself to lean back in the chair. With eyes closed, I tried to think calmly.

Okay, I can do this. Be positive, Stella, I told myself.
Well, the name could become a clue. Twisting Stars. Twisting. There was an old dance called the twist. That was the first thing that came to my mind. Wasn't the twist from the sixties, maybe seventies? These women were mostly older than me, Mom's age, so that would be a good clue. Let's see. The twist. Chubby Checker. I remembered he sang the song about the dance. I'd once gone to a retro sixties party and seen it.

Next, stars. What was another word, or a description, for stars? Um. I leafed through the dictionary. Celestial body.

I liked that connection to Cele. Chubby Checker weds Celestial.

It was the perfect clue!

Mom had told me that Sunday afternoon the students were supposed to start cutting the fabric. Maybe some clues about the shapes and sizes needed.

Hey, this wasn't so hard after all. In fact, it was fun.

I spread the notes across the desktop and ran my finger down the pages. As fast as I could, I listed details, and then I worked out a few clues about the sizes and shapes that they would be cutting tomorrow. Maybe mystery quilts really could be fun.

A hand came down on my shoulder.

I screamed, and Baby the cat yowled and jumped off the desk, taking half my notes with him.

Lori Billings jumped back, flapping her hands. "Geez, you scared me, Stella. The door wasn't latched. Sorry. Guess I'm kind of jumpy lately."

As she drew a deep breath, I noticed the dark circles under red-rimmed eyes, which Lori had attempted to disguise with powder.

"It's okay. Things have been kinda crazy. Uh, I should have told you before this how sorry I am for your loss." My tongue seemed to be having a hard time forming the words, and until this moment, I hadn't been alone with Lori to express the sentiment.

She waved her hand in a dismissive gesture. "I just wanted to tell you I'd help Cele if there was any way I could. Also, I'm not going to Nashville tomorrow. There's this stupid homeowners meeting. Well, Tom made it such a habit for us to go."

It surprised me she would offer to help Mom, but I noticed she hadn't said she thought Mom was innocent. It was beyond the limits of brashness for me to ask Lori her opinion on that, but there was something else I was too curious about.

"Lori, I was wondering if I could ask a question."

"Sure, shoot." Lori wandered around the room, stopping in front of the hutch. She stroked one of the tassels Cele had hung for decoration on the cabinet door handle. Next, her fingers played across the woodwork as if running scales on a piano. She seemed to be sleepwalking though. I had the impression of a woman working hard to hold herself together, who at any moment could collapse.

"Why would you want to stay in this class? Here in the cabin now?"

Didn't investigators always suspect the wife first?

"Geez, Stella. He married me for sex, and I went along for the money, but I liked the old coot. Why does everyone have such a problem with that?" She spun on her heel and glared for a second. "I like quilting. I need something to keep me busy." Her shoulders rose and fell.

Lori had the kind of face that men think is beautiful, but that women notice is over the top. The mouth was too wide, the nose petite enough for a child and the body—think Dolly Parton. Her hips swayed in an exaggerated motion when she glided across the room. She finally stopped in front of the window and turned her back to me.

I knew that at first she looked at her reflection because her hand smoothed the tight T-shirt across a flat stomach, but I believe then she slipped into a reverie. When she spoke, the voice was softer, and I could hardly hear the words. She talked while gazing out into darkness, rubbing her fingers back and forth over the glass as if trying to wipe away the rain streaking the other side of the pane. "You're older than me, Stella, by what? Eight years? But you remember my family, don't you? Dirty, stinking poor."

"Uh."

"I didn't see the harm in marrying Tom," she said. "I made him happy. Isn't it funny how old glass is ripply?" She pulled the sleeve of her sweater down over her hand and used it to wipe at the fingerprints she'd left on the pane. "I mean, Tom and I got together for all the wrong reasons, but we did love each other. We were happy."

"I'm sure you were, Lori. May-December romances can work." I wanted to soothe the distraught woman, keep her talking.

Lori spun around to face me. Her expression was fierce, glaring. "And now that he's dead I have nothing." She laughed with a sound that morphed into a cry of pain. "Hardly anybody knows that Tom made me sign a pre-nup. I get the house, but that's all. The amount I would get when he died was supposed to go up every five years, but we only got married less than a year ago. Without Tom, I'm back to being pretty much poor." Her gaze darted around the room.

"Gibb said Tom wanted Cele's business out of Mountaintops. Do you know why?" I asked.

"Had a bug about Cele is all I know. I think he wanted to get back at your mom. Never got over her dumping him all those years ago."

"What are you saying? Mom never dated Tom as far as I know. I thought he'd been married to Christine since the ark landed."

Her laugh grated. "Sure, but they, Tom and Cele, had an affair. Tom told me. Seeing your Mom always made him mad since she dumped him. I think that's what happened." She hurried to the door and jerked it open. "It didn't help that Tom was mad at me. He overheard Gibb say he still loved me."

The door closed behind her with a sharp click.

I fell back in my seat, stunned at her words. The force of my weight spun the chair in a wide arc.

When the spinning stopped, I saw Doodle Dog lying at my feet. He was eating a page of Mom's notes.

CHAPTER 12

Wiping Doodle Dog's spit off my hands onto my jeans, I paused to brace myself before stepping through the archway into the parlor. My nerves were still shaky from witnessing Lori's odd behavior. I would never have expected her to be so open about her odd marriage, and her words darted through my thoughts.

A shout of "Snail's Trail" from the room was followed by laughter. I couldn't remember what that particular pattern looked like. Where had all these strange, even bizarre, quilt pattern names come from? I mean, Melon Patch and Pickle Dish? Why would someone name a quilt pattern something silly like that?

"That's right," Leann said, picking herself up from the floor and dusting her slacks.

"Let's do one more," I said, snatching up a cookie and glass of tea because I still needed a minute to catch my breath and regroup after wrestling with the dog.

When I'd grabbed for the page of my notes, Doodle had thought it was a game. By the time we'd raced a few turns around the room with me plucking bits and pieces from his mouth, all that had remained of that page of instructions was a gooey spit-ball. How could I teach this class when I couldn't even hang onto the notes?

After solving the Tree of Life charade, Sherri Bane called, "Stella, clue time." A wolfish grin split her face.

"Let Stella have a turn playing the game," said Julie. "That's only fair."

Mrs. Littleton, who had arrived this afternoon, scowled. "You're only saying that because we're tied for points. We should each win some fabric."

"We can't have a tie," Sherri commanded. "Julie is right."

"Uh, that's okay with me," I said, but their expressions told me they weren't buying my decision. "Doesn't anyone else want to play?" I searched the faces.

"Everyone's had a turn," they chorused.

I edged to the middle of the room, feeling déjà vu from my days in the high school play. That was when my dreams of being a country singer died. Stage fright wiped my brain clean like a hard drive crash.

Traditional quilt pattern names. Traditional. I stalled for time by removing imaginary crumbs from the corners of my mouth until I finally had an idea.

My hands shook as I formed a ring with my thumb and fore-finger and slipped it over the third finger of my left hand, making the motion twice.

"Double Wedding Ring!" Julie jumped from her chair, pumped her fist in the air, but then looked sheepish and sat again.

"Too easy," Sherri said. "If we weren't so anxious for our clues, we'd make you do another."

When had Sherri started to speak for the group? The woman was so pushy.

I slipped the crumpled and still unfinished list of clues from my pocket, and at that moment the lights went out.

"Don't panic." My voice sounded raspy to my own ears.

"Who's panicking?" Sherri's disembodied voice pierced the blackness. "Just go and check the fuse box so we can finally get to the clues."

I could hear her crunching on a cookie as the others chattered about quilting while waiting for me to handle the situation.

With my first step, I banged my shin on the coffee table. By the time I hopped around howling for a minute, my eyes had adjusted to the darkness. A heavy cloud cover had brought rain showers off and on all day, but a full moon peeking between the clouds gave enough light to see the shapes of the women.

"Okay, everyone stay where you are. I'll be right back."

I shuffled my feet and felt along the plaster wall with my hands as I edged down the hallway to the kitchen. I thought I'd seen a flashlight in the pantry earlier.

My fingers wrapped around the plastic casing, and the light sprang on at the push of the switch. The beam was weak but enough to get me to the basement. I hoped. The door was just to my right in the corner of the kitchen, and it creaked like a horror movie ghoul when I swung it open.

I held my breath.

"For heaven's sake, Stellar. Be an adult," I whispered to myself. The path of the light ran to the bottom of the steps, revealing nothing out of the ordinary. There were no strange noises, moaning or groaning. No odd glowing orbs of ectoplasm. I pushed my toes over the edge and then started down.

Fourteen steep steps.

On the last stair I waved the light beam in an arc to find it wouldn't penetrate to the far reaches of the room. Why did the basements of old houses have to be so creepy? As a child I'd refused to play here, even when Gibb had built a fort in the corner. It had become his escape from me, his older, bossy sister. As an adult I hadn't been down here in two years since Mom had the flu right after Christmas, and I'd packed and stored her decorations. If I remembered correctly, the fuse box was to my left near the furnace.

I stepped carefully, sweeping the light back and forth in the hopes I'd see any spiders before they found me. Realizing the dry, hard-packed dirt floor wouldn't show footprints even if someone had been here ahead of me, I strained to listen. No mad men jumped out from behind an old dresser that Mom planned to refinish and give away. I crept forward, forcing one foot in front of the other.

Help is just a scream away, I thought.

The electrical box hung on the back wall amidst stacked boxes and an old table. I shoved against the table's top, managing to get it out of the way. I jammed the stiff latch of the breaker box up and swung the metal cover open. My gaze ran over the double rows of breaker switches to find that one was turned the opposite direction from all the others. I popped it over and heard faintly, from the floor above, a cheer from the ladies.

But the basement remained dark except for the weak

stream of my flashlight. Shue, I should have thought to flip on the stairwell light switch before coming down. I scurried back to the steps, following the narrow path of yellowed light, and hurried up the steps.

As I placed my foot on the kitchen floor, I breathed a sigh of relief and flicked off the flashlight. Then the basement door slammed shut in my face, forcing me backwards into a fall down the steps.

CHAPTER 13

"Would you quit squirming?" Gibb hissed in my ear so loudly it hurt. Several other Mountaintops home-owners attending this morning's meeting turned to glare at the two of us. From the expressions on the one hundred or so faces in the clubhouse, everyone was in a bad mood. The thin, warm breeze stirring the air didn't help. We were experiencing an abnormally hot Indian summer this year.

I tugged my earlobe and shifted from one hip to the other. I had bruises in places I hadn't known I had places. Maybe there was something to be said for a little bit of extra padding.

Last night, after skidding down a few steps, I'd dropped the flashlight but managed to stop my fall by clutching the handrail. The violent shove had still hurt though. One elbow was bruised, and the other wrist felt sprained. I'd wrenched my back and stubbed my toes. I didn't dare tell Gibb because he surely would try to make me go back to Nashville. He would send Mom's students packing, too, whether they wanted to go or not. I could picture him hauling their suitcases out to their cars for them despite loud protests.

The incident should have scared the wits out of me—well, actually, it had—but now I was mad. Someone had deliberately slammed that door on me. I hadn't screamed last night, and I was proud of myself. After collecting my wits and inventorying injuries, I'd searched the kitchen only to find the back door open. I'd returned to the parlor and acted as if nothing unusual had occurred, even though I was on the verge of tears. Only one other person knew what happened last night—whoever had shoved that door in my face.

It wasn't likely, in my mind, that one of the students gathered for the evening had wanted to hurt me. Sherri was obnoxious, but that trait didn't make her a criminal. Besides, the woman had no connection to Tom, no reason to murder a local resident. But that was just my guess. Maybe I should ask Gibb to run some kind of background check on her. Isn't that what the police did on television?

The most likely suspect was Lori. But she had left before the lights went out. Hadn't she? I realized I couldn't be sure. Even if I'd seen her drive off, which I hadn't, the woman could have parked out of sight and walked back.

The problem was Mom's home and how it was usually left open, unlocked, all day when there was a class in session. Last night was the perfect example. I hadn't locked up until after one in the morning, and Cele's strays were useless as watchdogs. They were constantly introduced to new people. In fact, once Mom rescued a dog that did bark and had backed a woman into a corner when she entered the house without Mom present. Cele found another good home for that terrier.

Gibb punched his elbow into my ribs in a not-so-subtle hint as I uncrossed and re-crossed my legs for the hundredth time. Darn chair felt like a bed of nails.

"Who is that woman?" I asked, watching a lady pace along the front row of chairs: sleek, citified, and out of place on the mountain. She'd been given the floor by the president of the board and was rattling on and on about flowers.

"Her name is Andrea Hudson. She and her husband moved here from Atlanta just this summer. Their house was under construction for two years. It's huge. On the cliff."

"How big is huge?" Living in Nashville for years, I thought my idea of big probably differed from Gibb's. He was still a country boy.

"Over eight thousand square feet. Mr. Post—he laid the tile—said the master bath is bigger than his whole house. The Hudsons must be stinking rich."

I gave a low whistle. That would be considered big any-where. Why build a mansion so large in Sewanee? No theaters, few restaurants. No shopping. Just good country.

Gibb's word choice reminded me of Lori's comment from last night. I'd yet to mention to him that I'd spoken to Tom's widow about matters other than quilting. I wasn't even sure whether I should tell Gibb what she'd said about his admis-sion of still loving her, but didn't Lori think I'd tell my brother? Had that been her purpose in being so open with me? When had this conversation with Gibb taken place, and how mad had Tom been?

I'd wanted to ask my brother this morning when he came to pick me up, but he was ready to burst with the news of his conversations with Ed Goody and Patty. The short drive from Wood's Edge to the clubhouse by the lake where meetings were held had been consumed with that topic.

It seems the library affair had been going on for almost a year and was common knowledge among many of the locals—except for Mrs. Fleck, Patty's husband, and Gibb, which had his feathers ruffled. The only interesting fact relating to the murder was that Ed swore he had not made a delivery to Mom's that day or, in fact, during the prior week. Ed speculated that someone had stolen the UPS truck, knowing the amorous pair was otherwise engaged. He sheepishly admitted to Gibb that he always left the keys in the ignition. A check with the UPS office and their computerized tracking system showed Mom signed for a package that day during the time when Ed was, well, busy.

Gibb said it could have been done in no more than thirty minutes. A man quickly changing into a pair of brown pants and shirt, the five-minute drive to the cabin, a few minutes with Mom, and back to the library. And, if he was lucky, no one would even notice.

Now at least we had some proof that another person had been in the locked office. Probably not Tom Billings, though, as Mom would have recognized him, even disguised as a delivery man. Gibb thought the fake UPS man unlocked the window and returned that night with Tom. What had they been after? Certainly not a mystery quilt pattern.

Thinking of our murder victim reminded me of something. I craned my neck, trying to find the first Mrs. Billings. I was anxious to ask her a few questions. There were a lot of gray heads here today, but not one matched my memory of the woman.

"Gibb, too bad Christine Billings didn't show up. I'd like to have a talk with her," I whispered. "Or did she change her last name after the divorce?"

"She is here," he said, shielding his words with a hand over his mouth. "To our left. Fifth row. Third chair in." He turned his attention back to the speaker and said out of the corner of his mouth, "She kept Tom's name, and leave the investigating to me."

I counted the rows and chairs and then counted a second and third time. The woman sitting it the space he'd indicated had beautiful auburn hair, shoulder length and styled for a shampoo commercial. The skin on the neck and cheek was as taut as a thirty-year-old, and the body was slim. The woman sat with tanned and toned arms crossed over her chest.

Suddenly, as if she'd felt my stare, Christine Billings turned and gazed at me with a look that seemed to say, *I look great, and I know it.*

Wow, plastic surgery could do wonders. Gone was the sixty-something, heavyset lady I'd last seen a year and a half ago shopping in *Piggly Wiggly*.

I leaned again toward Gibb. "Where's the old Christine?"

Before he could answer, Andrea Hudson stopped speaking and pointed her finger to the back of the room where Gibb and I sat.

"Would you be quiet? I have the floor," she said, planting fists on nonexistent hips.

Before Gibb or I could respond, Mr. Coffee, the president of the homeowner's association board, used the opportunity to break into Mrs. Hudson's diatribe on the lack of landscaping along the subdivision's private roads.

"Since we have no motion on the landscaping issue, let's move to the next item on today's agenda." Mr. Coffee slammed a gavel onto the tabletop so hard many of the people in the room jumped in their seats. Earlier, I'd heard a few soft snores and was sure those people had been awakened with a start.

Andrea Hudson, realizing she'd lost the floor, shot me a dirty look as she stalked to her seat on the first row. Several others in the audience gave my brother and me smiles and approving nods for ending their misery. The newcomer had been complaining for the last half hour.

After years living away, I still knew many of those in attendance. Turnover of property in the Mountaintops community wasn't especially fast since so many of the homeowners were retirees. Most had been friends and neighbors or neighbors and enemies of Mom's for years.

A voice from the other side of the room caught everyone's attention.

"Mr. President, may I be allowed to speak next?"

All heads swung as a handsome man stood. If his rugged good looks didn't bring him enough notice, the out-of-place suit did. Everyone else was in casual weekend attire. The clothes made me wonder what his profession was.

"Who's he?" I asked.

Gibb sat up straighter. "I have no idea."

The man didn't wait for permission to speak but continued. "Please, let me introduce myself. I'm Harley Morgan, a new resident of the community. Just last week bought the old Abbott cabin, and I'm looking forward to meeting each and every one of my new neighbors soon. Maybe a late barbecue." His smile widened.

Harley Morgan ran a hand down his jacket, checking that his tie was in place. I hoped this guy wasn't going to be like Mrs. Hudson, wasting everyone's time with some petty issue. I was so caught up in his sudden appearance that I didn't even catch what he was saying at first.

"... most concerned about the murder. I feel we need a committee to prepare a statement for the local newspaper. Maybe even for dissemination to adjacent cities." Mr. Morgan paused for effect. "Why, it could be devastating to the community, to our property values."

A gasp rolled through the crowd and grew in volume as it reverberated. Beside me Gibb snorted his disapproval as Mr. Coffee used his gavel to bring order back to the meeting.

"That seems a bit dramatic, sir," said Mr. Coffee. With his years of military bearing showing, Frank stood ramrod straight. "I think your suggestion is premature."

The murmur of whispers became a roar now until Frank's next words were buried under the avalanche. Within seconds people were out of their chairs and talking in smaller groups, many crowded around the newest resident of Mountaintops. The banging of the gavel finally died, defeated by the crowd. Mr. Coffee pushed through the residents as he bellowed, "Let's take a refreshment break. Fifteen minutes." He worked his way to Gibb and latched onto the younger man's arm.

"Gibb, boy, we'd best talk."

I watched their backs as they retreated to safety and privacy. I envied Gibb getting to leave, if only for a moment. As the hectic circles of conversation calmed, I could feel the gaze of one after another of my former neighbors settle on me. No one wanted to stand too near. Shoot. I'd grown up with these people. What was the matter with them, thinking Mom would hurt anyone? Who could be worried about property values at a time like this?

I eased past two men to reach the refreshment table, its paper tablecloth festooned with Halloween spiders, and grabbed a cookie.

"Don't let it upset you, dear. Gibb will get things worked out."

At the sound of a familiar voice, I turned to find an old family friend, Esther Pickens. I gave her a quick hug, being careful not to drop my snack or disturb her balance on metal crutches. As a child, polio had crippled her legs but not her spirit.

"I don't know what's the matter with these dang fools. How's Cele anyway?" Esther asked.

"Being Cele." I edged around to where I could watch the knot of people talking to the newcomer. "She's great actually. I'm the one who's a mess." I took another nibble of a store-bought pecan sandie. A little dry.

"You need a slice of my rhubarb pie to cheer you up, child." The mention of Esther's blue ribbon winner made my mouth water. When Gibb and I were little, Esther would make us a cake for every birthday, and she always had pie for anybody who might drop in to see her. The woman was one of the best bakers in Sewanee. Esther even reminded me of a confection herself, being short and round with a poufy head of powdered-sugar white hair worn in a swirling upsweep mimicking meringue. As far as the pie was concerned, I didn't need the calories, but she would know what was going on in Mountaintops better than anyone, being a long-time resident and one of Mom's oldest friends. And a tiny sliver of pie wouldn't hurt.

"Do you know that man?" I asked, pointing at the knot of people around Mr. Morgan.

"No, but I was talking to Eugena Colley yesterday. She's in real estate now. Eugena was the agent for the Abbotts, matter of fact. You recall that the property backs up to Cele's place?"

I nodded.

"He must be the new owner, so he's your closest neighbor now."

"Esther, how many are against Mom for having a business in Mountaintops?"

She frowned as she considered the question and raised a hand to wipe at perspiration on her upper lip. "More than half, I'd bet. I tried to warn Cele."

"Course that's the least of our problems now with the murder."

"Just figured they were one and the same. Tom was real riled. He'd been stomping around for months like a bear with a honey jar on his head." Esther pulled her crutches up. "I've got to get home and off my feet, honey. Come by anytime."

I put my hand on the old woman's arm. "One more question, please? What do you think Christine would say if I asked to visit her?"

Esther's frown deepened, pulling her wrinkles into deep tracks. "Best leave that badger alone, Stella."

"Okay." I didn't want to upset my friend. "What got into Christine? I wouldn't have recognized her on the street."

"Divorce got into her. Took up walking first, and now she jogs. Goes twice around this lake every afternoon at two." Esther twirled her finger around to indicate the path that edged the water outside the window and then moved her finger up in a small circle near her head in the universal sign for crazy.

"Thanks, Esther," I said as she shuffled away.

Maybe a jog this afternoon would be just the ticket. In that case, I could afford another cookie.

CHAPTER 14

Clearly the murder added plenty of fuel to the fire in the fight against Mom, and the meeting never did get back to being a meeting after the milling crowd split into two factions. It seemed there were plenty of Mountaintops residents wanting to investigate ways to get rid of Mom against a smaller circle of her friends. Esther had been right about the odds. Frank tried but couldn't get the two teams to sit and talk.

It really hurt me to hear people in the community talking badly about Mom, but as Gibb and I left the clubhouse, there had been many comments to overhear. I couldn't have missed them unless I'd stuffed my fingers in my ears and sung loudly all the way out to the car.

"Gibb, we can't let Mom lose her business and maybe even the cabin. We've got to do more than solve this murder." I rolled the window down and let my hand float in the air stream as Gibb drove me home. The police scanner mounted on the dash crackled occasionally, and Gibb had a mean-looking shotgun mounted ready for an emergency. Plus, no one gave cops tickets for speeding.

He braked as a deer ran in front of the car and bolted into the woods on the opposite side of the road. "I told you how I talked to her about moving her business to another location, but she was adamant."

"Of course she was." I sighed and then suddenly it was clear to me. I'd always wondered what an epiphany was. Now I knew. Mom had every right to run her business out of her home. Her father had created the Mountaintops community. The family had been here first. She wasn't hurting anyone. "Of course."

"You said that."

"Why should Mom have to change her life to suit those—I can't think of a bad enough word for the back-stabbers, but you know what I mean. It's her house. Her home. Her business." My voice grew louder with each word. "She's legally grandfathered, and they shouldn't be trying to weasel a way around that."

Gibb reached over and patted my knee. "Calm down, Stella."

I jerked my arm back into the car and used both hands to smack away his hand and platitude. I didn't want to calm down. I'd been calm all my life. Whenever someone told me I couldn't do something, I'd agree. I'd give in.

Look at Mom. She led her own life and ran her business on her terms. She'd tried hard to teach me to be my own woman. Well, the lessons finally made sense. I'd been stuck behind a keyboard for the last however-many years, and where was I going? Nowhere fast. I no longer even had a job, and certainly no career. No one was going to identify with me the way they did with my mother and her quilting.

"I am not going to calm down," I said. "I'm through being a wimp. From now on I'm going to be like Mom."

"Uh, I think being like Mom is what keeps her in trouble all the time. I kinda like you better the way you are, Stella."

I narrowed my eyes. "You like having a wimp for a sister? Nope. I'm officially changing. I'm going to be adventuresome and speak my mind, and I'm going to be creative. Uh, I'm going to try at least."

Gibb gave me a wary look as he slowed the car to turn in at the stone gates that marked the driveway to the cabin. Gravel popped and grated under the tires. I was glad the students were away on the field trip to Nashville because I definitely needed to think. I saw the problem, well, problems really, in a different light now.

When I swung the car door open, one of the cats, the little tabby, hopped up onto my lap. I scooped her and my tote into my arms and stood.

"What do you have planned? Are you thinking of getting into any trouble?" Gibb's frustration etched a wrinkle between his eyebrows.

"No thanks, I don't want any trouble today. I'm going to go jogging." I lifted my chin, wishing I could project some measure of nonchalance. I spun on my heel and headed toward the house.

Gibb called to my back, "Are you okay, Sis?"

"Yes." I tossed the word over my shoulder but didn't stop my march toward the back door. I listened to his departure with a twinge of regret but hurried on into the house. I vowed that from now on I might leave some ruffled feathers in my wake, but I wasn't ever going to bore anyone.

I paused to settle Baby on a kitchen chair and gave her a quick kiss. The house echoed with silence. Lam had told me he was going to work while the class was in Nashville, but just in case he'd changed his plans, I called his name loudly. I didn't want him to catch me in my plan. There was no answer except both dogs came racing into the kitchen wanting treats. I passed out several before running up to Mom's bedroom. I hadn't actually brought any clothes with me that would be appropriate for a workout, but I wasn't going to let that ruin my chance of talking with Christine.

Standing in Mom's closet, I stared down at my feet. Today I wore my favorite cowboy boots. They were red and white with lots of fancy topstitching. Once I'd seen a picture of Tammy Wynnette sporting something similar. Neither the boots nor my sandals would do for a jog though.

There were several pairs of athletic shoes on Mom's shoe rack since she loved to go on nature walks, but she wore a size seven, and I was an eight. Okay, eight and a half to be comfortable. Her tennis shoes would just have to do though. I plopped onto the floor and yanked at my boots. Mom's shoes were going to be a tight squeeze, but if I skipped the socks and curled my toes up, it might work.

Ten minutes later I was wearing the shoes, my cotton panties, and an old T-shirt of Cele's with *VEGAN'S ROCK* stretched tight across my bust, the letters rounded with the strain. But I hadn't been able to find a single pair of pants or shorts of Mom's size six that would fit over my behind. I kicked at the piles of clothing scattered on the floor.

Then I snapped my fingers. Lam. Why hadn't I thought

of that earlier? I peeked out the door to make sure I wouldn't be caught by Lam returning early and then hobbled across the hallway when I saw the coast was clear. His clothes were neatly folded into a duffle bag sitting on a chair in the corner of Gibb's room. The zipper slid quietly, but I glanced over my shoulder thinking he might come through the door at any moment. It was, after all, his bedroom for the time being. I shifted each item in the bag carefully, hoping not to find his underwear and trying to ignore the faint whiff of his cologne. Lord, my cheeks were on fire. Then bingo: shorts.

A pair of khaki cargo-style cut-offs slipped over my hips for a perfect fit. It would be embarrassing, but I didn't have time to worry about it now.

Once dressed and wishing I could make myself invisible, I tripped across the lawn, trying to ignore the pinching of the shoes. Lam was just getting out of his four-wheel drive and burst out laughing when he saw me.

"What are you doing wearing my shorts? Did you think I wouldn't notice?"

"Laugh and I won't give them back. For your information, I am going jogging," I said as I dipped behind the wheel of my station wagon.

Lam leaned in the window. "Please tell me you are really going for a run and you're not going to get yourself into some kind of trouble?"

I eased the car forward a few inches forcing Lam to back away from the car, and then shouted out the window as I roared down the drive: "I'm really going jogging." I left Lam in my dust.

"Why does everyone think I'm going to get into trouble?" I spoke to the trees overhanging the road.

I pulled back into the parking lot that I'd left barely an hour ago. The same lot served both the clubhouse and the lake in back of the cedar-shake building, and thankfully everyone from the earlier meeting had already left. There was only one car in sight. I drove to the far end, closest to the dock, to park right beside a white Mercedes sedan. It looked really expensive, even more so with my beat-up Ford beside it. I had no idea if it belonged to Christine Billings or not.

Pretending to do stretches, I casually looked in the window. A crisp white towel lay folded on the passenger seat, and a pair of women's sunglasses balanced on the center console. It was probably Christine's car.

I straightened and listened but heard nothing. The only noise was the wind in the dying leaves and the buzz of a dragonfly hovering where the gentle ripple of the lake lapped the ground. I saw no movement of a runner flashing through the trees as I gazed across the water, but the path that circled the lake meandered several feet into the woods in many places. I walked across a small beach of white sand that had been hauled in for the pleasure of the residents' children and visiting grandkids. It held dozens of footprints and a child's bucket and shovel left behind after an afternoon of fun.

Which way had Christine gone? It didn't matter. The circular path began and ended here. The way she looked I figured she probably made several circuits around the lake, each one probably being close to a mile long.

I started off at a slow jog. The first steps were okay, but I felt the pinch of the shoes on my little toes almost immediately. In twenty paces, as I entered the shelter of the trees, I slowed to ease the growing pain. The shade thickened quickly on the hard-packed dirt trail, and I watched the ground, hoping I wouldn't trip over a root.

Mom, Gibb, and I had walked this path thousands of times in the past, but I had never jogged it. Had never jogged for exercise in my life. Geez.

After what seemed like miles, my toes and heels felt as if they were raw. I slowed to a pace that any elderly person could best, and even at sixty-plus, with the muscles I'd seen, Christine certainly wasn't going to have any trouble lapping me.

I heard the approach of someone, their shoes slapping fast on the ground. Hurriedly I sat in the middle of the path and rubbed my calf. Christine rounded the curve and pounded toward me. Thinking she was going to barrel right into me, I threw my arms up to protect myself. At the last second the woman skidded to a stop.

"Well, Stella. What a coincidence." She drew a breath between each word. "I'm glad to see you've taken up jogging. You look like you could use some exercise."

Good Lord but that remark was mean. I bit back my retort.

Christine wore pink-and-white running shorts and a matching spandex tank top. Both fit like OJ's gloves. The outfit included a sweatband, wristbands, and shoes worthy of an Olympic marathoner. Definitely more impressive than my ragtag attire.

The Christine I remembered wore *Wal-Mart* poly pants and knit tops like the other locals. Mom had been Sewanee's only fashion standout with jeans and hand-painted silk or cotton tops in the summer months and hand-knit sweaters and quilted jackets for cold weather. Oh, and *Birkenstock* sandals that she'd had to mail order because no local store sold them.

"Um, yes. Just got a cramp though. In my calf." I started to massage one calf and realized I'd been rubbing the other one previously. Maybe Christine hadn't noticed.

"You're okay then. See ya." She was ready to dart off.

"No. Wait!" I stood and faked a limp for a few steps. "I think maybe I'm going to need some help getting back to my car. Ow. Ow. It hurts."

Christine's eyes narrowed and her lips compressed, but she didn't say anything. She pulled a tissue from her waistband and dabbed at her wrinkle-free, immobile brow. Botox?

I pretended to try another step. Why hadn't I decided what questions I wanted to ask before getting to this point? Maybe some flattery to get the ball rolling would be helpful.

"You look great, Christine," I gushed, "for your age—" I slapped my hand over my mouth. "I didn't mean it like that. For a woman of any age. I mean you look better than me." The flow of words limped to a halt.

Christine crossed toned arms over her chest. "Better than that tart. Right?"

"Tart?"

"Lori. The tart. Except I didn't get the bigger boobs like Tom bought for her."

"Uh, boobs?"

"Stella, have you gone simple since I spoke to you last?"

"No. Not simple." I forced my mouth closed.

"How's Cele?"

"Uh, okay, but Christine, I'm sure Mom didn't kill Tom. You know that, don't you?"

Christine smiled for the first time. It wasn't pleasant, rather like a snarl. "Are you sure? Who else could have done it? Unfortunately, I know it wasn't Lori."

She looked so smug I wanted to slap her.

"Did Tom have any enemies?" I asked instead.

"Everyone needed Tom's business. That brought in a lot of money, and he was one of the most respected men on the mountain."

I noticed she hadn't answered my question. I said, "Someone wanted him dead. It had to have been planned."

Christine looked thoughtful for a moment. "You're right, Stella. I need to think about this."

"Is there anything that Gibb needs to know that could help the investigation?"

"Tom was going to leave Lori and come back to me."

"Really? Did anyone besides Lori know? Or did she know?"

"What are you doing, Stella? Playing detective for your little brother, Lori's special friend?" she said, her words taking on a mocking sing-song rhythm. Now the smile disappeared and there was no mistaking the emotion, the hatred, behind the lips curled back from the woman's teeth. "There's an election coming up, you know," she added, the words a low growl.

As I was thinking through what she meant by that comment, Christine lunged forward toward me. I jumped back with a startled shriek, but the woman only dipped into a stretching motion, one foot forward, knee bent, and hands on her thigh.

"Got to keep the hamstrings from tightening. You seem okay to walk." With those words, Christine straightened and loped away, arms pumping.

I lifted the hem of Mom's tee shirt to wipe the sweat from my face and left a streak of blush smeared on the white knit fabric. Detective work was harder than it looked on television.

CHAPTER 15

The drive to the jail gave me time to cool down from my short jog, although a glance at my reflection in the rearview mirror showed cheeks still flushed from the encounter with Christine.

I braked as a farm truck loaded with pumpkins pulled onto the road ahead of me. It moved along at about ten miles an hour, the bed lifting to the left and threatening to dump its load with each bump. I pressed my bare foot on the brake pedal and increased the distance between the truck and my little station wagon. I wanted to keep it safe for at least a few months. The body shop was its home-away-from-home, and I had put the garage owner's three children through college all by myself.

Ahead of me, the truck's brake lights flashed as the driver slowed and then stopped for Sewanee's one traffic light. The police station was on the opposite side of the road across the intersection. The front of the building was visible, and as I watched, the door swung open and Lori Billings stepped out. Gibb was right behind her, his hand on the small of her back. He stopped though, remaining framed in the doorway, while she crossed the sidewalk. Her long blond hair was all shine and swing, matching the rhythm of her sashay. The woman slipped behind the wheel of her car, a flame-red, two-seat roadster. For that matter, her dress was red and skin-tight, too. Did she always dress like that for a trip to the jailhouse? Or was the sizzle meant for Gibb's eyes?

My brother disappeared back into the building, but Lori's car didn't move. I could see her sitting behind the wheel waiting on something. Maybe she was adjusting the radio.

The pumpkin truck rolled forward with a belch of exhaust. Without thinking, I swung the steering wheel hard and whipped into the parking lot of an old motel called Jim's Motor Lodge. Rather than pull into a space where Lori might see me, I double parked behind a delivery van and inched my car forward until I could spy on Tom's widow.

I wasn't sure what I was waiting on.

At that moment the sheriff's Crown Victoria came around from the lot behind the jail house. Through the windshield I could see my brother look both ways before pulling onto the roadway. As he accelerated, Lori's car pulled away from the curb going in the same direction.

Should I follow them?

I knew if I hesitated, the decision would be out of my hands in seconds. With a silent curse, I bumped over the curb and sped forward, hoping to keep both cars in sight yet praying neither saw me. Two days had given me more respect for detectives.

Gibb slowed as if to make it easier for Lori to follow. She

stayed about ten car lengths behind the police car, but after a couple of miles and two turns, it was obvious she was following Gibb.

I had a sick feeling in my stomach that worsened as each mile passed. Our little convoy was heading toward the house Gibb rented.

Please, little brother, drive past. Don't take Lori to your home sweet home. I tried to will my brother to continue driving. I knew if I had caught the two together, others would also.

"Please, Gibb. Keep going. Don't be stupid, little brother." One at a time, I took my hands from the wheel and wiped sweaty palms on my T-shirt.

Gibb slowed and turned off the road onto his own driveway. My heart sank when seconds later Lori followed.

Oh no. Suddenly I realized they might see me if I continued on past the house. Gibb would recognize my purple car. I jammed on the brakes and wheeled into a U-turn. There was traffic coming toward me and a car behind me. Brakes squealed, cars swerved, and I watched in the mirror as a minivan ran off the highway, speeding through a field of corn stalk stubble before bouncing back onto the pavement.

When I turned my gaze back to the road, it was too late. I'd veered to the right and was heading straight toward a mailbox. I jerked the wheel hard, bouncing the car as the tires hit the shoulder. I swerved and managed to avoid that obstacle but clipped a tree just beyond the post. There was a ripping noise as my station wagon bucked and shuddered, but I didn't stop. I sped away hoping no one had seen my face.

Why me? Maybe my next car should be a tank. No, I wasn't

going to take the blame for this accident. It was Gibb's fault.

He was going to talk about what he was doing whether he wanted to or not. He owed me now. As soon as possible, I was going to corner my brother and force him to tell me what was going on with him and the tart—I mean Lori.

For now, I was going straight to Mother to tattle.

I drove directly to the police station and parked on the street, but as quickly as I had opened the car door, I slammed it shut again. If anyone saw me dressed as I was, and dirty to boot, I'd die of embarrassment. I circled to the back of the building. After all, I knew the combination to the back door. I'd let myself in.

With a glance around, I darted to the back door and punched in the birthday combination. The lock mechanism clicked. Feeling like I was breaking and entering, which I guess I was, I tiptoed down the hallway.

The first cell was empty, the door open. Evidently, William was sober and back to painting houses. Another three steps and I could see that Mom's cell door also stood open. I called her name even though a glance proved the cell was empty.

"What?" Cele spoke from behind me.

I jumped. "What are you doing? Shue, you scared the life out of me." I patted my chest.

Mom slipped past me and sat on the bed, drawing her legs and bare feet underneath her. She pulled a spoon out of her pocket and peeled the foil top off of a container of yogurt.

"Where were you?" I asked.

"Getting a snack from the break room," she said as if it were obvious. "Barney knows I'm not going to run away." She tasted the pink cream. "Not bad for non-organic."

She looked different today.

"You fixed the pumpkin suit. It looks great," I said.

She hopped to her feet and spun around, posing. "Like it?" She'd tailored the jumper to properly fit her slim figure and added some sort of red fabric decoration on the front. Instead of clashing against the orange, the ornamentation looked perfect.

"It's wonderful. What's this?" I fingered red triangles of fabric. I noticed she was no longer wearing earrings, and crimson beads also embellished the shirt front.

"I cut up my bandana and made prairie points that I edged with the beads."

"Wow. I'd like to learn how—" I threw my hands into the air and paced around the cell. "What am I saying? Am I the only sane member of this family?"

Mom eyed my outfit, and after my last question, I didn't want to go there. Before she could ask why I was dressed in her and Lam's clothing, I said, "Mom, I saw Gibb and Lori together not ten minutes ago."

She frowned. "I warned him to stay away from her. This is worrisome." She crossed to the sink and placed the yogurt container on the ledge of the stainless steel bowl. Mom tapped the spoon against her chin, deep in thought.

"Worrisome." My voice bounced off the walls to echo back at us. "You're under arrest for murder, and my brother is playing loose with the widow. Did you know he told her before the murder that he still loved her?"

"Why do you say that? Even before Lori latched onto Tom, Gibb had been working up his nerve to break up with her. He talked to me about it. He said he felt that Lori wanted to be around me more than she wanted to be with him. I even wondered if she suspected he wanted out. That was probably why Lori was already searching for her next boyfriend."

"Lori told me Gibb made the confession and Tom overheard. Anybody hearing her story will think Gibb had motive to murder her husband."

"People shouldn't believe everything they hear."

"Mom." I took her hand and pulled her down to sit beside me on the cot. "Tom told Lori that you and he had an affair. Years ago."

My mother leapt from the bed. "He lied."

"Maybe it wasn't Tom who lied."

"Lori?"

"Sure. We only have her word that Tom made the claim. Mom, you said Gibb thought Lori wanted to be around you. What did you mean?"

"When Gibb would ask Lori where she wanted to go on a date, she often wanted to come over to the cabin and just hang out. I mean, I guess I was flattered, but Gibb got tired of Lori only wanting to talk about quilting and needlecrafts."

"That's pretty odd. Don't you think?"

"I suppose I thought she wanted to impress me. You know, just hoping I'd be the future mother-in-law and wanting to get off on the right foot."

"So she really likes crafting."

"No. Like isn't a strong enough word. Lori loves crafting. But she's a novice and clumsy. She never finished high school, and I'd even started to wonder if she had some trouble reading the patterns and instructions. It's a shame."

"Guess that's why she stayed in the class after Tom was killed. I mean to be close to you. I still think it's strange though.

How in the world could she want to be there? But when I think about it, the key is that they, Tom and Lori, weren't really that close."

"I think she found being around me comforting. I can understand why she wanted to stay."

"Makes sense."

Mom paced the cell, head bowed while I watched her. She was a beautiful woman, in a natural way, for her age. Heck, because of her age. Slim and in great shape, she power walked most days and ran a business. I knew she'd be basically the same in twenty years.

She snorted. "Gibb told me about the library books. That's good news. I told him I didn't recognize the delivery man that day. I asked the guy if Ed was sick, but he pretty much limited his response to grunts."

"What did he look like?"

"Weird, now that I know he was an impostor. His hair looked like it had been dyed black with shoe polish, and he kept his dark sunglasses on in the house. Reminded me of Elvis. Oh, and he insisted on carrying the one box into the office for me. And the sweat. You wouldn't believe. His shirt was so wet I wanted to offer to get him a bucket. When he wanted to carry the one little box inside for me, I didn't think too much about it because I had my hands full when he drove up."

"Did anything unusual happen while he was in the cabin?"

"When he handed me that tablet to sign for the package, he dropped the pen. You know that electronic pen thing. Gibb says he probably unlocked the window when I bent to retrieve it."

"At least now Gibb has opened up the possibility to other suspects."

"Gibb? Much as I think my son's good at his job, you did it, honey."

For a second, I just stared at her and then we both grinned at the same time. I had made that happen, hadn't I?

"The girls say you're doing a fantastic job with the camp," Cele added. "They called and passed me a message. I really miss getting to see them."

I wanted to bask in the glow of her praise, but that was the first word of complaint I'd heard from Mom, and it brought tears to my eyes. I needed to work faster, but there were too many questions spinning in my head.

"Mom, I talked to Christine earlier. She sort of threatened Gibb. You know about the election. Or maybe she did. I'm not sure."

She sat again beside me and took my hand in hers.

"We need to be careful, sweetie. Christine has a lot of pull in Sewanee now that she runs Tom's business all by herself. I remember she took the divorce real hard."

"She told me Tom was going to leave Lori and come back to her."

"I wouldn't doubt it. Lori and Tom had nothing in common. He just wanted some excitement in his life. It happens to a lot of men as they age. After that, Christine just got off her butt and started running." Cele sniffed. "Although I don't believe in plastic surgery, she certainly does look good now."

Christine did look good. I pinched the roll of fat at my middle. Was it smaller than the last time I'd done the spare tire test?

I asked, "Had you heard anything lately about Tom going back to Christine?"

"No, but I don't often hear the local gossip. You might ask Esther."

"I will. She invited me to visit anyway, and she asked how you were." I took her hand and squeezed. "I don't think you should have to move the quilt camp. I'll help you, Mom."

She smiled but also looked surprised. "Thanks, honey. Gibb thinks I should just rent a building in town and move the business. I figured you would agree with him."

I opened my mouth to defend myself but stopped. Mom was right, or two days ago she'd have guessed correctly. What had changed? Maybe everything.

"No, we're going to fight this, not just the murder but the homeowners' association. I'll think of something." I gave her a quick hug, planning to leave, but I needed to tell her something else. "I have had one little problem." I held my thumb and finger about an inch apart and peered at her through the space. "I'm, uh, missing a page, maybe two, of the notes. See, there was this accident. Uh, Doodle Dog."

"Doodle. I should have warned you about that scavenger. Don't let him near the toilet paper or any paper for that matter. Just look at the finished quilt. You'll be able to figure out the pattern. I trust you." She retrieved the yogurt cup and ate a spoonful.

"Finished quilt? You made a Twisting Stars quilt?"

"Of course. Lap size."

"Of course."

CHAPTER 16

I hobbled back toward my car.

Oh, no. I'd expected a dent from hitting the tree earlier, but now I noticed that the accident had torn the back bumper clean off. There were two jagged holes in the metal frame where the bumper had been attached and plenty of scrapes on the paint job. I plucked a twig off the mangled tailpipe.

Now I had no job, a banged up car that would need fixing, and I hadn't told Mom that I'd quit my job. Shue, I dreaded that conversation.

I wheeled my car back onto the road, planning to go back to the cabin and change clothes. I would barely have time to visit Esther before the students returned around six. Supper would be the first order of business then.

Wait. I'd missed lunch, and the two cookies didn't count. I'd be able to have more than a sliver of pie, and maybe Esther might have some of her famous biscuits left over from breakfast.

Surely she'd have some salt-cured ham in her fridge too.

I didn't slow the car for a mile until I turned off at the security gate for the Mountaintops subdivision. I waved at Susan and shoved Mom's plastic pass into the slot of the electronic gate-keeper.

Mountaintops was a beautiful development, more like a national forest or state park than a subdivision. All the common areas were wooded with old-growth forest, the roads were overhung with a living canopy of leaves, and homes sat back out of sight in the foliage. Each home was burrowed in its own hundred-acre hideaway.

I drove through the beauty, slumped in the seat, wishing the serenity of the setting would cheer me up. The sight of a red-tailed hawk dipping between the trees ahead distracted me, and I slowed to watch. My breathing evened out as I watched him ride the wind.

For the most part, the residents were nice people who just liked the quiet life. All loved nature, or they wouldn't be here. The combination might prove to be Mom's downfall as a business in their midst was the antithesis of Mountaintops living. It wouldn't matter that the essence of Cele and her family was the thing that had given birth to the development. Some of the newer homeowners probably didn't even know Cele Hill.

It had been fun growing up on the mountain. Our property, being so much larger than any other lot, meant privacy for two children to explore and pretend they owned the whole plateau. But the isolation had separated our mother from the fold. She wasn't a local, and she wasn't quite a member of the Mountaintops community either. Her friends were the quilters.

The bird dived, missed his prey, and rose on the autumn

breeze to circle and wait for another chance.

The shape of Mountaintops was long and narrow with the family cabin on the east end of the development. I wondered if there would be some chance of getting the covenants that governed the homeowners' association changed to allow Mom to break her property away from the subdivision. It seemed a win-win solution to me. Mountaintops would only lose a headache and not money, since she didn't pay association dues anyway. Her property was grandfathered, having been here before the creation of the subdivision, and she didn't care about the snob factor of being a part of the exclusive community. All she'd need would be a driveway to the two-lane state road so her customers could bypass the gate house. I'd run my idea by her tomorrow.

At the last second, I bypassed the turn that led to Esther's house, knowing I needed to clean up before the students returned from the quilt show. I groaned. Biscuits and pie would have to wait.

As far as running the quilt camp was concerned, I was less worried now that I knew Mom had made a sample quilt in the Twisting Stars pattern she'd designed. But I knew it wasn't in the office as I'd already turned that room inside out and upside down. Maybe the lap quilt was in the quilting studio or Mom's bedroom. At this point, I'd barely had time to stick my nose in the studio. Today when I'd ransacked Mom's closet, I hadn't seen the quilt, but I hadn't been looking either. I didn't even know the colors of the little quilt since I'd forgotten to ask, and Mom's room was full of quilts. The whole house was.

I parked near the back door and spent a minute petting Doodle Dog and Carly. My tote bag seemed to weigh a ton as

I slid it onto my shoulder and crossed the lawn with my head bowed and the dogs on my heels. I needed a hot shower and something to eat, and not in that order. Getting out of these torturous shoes was first on my list. Once in the kitchen, I kicked them off, wiggling my toes.

I buried my head in the refrigerator, shuffling Tupperware bowls in search of something appetizing.

"Hey," a voice called from behind me.

I bumped my head on the top shelf. Retreating from the appliance, I rubbed the back of my head with one hand while hanging onto a container of lasagna with the other. Lam stood in the kitchen doorway.

"Sorry. Vegetable."

"What?" I asked.

Lam leaned against the doorframe with his arms crossed over his chest. He wore a sweater in a blue that matched his sexy eyes, and it appeared so soft that I'd bet it was cashmere. Probably a hopeful gift from one of his many girlfriends. He pointed to the plastic bowl I held.

"Vegetable. Cele's cooking."

"Oh." I shoved the container back into the far reaches of the refrigerator.

"Your mother's a lovely woman, but she can't cook. I've known that since I was six."

I tried to hold back the tears.

Maybe if I had a spoonful of real lasagna with Italian sausage in a spicy sauce with thick noodles, I could do it, but I wasn't eating something good. Plus, I was dressed to look like a ridiculous teenager, and I was dirty. I burst into tears.

Lam's smile vanished, and he crossed the room to fold me into an embrace. I discovered that the sweater was just as soft as it looked and that beneath the knit fabric, his chest and arms were hard and comforting. I snuggled close and sobbed.

"Hey, darlin', tell Lam what's wrong." He placed a finger under my chin and tipped my face up.

I balanced on my tiptoes and kissed him. Nice didn't begin to describe his lips, but somewhere in the back of my mind sanity and panic raised an alarm. I ran out of the room. In the foyer I took the steps two at a time, my bare feet slapping against the wooden treads. The door to Mom's bedroom slammed behind me with a soul-satisfying crash that rattled every window in the house.

The closet was just as I'd left it with clothes strewn in heaps. I kicked at the piles several times before collapsing in a good imitation of an abandoned rag doll only to land on something hard and uncomfortable. I reached back and pulled one of my cowboy boots from underneath my butt. I put it behind my head for a pillow and lay there on my back, staring up at Mom's clothing hung around the closet walls on wire racks. It was the first time I'd noticed my mother was partial to blue. Wasn't red her favorite color? Maybe orange? She used those hues often in her quilts.

I heard the bedroom door open and close.

"Decent?" Lam asked.

"Would that stop you?"

"Not really." He stepped near, wearing a wide grin as he gazed down at me.

"What's Mom's favorite color?" I asked.

He looked surprised at the direction of the conversation, but without having to consider his answer, said, "Blue. Why?"

When I didn't respond right away, he asked, "Did I pass?"

"I would have guessed red. How come I didn't know?" I sniffled.

Lam folded long legs to sit Indian-style on the floor next to me. "Because you're normal, Stella. Relax. You're just a busy, happy career gal."

"I quit my job probably seconds ahead of getting fired." I scooted to a sitting position, leaning against the closet door frame. "It's been a madhouse at work for months, and there I was, asking for time off. I didn't even know when I would get back. We argued. I mean my boss and me. Everybody calls her the Wicked Witch. Her voice got all loud, and then...then I started to cry and I just quit. I didn't even try to work it out. Why did I do that, Lam?"

"Temporary insanity? Do you want the job back? Maybe it's not too late if you're prepared for some major begging." He rested his hand on my knee. "Maybe you wanted out anyway. Had you thought of quitting before?"

"No." I drew the word out on a sigh. "Maybe."

"Sounds like you have some thinking to do, and the mountain is the best place for that."

I only nodded, not trusting my voice or the spigot holding back my tears.

"I'd like to see you stay, Stella."

He leaned in closer. I didn't understand what was happening with Lam, and I hadn't had any time to think about it. My thoughts rode a tornado of fear and uncertainty right now. I twisted my face away just a fraction.

Lam must be good at reading women's body language because he leaned back to a safe distance. It was odd that such an old and loved friend could seem so dangerous to me.

"Do you remember when we were little?" I asked Lam.

"How we used to play house. Do you think you've never gotten married because I made you spend so much time as my husband in that tree house?"

I watched a smile start in Lam's eye's and spread across his face. "I hadn't thought about that in years." Suddenly his face darkened. "No, I'd say it had more to do with watching my dad go through wives at the speed of light. When all this is over, I'll catch you up on the latest doings."

I started to speak, but he shushed me and said, "Listen. Wash up. The students will be back any minute. I'll go and pick up pizza for tonight. I'm finally tired of cooking. Never thought I'd hear myself say that. I'll just be content to sit on the porch with my shotgun across my knees tonight."

I called to his back, "Lam, where's that lap quilt Mom made for the class?"

"The little orange and red and blue one?"

"I don't know what it looks like. Mom just remembered today to tell me she'd made a sample."

"It must be in the office. Probably in that hutch."

"No. I've been through everything in that room."

"Sorry. I don't know then."

After Lam left and I'd showered and changed clothes, I searched every inch of Mom's bedroom, even the linen closet in the bathroom. I'd hoped maybe to find the sample hidden among the folded towels and extra set of sheets.

No sample quilt. The only surprise, and it was a big one, had come when I'd gone through a chest sitting at the foot of Mom's bed. There were a couple of bed-sized quilts lying on top. Both had been made by Mom, but neither could have been mistaken for the sample. Beneath those there were four more folded quilts that were instantly recognizable to me, and the fact that they'd been saved by mom brought me to tears yet again.

They were the quilts I'd made as a teenager. The full-bed, wedding ring coverlet, nestled in crisp tissue paper, had to be the ugliest thing I'd ever seen. Even my memories didn't do it justice. I spread it over the bed. Its hills and valleys resembled the Tennessee landscape. Each seam I examined looked worse than the next. A few of them had even opened up, though it had never seen any use on a bed. I felt repulsed, tossed it back into some semblance of Mom's orderly folding, and threw it back into the chest.

I'd been just as disgusted the day I had jerked the lid off the trash can and dumped my work into the depths. Mom had retrieved it, and, what's more, she had never said a word. The other three quilts surprised me in that they weren't too bad. Looking at them together, a collection in the blanket chest, I could see that my color choices were bland but not too bad.

My second attempt, a more reasonable split-rail pattern, lay flat, and the intersections of patches met in fairly nice points. A memory I hadn't revisited for years surfaced. Mom had taught me to make mitered corners on the borders. She'd volunteered, and we'd spent an entire day deciding on the width, marking the fabric, and cutting it out with scissors. She'd let me sew the borders on without a single critical comment. Then she'd demonstrated how to sew on a binding and left me to finish up alone, a sure sign of trust for her. My mother had bragged so hard to Esther about the end result that I'd been embarrassed.

I lowered the lid of the chest and patted the top. I'd find the killer so that Mom could come home. I thought maybe it was time for the two of us to have another quilting lesson.

CHAPTER 17

No. This couldn't be happening. There was no quilt, lap or otherwise, in the log cabin. I'd taken the office apart again, unfolded every scrap of fabric, emptied a dozen boxes, dumped the contents of every drawer. I'd even looked under the braided seat cushion on the desk chair. Before that I'd peeked through the other bedrooms. I'd even crept down to the basement, thinking that perhaps she'd hidden it there from the students.

I flopped onto the desk chair and stared up at the ceiling. Nope. No quilt there either.

The door swung open.

"Want some pizza, Stella?" Julie entered carrying a plate with two slices of pepperoni pie, smelling like heaven.

"Sure, thanks." I let the chair flip forward and accepted the meal from her. "Have a seat." I looked around for the other chair, not immediately able to find it in the jumble I'd created.

Julie scooped folds of fabric from the caned-bottom chair

and looked around for an uncluttered spot. Finding none, she finally draped everything over the ironing board standing in the corner.

"You're not quite as neat as Cele. No offense. Camp is just wonderful, Stella," Julie said with a blush. "To think I was afraid to sign up. I was so nervous when we first got here, but you've really put me at ease. I've never ever made a quilt before, so I'm learning tons."

"Cele is a great teacher."

She blinked. "Well, I guess, but you're a wonderful teacher, too."

I sputtered and brushed at my shirt front, hoping I hadn't sprayed sauce on myself. "Mom will return Monday. You'll see how fantastic she is."

"We were all hoping you'd stay on. I mean to work with your mother. Everyone agreed."

"Even Sherri?" I asked, flabbergasted that I'd made a good impression on the group. Hadn't they noticed I was a quilting novice and a klutz?

Julie pulled her chair closer to mine, looking over her shoulder as if she were afraid that brash woman would overhear.

"I think you need to know something about Ms. Bane. She let slip today on the bus that she's not really a quilter. I mean, she's a quilter, but that's not why the woman's here at camp. She's taking the class under false pretenses," Julie whispered with her hand cupped beside her mouth.

"Why is she here?" I asked, the murder immediately springing to my mind.

"She's scouting to hire a TV host for a quilting show she's developing."

"I don't understand."

"She's a television producer for the Artisans and Crafter Channel," Julie said. "It's my favorite."

"You mean the one I watch on TV?" I pointed at the set in the corner.

"Stella, you look like you're in shock."

"I am." I took another bite of pizza and chewed slowly. "Mom would love that."

Julie grinned. "Sherri is considering you now, Stella." She reached out and patted me on the knee. "I mean, you deserve it after years of working on your craft and you're, well, just so, so dynamic."

The blood drained from my face. My frazzled state of panic was being mistaken for dynamism. I tried to think of an intelligent response but was interrupted when the door creaked open a few inches. Sherri Bane peered at me through the crack.

"Class time, Stella," she said.

"Class?" I swallowed pepperoni and fear. "Oh, yeah, we'll be right there."

Sherri gave Julie a hard, suspicious stare. I hoped Julie would just keep quiet, but I could practically see her breaking down under the brash woman's scrutiny.

"Stella was answering my question about, uh, about borders," the younger woman stammered.

"Well, I could always use advice with finishing my quilts." Sherri slid into the room and leaned against the wall with her arms crossed over her chest.

This evening Sherri wore a beautiful and obviously artistically handmade jacket. Several shades of blue fabric were combined in a pleasing geometric pattern then overlaid with some type of sheer rose-colored fabric. The combination resulted in purples that seemed to change as Sherri moved. A gold metallic thread flittered over the surface, quilting the layers together. As I examined the path of the sewing, I picked out the shapes of dragonflies subtly outlined in the design.

"Sherri, your jacket is gorgeous." I gushed.

"Thanks."

"I'd love to know how to do that." I knew I'd made a mistake as soon as the words escaped my mouth. Surely Mom was an expert in every technique the jacket required.

Sherri's eyes narrowed. "It wasn't hard."

"I mean the fitting." I searched for an excuse. "I'm not very good at tailoring myself, but you've done an exceptional job."

Sherri seemed to consider that and gave a slight nod as she accepted my praise.

"Julie, what was your question for Stella?" Sherri asked. If she was suspicious Julie had revealed her secret, she wasn't going to be deterred by my compliment.

To her credit, the expression on Julie's face made it clear she wasn't a good liar.

"Oh. Scallops. Right. Scallops." Julie beamed at me. "How do you figure out how many of those pretty scallops you can have along the edge? You know, so it comes out even."

Julie gave a sigh of relief at passing the problem to me.

"Ah." I tried to inject wisdom into my voice then realized with surprise that I could answer the question—or at least divert them with an answer that would sound as if it might work. Two weeks ago I'd taken my turn as the Sunday school teacher at my church. For the preschoolers it was more a babysitting job, but one I enjoyed. To entertain the youngsters, I'd cut a chain of dolls out of folded paper and let them color and tape the decorations on the walls.

"I like to make a paper, uh, full-size pattern," I said.

Sherri's eyes narrowed again. "You mean a template."

"Right," I said. I ripped a sheet off a legal pad lying on the desk top. "Pretend this is the width of the border and the length of the quilt. Just fold," I said, fan-folding the paper in half lengthwise and then again. "Do that as many times as needed till you get the number scallops you think looks good."

"But how do you get the curved shape?" Julie asked.

"Here, let's use this mug." I grabbed a pen where it rested in a ceramic coffee cup and set it on top of the folded page. I traced a half-circle around the bottom edge and then began cutting on the line with small scissors.

"See." I unfolded the paper. "Perfect scallops." Something didn't sound quite right though about my explanation, and then I realized what was wrong. "But you'll have to change the pattern of the scallops to go around the corners." I was thinking of what Mom had taught me about mitered borders. "Cut a forty-five degree angle here, and combine two half scallops to turn the corners."

Sherri tipped her head to stare for a second. "I like it. So let's get started with painting class." She rubbed her hands together.

"Painting?" I felt like Alice in Wonderland.

Sherri gave me another sharp look. "Isn't tonight the special bonus class 'Painting on Fabric?' I'm sure I read the schedule correctly."

"That's right," Julie said, always helpful.

"Oh yeah. Sorry." I stood, and as I paused to pick up my

plate, Julie left the room and Sherri stepped in front of me blocking the doorway.

"I have a complaint."

"Sure." I bit my lip, realizing that I'd probably removed most of my pink-frosted lipstick hours ago. "What's wrong?"

"I saw Lori already cutting her fabrics. I don't think she should be getting a jump on the rest of us."

"Well, we'll all be starting tomorrow anyway." I tried to brush past Sherri, but she bunched her shoulders and stood her ground.

"It's not fair. Did you give her extra clues?"

"No, of course not."

"The rest of us still don't have all the clues yet," Sherri said with a whine that would do my Sunday school kids proud.

"I've got them ready now." I turned and grabbed my notebook, waved it in her face, and then tucked it under my arm. I'd spent an hour picking out the remaining cutting instructions from the notes I'd taken in the jail. How Mom had remembered all the sizes that needed to be cut was beyond comprehension, but she had seemed confident.

"Maybe Lori came in here and has already seen the clues." Sherri's face lit up with the thought that she'd solved her own mystery. "How else would Lori know what needs to be cut?"

"That's not possible, Sherri." I snapped the key holder, gently this time, against my wrist. "The key hasn't been out of my sight. Lori could be working on another project. Did you ask her?"

Sherri shook her head to indicate she hadn't, but her expression started to look more quizzical than angry. "Maybe," she said.

"Look, Sherri, the woman's husband was murdered. Lori's probably just trying to distract herself."

"Oh, Tennessee bull. I'm not sure where you and Cele are going with this mystery murder, but I'm game for something new and exciting."

I sighed. I refused to try again to convince any of the students that a real murder had occurred in this room.

"It'll be fun. I promise," I said with what I hoped was an enigmatic expression.

Let this television scout think I had something planned, that I knew what I was doing. Hopefully I could keep stringing Sherri along until Mom could get back in the game and demonstrated that she'd be a great television show host.

Sherri looked as if she might protest again, but the telephone rang before she could speak.

"Go on to the studio, please," I said, "and tell the others I'll be along in a second." I paused with my hand on the receiver until Sherri turned and left. I watched until she was halfway down the hall before I picked up the receiver.

"Hill residence," I said.

A gruff voice that sounded as if it were being filtered through a handkerchief said, "You're investigating Tom Billing's murder."

"No. How could you think that? I'm not." I hoped I sounded believable. I didn't want word to spread and get back to Gibb that I was doing exactly what he'd forbidden me to do. Who was this anyway?

"Okay. Since you're not investigating the murder, I thought you might want to know a little more about Tom's business." The voice sounded amused at the clever response. "Did you know Christine was half owner of Billing's Hardware and

Rental while Tom was alive? Even after the divorce."

"No, I didn't realize. Does Gibb, I mean, does the sheriff know?"

"Of course." There was a long pause. "Come on, Stella. You should ask me who inherited Tom's share."

The connection buzzed as the person waited until I asked, "Okay, who owns his half now?"

"Why don't you meet me tomorrow, and I'll tell you." A hoarse laugh snapped over the phone line.

"Who is this?"

"Go to church early tomorrow. The old Sewanee Baptist Church is being rebuilt. Drive around, and park on the side where the construction work is being done so we can have some privacy. Say nine."

With a click the phone went dead in my hand.

Who could it have been? I couldn't even identify the voice as that of a man or a woman. Who else wanted Tom's murderer found? And was everybody an early riser but me? I tapped the spiral edge of the notebook against my chin. Something Sherri had said minutes ago rang a warning bell in my head. She'd suggested that Lori might have sneaked into the office to steal clues. To find the clues for a mystery quilt or to kill her husband and pin the crime on someone else? Could that be her way to get back at Gibb? Could she want revenge?

No, that was wrong. Neither Lori nor Christine could be considered suspects. Christine said they'd been together, and the person who tricked Mom, the UPS impostor, was a man. Just how many people had come into this room through the unlocked window? Tom obviously. He'd entered and been murdered. So at least two people had come in, and the murderer didn't have to be the UPS impostor. If two had crawled in, well, a third person could have been here.

Oh, this was getting complicated and scary. I looked over my shoulder at the window. The latch was in the lock position. And Lam was here. He really was out on the porch, not with a shotgun, but with a beer in one hand and a book in the other.

Another alarm sounded in my mind. Mom had said you couldn't believe everything people said. Now what had I been told so far?

I flipped open the notebook to a clean page.

Lori had told me that she'd married Tom for money and that he'd done it for the excitement. Basically, he'd wanted a trophy wife. I started my list with that tidbit.

The young woman had also indicated they'd been happy despite marrying for the wrong reasons and that, due to the pre-nuptial agreement, she got next to nothing if Tom left her or died early in their marriage. So Lori would have been better off with Tom alive.

There was still the business involving Gibb though. So far I had only Lori's word that Gibb had made his declaration of love, and Cele disputed that possibility. Soon I would have to ask Gibb for the truth, but I dreaded that moment because I wasn't sure I would get the truth from him. I didn't blame him. It was none of my business.

But I had seen them together, said the little devil part of my mind. Had Gibb's feelings for Lori flared over the months? Oh, shue, I certainly wasn't going to believe my brother had anything to do with murder. But Gibb could have told Lori his feelings, hoping she would leave the other man. Could that have somehow led to Tom's demise?

Okay. What else had I been told that I couldn't be sure was true?

Christine had declared that Tom was coming back to her. Wait a minute. That left Christine better off with Tom alive as well. Did those facts eliminate both wives, former and current, as suspects?

No, the fact that the two women had been together during the evening meant they shouldn't be on the list of suspects. Were they telling the truth about being together? Wouldn't both have to be lying? And, if one was a murderess, then both would have had to be involved. They wouldn't be working together, not as much as they hated each other.

The only thing I knew for sure was that my head was spinning. One thing I knew to be true, I needed a starting point. I thought back to being called naïve. I always believed the best about people, and I couldn't tell when someone was lying to my face. So what fact did I know for sure?

Mom did not have an affair with Tom Billings. That was the truth because she'd told me so. That meant Lori had lied. Or Tom had.

Shoot.

"Stella," chorused the ladies. The students were crowded into the hallway, calling my name. "Time for class."

CHAPTER 18

"Wow, this is fun!" I said, dabbing a foam brush loaded with fabric paint onto the surface of a rubber stamp. I pressed the stamp's colorful surface to a square of muslin laid on the work table in the teaching studio. "Lean on it, gals! Isn't this fun? Better exercise than weight-lifting." I released the pressure on the stamp and peeled it off the cloth, leaving a perfect purple pear print.

"Look, Stella!" Claire waved her first try, which sported a red leaf. "This is great. My quilts will never be the same again."

"Great, Claire!" I pushed my bangs back.

Laughter erupted.

Julie stepped around her work station and wiped at my forehead with a tissue. It came away with a smear of purple.

"Oh no. Is it in my hair, too?" I asked Julie.

"Just a little."

"Everybody keep stamping while I clean up." I ran water at the sink in the corner until it warmed, and swiped at the paint with a dampened paper towel. I continued to work blindly until I decided a bit of color wasn't going to do me any harm.

I glanced around the large room set up as the teaching studio. It was a wonderful space. How come I'd never known Mom was having so much fun? Guess I'd been too busy being the perfect office worker, sitting in my stuffy cubicle typing all day.

Scattered around this third-floor attic space were thirteen stations, twelve for students and one for Cele. Each space had a sewing machine in a cabinet with plenty of drawers and a Formica tabletop. The room was pretty crowded with people milling about, but once everyone was seated in front of a machine, it was open and efficient.

The walls of the room were crowded with cabinets and racks holding wire baskets stuffed with fabric in every hue and print ever designed—or so it seemed to my novice eyes.

Throwing open one of the storage cabinet doors was like tearing away Christmas wrapping. Mom owned a vast array of crafting supplies all neatly labeled and arranged on the shelves. The tubes and bottles of paint and ink made my mouth water, the colors attacking my senses. I felt as if I'd stepped inside a rainbow.

If there was a crafting heaven, this was it.

I'd always loved working with my hands as a kid, making things, but crafting for me had ended with college and a job. I'd never considered myself artistic, but I did know my way around a paintbrush.

The students were all intent on their projects. I walked

around looking over the women's shoulders, marveling at how creative they were. Some were bolder in style and color choices, but all obviously felt a distinct enjoyment in the work. Except the new widow.

Lori sat hunched over her work surface, eyes inches from the fabric, the tip of her tongue caught between her teeth.

"Are you doing alright, Lori?" I stopped at her side.

"I didn't do it right. Guess I didn't have enough paint on my stamp," she sounded close to tears, "or press hard enough."

"It really doesn't look bad. Kind of antique like." I held her work up and squinted. She had tried to print a seashell in gold but had only left a ghost of the stamped image behind.

"I was trying to line the stamp up to press again, but that's hard to do."

"Right. That's next to impossible. Let's try something else to fix it," I said. I slipped her foam brush from her finger, dipped it into a medium pink, and then removed the excess. I pounced the almost dry brush on the image, laying a lighter hue over the original darker color. The result was a subtle blend, which I pressed onto the fabric square.

"Now let's go over some of the edges with a pen." I marched to one of the cabinets and grabbed a fistful of markers I'd noticed earlier.

"This is just like coloring when you were a kid, Lori," I said, working a silver marker in short strokes across the fabric but only along one edge, like a metallic shadow.

"That's so artistic, Stella. Guess you learned all this from Cele." Lori's voice held an edge of jealousy.

"No. Well, yes. I guess I just absorbed it." I didn't elaborate when she gave me a puzzled look, and finally she dropped her head back to her work. I felt ashamed now to remember how I'd just wanted to be different from my mother. I should have been proud to learn from her.

Before moving on, I glanced around Lori's work station. Her sewing machine was turned on, and a cutting mat was laid out on the table, although pushed aside. Tonight's class was only painting, so she must have been cutting and sewing earlier.

Sherri had been telling the truth.

Lori's large tote bag was on the floor, leaning against the table leg. As I stepped away, I reached out with my toe and kicked the bag over. The contents spilled out, and I knelt quickly to examine everything before Lori could bend to gather her possessions.

I scooped up a lipstick, powder compact, rotary cutter, ruler, and dozens of pieces of fabric cut into squares and triangles. The bag also held a needlepoint canvas and small skeins of wool yarn in a lovely palette of colors.

"Stop. I'll get it," Lori said.

She snatched at the items in my hands as I tried to sort through the bits of cloth, although I should have realized I wouldn't be able tell what project the woman had been working on. Was it the Twisting Stars quilt? I didn't even know what the pattern looked like myself. Too bad I hadn't been paying attention the night I'd had Mom's sample blocks in my hands.

So much for this attempt at being a detective.

I moved on to help Mrs. Littleton but saw a small scrap of fabric lying behind Lori's chair and out of her line of sight. I stooped and retrieved the piece, which was about three inches square. It was a navy print. I squinted at the pattern on the surface, a scattering of tiny silver stars across the weave.

I let the class go longer than the planned hour. It was better than being badgered for more clues. Earlier, I'd given out the last of the cutting instructions, and I had no idea if they needed anything else right now. When I offered to do all the cleanup, the ladies left in a merry mood. I heard one of them say that she had a travel bag full of chocolate, and she was willing to share.

It surprised me how much fun the painting class had been. It was even worth painting my hair, which made me think maybe it was time to update my style anyway. Maybe go for the Trisha Yearwood look. After all, quitting my job was going to require many changes. Did I want to stay in Nashville? That thought made my stomach twist. I had friends there, but coming home seemed to be the right answer if I could find work here.

I rinsed a fistful of foam brushes in the sink and placed them on the counter to dry. That was the last of the cleanup. I'd be in bed tonight at a reasonable hour at least. I hung my work apron on the pegboard by the door and snapped off the lights. As I went down the stairs, I ran a mental checklist of everything I needed to do tomorrow. First things first. Meet with the strange caller who might be the murderer.

I shivered at my own joke.

When I reached the foyer, Mom's little dog Carly came up to me, wanting to be petted. I happily obliged, stroking the soft black fur. After a minute, I straightened, ready to head to the kitchen for a snack, but the dog sat down in front of the door and gave me a beseeching look.

"Do you need a quick trip out? Okay, baby."

Carly scampered out onto the lawn, and I followed her as far as the porch. All the rockers sat empty. Lam had gone in, and I thought he was in his bedroom. Probably still reading.

I drew in several deep breaths. It felt good to be back on the mountain, and I knew my decision as to what to do next was already made. I supposed I'd known all along that I was going to stay. I'd just have to find work.

Who could leave this place, I thought as I looked up at the millions of stars that seemed to shine tonight just for me.

I heard Carly whimper softly and wondered if she'd found something. Sometimes the dogs would find a raccoon or possum wandering too close to the cabin. Doodle enjoyed chasing the wildlife, but Carly was often frightened and cowered, too scared to run even. I tiptoed down the steps and edged along the front of the house. Carly stood near the garage, staring at something just out of sight around the corner. The soft grass muffled any sounds as I moved toward Carly and then a step beyond. I rounded the corner of the old wooden garage running straight into the arms of a man.

I screamed.

He yelled and started to run.

Well, how dangerous could the man be if he screamed like a girl? I chased him across the darkened lawn, and just before he could make his escape into the forest, I tackled him. We rolled on the dew-slick grass several times, and the tumble stopped with him on top.

"Yowee. What a way to meet my neighbor," the man said with a booming laugh mere inches from my face.

"Harley Morgan?"

"The one and the same. Hot dog, babe, you feel good. Soft in all the right places."

The voice matched, yet this didn't sound at all like the stuffy man who had spoken only this morning at the home-owners' meeting. Could he be drunk? I dug my elbow into the ground and levered myself onto my right side, flipping his body off of mine. Four years of self-defense classes in action. He landed with a thump on his back.

I sat up. "What are you doing snooping around Mom's house?"

"Sorry. I was, er, searching for my cat."

"In the dark?"

"Well, he's only a kitten. I've got a flashlight, but I dropped it and broke the bulb. Right before you ran into me."
He sat up, and as a cloud cleared the moon, his face became visible. His eyes leveled on my chest.

I glanced down to see that the neckline of my blouse was pulled down, exposing plenty of cleavage.

"Cat?" I asked, tugging the knit up.

"Yes, ma'am. Little, uh, Smoky."

Did he pause because he was lying?

"So you bought Ida Abbott's cabin?"

"Yes ma'am, and I think I'm going to like living next door to you. Liven things up a bit."

I gave my head a shake. "I'm Stella, not Cele. And if my life gets any more lively, I might end up in the hospital."

"Hey, I know who you are. Saw you at the meeting this morning."

"What were you doing stirring people up against my mother?"

The man had the good manners to look ashamed. "I'm new. Guess I didn't realize there was already a bellyache against your mama." He stood. "I'd better git." He started off towards the edge of the forest.

"Wait up," I called to his back.

His face was in darkness now as he looked back at me over his shoulder.

"I'll give you a ride home," I said. "You can't walk back through the woods in the dark.

I dusted myself off.

As we walked toward my car, Harley Morgan stopped short.

"Wow. You weren't kidding about living an exciting life." He gave a low whistle.

"What?" I followed his gaze and in the moonlight saw the back of my car. "Oh. I'd forgotten about that already." I groaned, thinking about what this would do to my insurance rate.

CHAPTER 19

"Turn off that alarm."

The alarm penetrated my sleep-addled brain, and I realized I'd spoken those words out loud. I couldn't seem to pry my eyes open. With a flailing arm, I shut off the clock's incessant screams, promising myself I would rise from the oh-so-warm and comfortable bed. Just one more little minute.

I opened my eyes and stretched until my arms felt like they were going to pop out of their sockets. I felt so much better. All I'd needed was that extra bit of sleep. When I turned my head, the bedside clock numbers glowed eight, three, zero in bright red. Eight-thirty.

No, no, that couldn't be right. I'd set the alarm for seven. I needed to rampage through Mom's closet with the slim hope of finding something nice to wear to church that I could fit into. I had to shower. I liked to wear make-up to services.

That alone took me twenty minutes.

I had to meet last night's mystery caller. Gibb would be furious if I went, but how could I let the chance to learn something about the murder slip through my fingers? Should I be frightened though? I didn't see how meeting someone outside the church on a bright Sunday morning could be dangerous. I'd die of curiosity if I didn't find out who that rough voice belonged to.

The only luxury I allowed myself was a splash of hot water on my face and running the toothbrush quickly around my mouth. I jerked on a pair of my jeans and a cotton tee that I covered with my denim jacket. It was hardly fit for church, but the Lord wouldn't mind. Of course, the congregation was a different matter.

I ran a brush through my hair and hurried out of the cabin, slipping unnoticed out the front door. Crossing the yard, I was glad to see that none of the other ladies were out yet. One or two would be sleeping, but most were probably sitting in the dining room enjoying Lam's cooking before dividing up to carpool to the various churches of their choice. Sitting in the driveway, my car looked ridiculous without the back bumper. I gave the wagon's rear tire a couple of kicks in frustration. Well, I didn't have time to worry about it now. I hopped behind the wheel and roared down the driveway.

Mom had never been a churchgoer, claiming she was spiritual but not religious. Even as an adult I wasn't sure what that meant. I'd gotten my first taste of the Baptist church after sleepovers with various friends growing up, and it had been an important part of my blending-in campaign. Discovering that I could sing had been a bonus.

I looked forward to seeing some of my old friends today

after the sermon. A couple of girls I'd gone through high school with were still in town. Every one of them was married and a mother by now. That's why we didn't get together anymore. They were all too busy.

After church, I intended to visit Mom. The tension caused by her being locked in a cell was growing in me by the day. It wasn't just the students or the teaching, but that I couldn't bear to think of her there. I knew she could handle it, as she always took care of everything life handed her, but I could barely stand the thought. Mom had to be freed, even if it did hurt Gibb's chances of re-election.

As I made my way westward to the outskirts of Sewanee, a white wooden steeple peeked over the trees. The old Baptist church had definitely seen better days. The boards were in need of whitewash, and the roof shingles were sun bleached and curling. But the new red-brick structure, half complete and hulking over the smaller sleepy country church, seemed uninviting to me, lacking in charm. It appeared too solid and weighty, as if it would hold in the spirit and keep it from soaring with the hymns.

I frowned. The new construction was farther from the old building than I'd expected.

I drove through the church lot. There were only three cars since it was too early for services yet. I rolled slowly to the far side of the lot where a few construction vehicles were lined up, waiting for Monday morning. The remainder of the graveled parking area was littered with bits of building debris that I was concerned might puncture a tire.

There was no one else around.

I shut off the engine, but left the switch on so I could listen to the radio. With the window rolled down, the autumn breeze chased its tail in one side of the car and out the other. After several stabs at the radio's seek button, an old-time bluegrass song rang out. The fiddle and nasal twang cut through the morning quiet, and I turned the volume down so that the music played just in the background.

I couldn't see the original church from my space tucked into the L-shape of the new building. Only the red brick masonry and spaces left for the windows were visible for scenery. I hoped there would be stained glass windows, something the old building had never had. Through the holes I could see that scaffolding filled much of the sanctuary.

In my rush to dress, I'd forgotten my cell phone, but a glance at the radio showed me it was only ten minutes until nine. I let my head fall back against the headrest, and my eyes closed as the glint of sun off the hood warmed my skin. The music and the hum of a bee lulled me almost to the point of falling asleep. The buzzing grew louder, and I could feel my mind slipping deeper.

The rocking of the car had me dreaming I was in a boat.

Rocking. My eyes flew open, and I pushed open the car door to find that the ground was six feet beneath the car. I tried to rear back away from the drop but it was too late. My momentum propelled me forward, and I fell to the gravel. Although I hadn't fallen far, landing on the hard ground hurt. Luckily the tough denim jeans and jacket gave me some protection. I rolled to a sitting position, dazed.

What was going on?

I glanced up to see my car suspended from the wide bucket of a bulldozer idling in front of me.

I froze, sprawled there in the parking lot, a car balanced in the air above me, and a piece of construction equipment much too close for comfort. The engine of the dozer revved like a growling monster and lurched forward a few feet, carrying its load. The weight was now directly over my head. I scrambled to get away just as the equipment shifted again. The bucket was tipping to dump my car.

I tried to stand but slipped on the loose gravel and landed spread-eagle on my back.

The wrenching sound of metal tore through the air. I covered my head with my hands as if that puny effort could protect me from the weight of an automobile.

Nothing happened. No great weight crushed me.

The bulldozer's engine stopped, and I heard footsteps running away in the direction of the rear of the new church building. From my fetal position, I saw nothing.

I rolled to my back. My car dangled from the lip of the dozer bucket, caught on the back axle. The sound of tearing metal screeched against my eardrums and the station wagon swung lazily.

I inched backward on my heels and elbows. I couldn't seem to rip my gaze from the sight of the undercarriage of my car.

Just when I could see I was clear of danger and breathed a sigh of relief, I heard footsteps behind me and felt hands roughly twist into the collar of my jacket. Someone was trying to help, not realizing I'd already gained safety. Whoever it was drug me at least six feet back across the ground.

With a final tear, the car fell. It bounced and landed where my legs had been seconds before. The driver's door popped open and hung at a drunken angle, one hinge broken. The front tire rested three inches from my toes, hissing as the air leaked out. All the glass had broken and scattered on the ground around me, looking like winter ice. The fiddle music played on, though.

"What happened?" asked a voice from behind me.

The words came with a rasping gasp so husky, I couldn't identify my rescuer. I looked over my shoulder to see Harley Morgan sitting on his butt where he'd landed after dragging me to safety. He stared at my car with eyes round as the hub caps, one of which was spinning off across the parking lot.

Harley and I sat in silence for a few seconds, and then he stood and helped me to my feet. He dusted off my back, which I was grateful for until his hands moved down to swat the dirt off the seat of my pants.

"Stop it. What are you doing?"

"I just saved your life," Harley said.

I gave a loud humph, but the rest of my response was interrupted by a shout which caused us both to turn.

"Stella." Gibb skidded to a stop by my side. He gathered me into a breath-stopping hug. "What happened?"

Reverend Mills, Christine, and two other parishioners followed at a slower pace.

"I don't know," I stuttered. "It was crazy." I tried to push back from Gibb, but he kept me in the circle of his arms.

"You don't know what happened?" Christine sounded incredulous. "Looks to me like someone tried to kill you."

"I didn't see anyone. I was waiting on, uh, I was early and just wanted to see the new building." I escaped from Gibb's embrace but refused to meet his gaze.

Christine frowned as she stared at my car.

Gibb left my side and walked around to where the bulldozer sat with the scoop lifted high in the air but angled down where the operator had tried to dump the load.

"Do you own this piece of equipment, Christine?"

"Sure, but I was at the store. I got a call this morning from a customer who needed a tractor part. I was there until just five minutes ago."

"I'm not accusing you," Gibb growled. He pulled his phone out of his shirt pocket and stepped away to speak softly into it. When he turned back to us, he spoke to Reverend Mills. "Could you see if Esther Pickens is here yet? Ask her if she'll give Stella a ride home."

The preacher nodded and trotted away toward the old church.

"But my car," I said.

"I don't believe it's drivable, Sis."

Christine walked over to stand beside the huge dozer. She leaned toward the engine compartment, being careful not to brush her white dress against anything dirty. "Hot-wired."

"Don't touch anything," Gibb said.

"I'm not stupid, Sheriff," she said, rejoining the group.

"Tell me what happened, Stella," my brother said calmly.

I ran through the story, surprised to hear my voice become shaky when I got to the part about the dozer advancing to hold my own car over my head.

"And how'd you know to arrive in the nick of time, Mr. Morgan?" Gibb gave Harley a hard look.

"I heard a scream." He shrugged. "I was just walking up the steps to the church. He hooked his thumb over his shoulder.

"But—" I started to say that I hadn't called out, but did I know for sure? I could have screamed. I'd never know. The events were already jumbled in my memory.

"What?" Gibb asked as his gaze searched my face.

"Nothing." I shook my head.

"You're new here, sir. What do you do for a living?" Gibb eyed Harley again.

"Uh. I'm a lawyer," the man said with a grimace.

For the first time, I noticed Harley was back in a suit and sounding every bit the high-priced professional. No *yowees* or *hot dogs* today.

"Did you see who was in the cab of the dozer?" Gibb whispered in my ear as he led me a few feet away for privacy. I shook my head again. I'd been too busy watching my station wagon.

Two vehicles pulled into the parking lot at that moment, and we walked back to the others. One of Gibb's deputies stepped out of an official county car while Esther remained behind the wheel of an older Toyota.

"Oh my," Esther said, following with a series of tsks and shaking of her head as she gazed at my smashed car. "Get in, child."

Gibb placed his hand on my right elbow at the same instant that Harley took my left arm. Both tugged on me, then glared at the other.

"I can walk." I shook them off and wobbled over to Esther's car.

Gibb followed, opened the door, and then knelt to face me after I lowered myself to the seat with a groan and a sigh. He took one of my hands in his and said, "I was looking for you this morning to give you some bad news." His normally smiling face looked grave.

"Mom is gone," he said in a hushed tone.

I gasped and threw my hands over my face. "Dead!"

"God, no, you ninny! Gone. Run off. Skedaddled."

I punched Gibb in the arm. "Don't ever scare me like that again. You just took years off my life, and what are you talking about? Gone. You had her locked in jail. Where could she go besides the break room?"

"Judge Marcum came back to town and signed the paperwork last night. He set bail at ten dollars and paid it himself. Barney—uh, I mean Harold—said they left together. Harold called me with the news, but I just figured the judge gave Mom a ride home. I didn't want to wake you, Stella. Thought I'd let you sleep."

"You should have called," I huffed.

"I had my hands full with a bar fight."

I supposed I'd been acting like the world had stopped spinning while I ran quilt camp. Gibb still had responsibilities he couldn't let go of.

"But you're sure she's not at home?" I asked. "Maybe she was still in bed when I left."

"I went over to the house earlier, thinking I'd catch you there before church and talk to Mom. I didn't think you'd be leaving early." Gibb's voice was reproachful, but he continued. "Lam says he hasn't seen Mom, and I checked her bedroom. Nobody answers at the judge's number."

"No. No. No." I pressed my hands over my ears. "Don't even tell me she left with the judge. This is too crazy, even for our mother. Why would she do that? They don't get along."

Beside me, behind the wheel, Esther snorted. "Where you find one of them, you're going to find the other."

I remembered Mom's comment from a few days ago when she'd called the judge an old coot. When Gibb had asked what the rift was between them, she had only said it was ancient business.

Gibb and I both stared at Esther while this tidbit sunk in.

"Did you check the judge's house? He's not married is he?" I asked with a shudder.

Esther answered for Gibb. "Man couldn't stay married. Tried it twice, but he's been single for the last five years. Children, don't worry about those two. One of them will get their head on straight today and call. I'm sure of it."

Gibb leaned around me. "Thanks, Esther. Sorry to make you miss church, but I've got to stay and conduct the investigation and track down Mom. If I can." He sighed. "Don't let this one out of your sight except to hand her over to Lam." His gaze swung to me. "I'll stop by the cabin as soon as I'm done here."

"I want Esther to take me to her house," I said. Suddenly, rhubarb pie seemed like the only thing in the world that could possibly make me feel better.

Gibb looked thoughtful. "Sure. Maybe you could use a quick break. I'll call Lam and ask him to pick you up there in an hour. Is that okay?"

I sighed and nodded. "Do you think you'll be able to find anything?" I asked.

"Probably not, but I'll try, Sis." He stood as he closed the door.

Esther started the car forward, and I stabbed the button that lowered the window. I called to Gibb, "You've got to find Mom, or I'm doomed."

CHAPTER 20

"My granny always said it was bad luck to eat dessert first." Esther split open two biscuits and picked up a slice of ham, dark and dry, from a plate. She used her fingers to tear the salt-cured meat into smaller pieces, spreading the bites over two of the halves of the bread. "Mustard or honey?"

"Um, honey." I spoke around a mouthful of tart rhubarb pie. "Just a touch, Esther," I said after I'd swallowed.

Esther's warm and inviting kitchen put me right at ease, and for the first time today I felt truly safe. I'd decided that country cooking was just what the doctor ordered to soothe my frayed nerves. Although I couldn't put it off for long, I dreaded leaving the warmth and comfort of my friend's house. But the real world and all my problems could wait for another few minutes.

"Right." Esther smiled as she pulled the wooden honey

dipper from the jar and drizzled a liberal amount of golden liquid sugar on top of the ham.

For a second I debated asking the older woman if she had any vanilla ice cream to top the pie, but decided she might take the request as criticism. Anyway the dish was heavenly as it was. I licked the spoon after swallowing the last bite and rubbed my stomach.

Hmm. Had I lost a few pounds? I had missed a couple of meals in the last few days and maybe worrying burned calories. I realized Esther was saying something.

"You stick close to Gibb or Lam. Hear me?" Esther wagged a finger after setting the plate of biscuits on the table in front of me. "What happened this morning was dangerous business. I'm worried."

I shuddered and tried to blank out the image of the undercarriage of the car hanging over my head. Then there was the earlier incident with the basement door to consider. No one else knew about that. Should I tell Gibb? He'd surely want me to go back to Nashville, and that wasn't happening except to rent a truck and move my things out of my apartment.

"I hear. I realize I could have been a pancake now. Esther, you think Mom and the judge are together, don't you?"

"Oh, of course. They had a torrid affair years ago. She kept it quiet from you kids."

A blush scorched my face with her overly rich description. I searched my memory but didn't remember him ever coming to our house. Mom really did keep it away from Gibb and me.

Esther continued. "You know your mama. You young'uns always came first, but she's a wild one. Always was." Esther balanced her crutches against the kitchen counter and eased her bulk onto the chair opposite me. She pushed the glass of milk she'd poured closer to my plate.

"Who do you think murdered Tom Billings?" I stared into Esther's eyes.

She pursed her lips as she interlaced her fingers on top of her stomach. "You know, it's funny. When I heard the news, my first thought was that Christine killed him. But then came the part that Lori and Christine were together." Esther closed her eyes and leaned her head back in deep thought. She pursed her lips. "Tom was such a big part of the mountain community. Some liked him, some not so much, but he didn't have any real enemies that I'd heard of. He was a fair businessman."

"People talked well of him?"

"Always had, but since he remarried maybe things was shifting some. Did you ever get this tickle in the back of your mind that something ain't right?" Esther rocked forward with her last words. "But most important, Gibb's got to prove Cele didn't do it."

"Finding out about the UPS truck being stolen and the wrong package delivered will help, but it was still Mom's scissors in the man's back," I said.

"I think Gibb needs to find out if somebody lured Tom there or if he came of his own will. Did he bring the killer along without knowing he was putting himself in danger?"

"Which do you think it was?" I knew Esther's impression might be the most valuable clue yet. I wished I'd made it over for a visit sooner.

"Well, way I heard it, Tom was definitely killed in that room. Expect Gibb's already told you that much, so I think

Tom wanted to be in Cele's office. He was the kind of man who was hard to make do things he didn't want to do."

"But how can Gibb find out for sure?"

Esther lifted her hands and let them drop back to rest again on her ample belly. "What does your mama keep in the room that someone would want?"

I grinned. "Now that's a good question. Not just some-one—Tom Billings. He wasn't just any ol' thief." I chewed a bite of the tough but flavorful meat. "I've been through ev-erything in the room over the last three days. It's mostly full of quilting supplies. Let's see, a TV and VCR, dozens of tapes, books, and that includes Mom's business books."

Esther and I stared at each other.

"Getting Cele's business out of Mountaintops—" I said, "was centered around Mom making money off her teaching. What if Tom wanted a look at the books?"

"That sounds reasonable to me."

"Why did he want to hurt Mom?" Tears filled my eyes at the thought of someone hating my mother.

"It was funny. It didn't start until he married Lori."

"But Lori is worse off for Tom being killed. She told me about the pre-nup they'd signed."

"Hadn't heard about that. Silly business. People ought to get married for better or worse."

Esther and her husband had been together for fifty-two years before he'd died of cancer. How nice that they shared over half a century of marital bliss.

The clock over the sink chimed. Eleven o'clock. I couldn't help but smile. The timepiece was the same one that had hung there for years, fascinating every child who saw it. It was a black plastic cat with rhinestones for eyes and a swinging tail for a pendulum. The country décor made me realize how much I'd missed this simple way of living.

I rubbed my hand across the handcrafted placemat under my plate of biscuits, seeing it for the first time. It was quilted orange pumpkins with their carved faces appliquéd in black fabric. A gold thread raced in a curlicue leaf pattern to quilt the layers together. There were four of them spaced around the oak tabletop.

"Cele made those for me," Esther said.

"Don't you quilt, Esther? I've never seen you sew."

"Lord, no. Don't have the patience. Too busy raising young'uns, working the store, and cooking. Besides Cele was always giving me a quilt or gifts like these." She tapped the placemat in front of her.

Mom was so good to her friends. I had to clear her name.

"Christine and Lori were together during the time of the murder," I said half to myself.

"There's no love lost between those two. I didn't even think they spoke. Far as I know, that pair wouldn't get caught in the same room except for association meetings. Tom would always set Lori down as far from Mrs. Number One as he could manage without leaving her in the car."

"Christine told Gibb she was with Lori trying to iron things out."

"Uh-huh. Pretty late at night to be working on that problem." Esther frowned. "And darn right convenient."

"I hadn't thought about that part of it. Something isn't adding up. Lori says she's back to being poor now that Tom's dead. Christine told me Tom was coming back to her. That would make Lori poor too. Do you know if that was true, Esther? Somebody's lying."

"I hadn't heard, but that don't mean anything. Want another biscuit, honey? You need some meat on your bones."

"No way," I said, smiling at the thought.

"Anybody home?" Lam's voice called through the screen door.

"Hey, sugar, come on in." Esther twisted her head to speak to him but didn't rise.

"Here's my favorite lady." He leaned over the older woman's shoulder and gave her a quick kiss on a rosy cheek, then looked across the table. "Gibb called. He asked if I could come over and give you a ride. He wanted you to unwind here for a bit, and it looks like it worked."

Lam dropped with a sigh into the chair between Esther and me. "Are you okay sweet Stella"? He took my hand and rubbed it between his.

From the corner of my eye, I watched a tiny smile twitch on Esther's lips.

"Physically. Just a few bruises and a skinned elbow." I twisted my arm, trying to get a good look.

"Lord, child, I didn't know you was hurt." Esther worked herself to her feet and got a wet washcloth and tube of antibiotic cream. Lam took the items and cleaned the minor wound.

When he finished doctoring, he said, "Cele called the house."

"Where is Mom?" I wanted to yell but tried for a calm tone.

"Las Vegas. Says she's getting married."

"Hitched." Esther hooted and slapped her knee.

I opened and closed my mouth. Mom couldn't. She wouldn't. Would she?

"When will she be home? Should she be out of the state? I mean, there's still a murder charge against her. Don't they always say don't leave town." My mind was spinning, fear for Mom, and myself, churning my thoughts.

"Oh, Cele said she's safe with her companion. She'll be back tomorrow morning on the red-eye. Told me to tell you to hang on, Stella."

"Would you like a piece of pie?" Esther asked Lam.

"I'll come back for it later." He winked.

"I'll have an extra big piece in foil ready when you bring that cord of firewood by," Esther said. "The nights are starting to get cool."

Lam tried to quiet Esther.

"Lord, don't shush me." She turned to face me. "Lam keeps me supplied all winter and won't take a penny."

I wondered why he didn't want me to know that he helped an old woman. I knew Esther didn't have a lot of money and the free wood must mean a great deal to her. But to help Lam out I changed the subject.

"Lam, are you going to move out now that—"

"Cele's almost home? No, I'm sticking around to help you till she sets foot in the house. I wouldn't miss this show for the world." He gave a smile that softened the words. "Actually, I plan on keeping watch until the murderer is caught."

I grunted, slightly offended at being labeled a show, but I needed his help, and frankly I'd gotten used to the man being around. It was going to be a shock to have him leave the cabin sometime in the near future. Maybe I'd be seeing more of him. I hoped so.

"Well, I need to get the teacher back." Lam pushed his chair away from the table and stood. "She's got a class right after lunch, which, by the way, it being Sunday, is fried chicken."

"Shoot. Why did Mom schedule work on Sunday?"

"Darlin', quilting isn't work to Cele and the gals. It's fun."

Lam laughed.

"You're laughing at me again."

CHAPTER 21

I snapped on the overhead lights in the studio and saw a figure at Mom's sewing station. My body jerked in fright before recognizing who it was.

"Lori? What are you doing in here?"

"Just waiting on class to start, Stella."

Lori's voice sounded sleepy, drugged, and her face seemed drained of life. She ran her hands over the sewing machine, her fingers tracing the florid gold decals. Her feet pumped the old treadle, causing the threadless needle to rise up and glide down, the bobbin clacking under its throatplate.

Her movements brought to mind a marionette. Was someone controlling Lori or forcing her to do their bidding?

"So beautiful," she said, as if speaking to the inanimate object. "Cele told me once that her grandmother passed this down to her. Stella, do you ever think about how this will be yours one day?" She dropped her hands to her lap, folding them primly. "Like this cabin. Or will Gibb get the house? Do you know, Stella?"

"No. I've never wanted to think about that. It doesn't matter." I shifted on my feet and hugged the class notes to my chest. Her question was like a gust of cold air from a crypt blowing through the cozy room.

Lori nodded as if processing the information. "Yeah, I'll miss Momma when she's gone, but she's got nothing to leave behind. No heritage." Suddenly, Lori popped up from her chair. "Well, what's the matter with me? I've just got to pull out of this funk." She smiled and then hurried to the sewing station she had been using before, one nearer to the back of the room.

I watched Lori reach out an arm and carelessly sweep pieces of fabric into her tote bag. The different colors of cloth—navy, red, yellow—flashed under the fluorescent lights. Some memory tugged at the back of my mind but wouldn't surface.

"You don't have to put your stuff away, Lori," I said. "You'll just have to get everything out again in a few minutes." I walked casually toward her, hoping to see into the bag.

"I was working on a different project." The woman's face crumpled. "It's so quiet at our—at my house. I need to keep busy. Why, I must have a dozen projects going and I always finish them, every one."

Sudden sympathy for the widow made me feel guilty for my suspicions. Did Sherri Bane have me reading something into Lori's actions that were completely innocent?

Lori pulled a paper bag from underneath the table. I saw that the side was imprinted with the words *Mimi's Quilt*

Castle. "Here's my fabric for the mystery project," Lori said. "This is so exciting. I've wanted to take one of Cele's classes for a long time. No offense, Stella, but I wish she were here."

I watched as she unfolded several pieces of fabric, snapping them up into the air to unfurl the lengths.

"You okay, Stella? Aren't you excited about teaching the class? I guess it gets kinda old."

I hiked my hip up onto the corner of the table. "No. Guess I'm just worried about Mom. I wish she were here, too." I needed to get some information from Lori. Now, while I had her alone, would be the best time.

"Do you have any idea why Tom would have been in Mom's office?" Thinking that it wouldn't do to hulk over the vulnerable woman while I was trying to interrogate her, I slid off the table and hooked the back of the chair from the next table. I hoped I looked sincere and caring. "I mean, what would be so important to him that he'd commit a crime? He did break into Mom's home."

Tom's widow fingered the selvage edge of a pale blue cotton dotted with wisps of white cloud. She shrugged.

"Tom's known for years that Mom had a business here. Why did it suddenly start to bother him?"

"Stella, I just don't have a head for business. Tom never talked to me about money matters. I never even finished high school."

I opened and closed my mouth. I hadn't known that because Lori was so much younger. I would have been living in Nashville by that time, but her admission brought back the memory of Lori's older sister and brother. I remembered that neither of them had graduated either.

"Cele says she doesn't make money off the business. Says

she gives the profits to charity," Lori said. "Just for the last five years. Cele said so at one of the association meetings a few months ago. Tom didn't believe her."

"Gives the money to charity?" What in the world was Lori talking about? Had Mother lied to the homeowners of Mountaintops? Was it some tactic to avert a showdown? "But that still doesn't explain why he cared in the first place." I reached my hand across the table and placed it on Lori's arm.

"Trying to be friendly, Stella? I've been grilled enough by your brother." She frowned. "I don't know why Tom wanted this place." Lori pushed back from the table, the chair's metal feet protesting against the linoleum.

"Sorry, Lori," I said. The woman looked twitchy, ready to bolt. "Would you mind giving Lam a hand in the kitchen for a few minutes?" I tried to give Lori a sincere smile. I was afraid if I didn't calm her, she might leave for good. Although I was a little afraid of Lori, having her around was too good an opportunity to lose. If I was going to solve the murder, I needed more information.

She seemed happy to get away from me, hopping to her feet and hurrying out of the room.

I realized I still didn't know who had inherited Tom's half of the business. That had been the whole purpose of my meeting this morning. At least that had been my reason for going. Evidently someone else had wanted to protect themselves from murder charges. So far I hadn't let myself think too much about my run-in with the dozer. I remembered my car's axle caught on the edge of the scoop. It had been like seeing a metal monster with its prey, a little purple mouse, dangling from a huge mouth lined with sharp teeth.

I laughed, but it wasn't a pleasant sound, just a gurgle of fear. I'd told no one about the planned meeting.

Could it have been Lori? I dismissed that idea. She didn't seem the type to know how to operate a bulldozer, much less hot-wire one.

I'd bet my favorite cowboy boots that Christine knew how, but that woman wouldn't say she had been called to the store if the alibi wasn't true. She was too smart to lie about something that Gibb could, and would, check out. A smart woman. A smart business woman.

What was it Lori had told me a few minutes ago? She'd said she didn't have a head for business. Said Tom didn't discuss money matters with her but he would have had to talk about business with his ex-wife. Christine was his business partner.

Had that arrangement brought the couple back together? Wait a minute. Lori had said something else important. She'd said she didn't know why Tom wanted Mom's home and property. I'd thought Tom had merely wanted the business closed or moved out of the subdivision. No one had said anything about the man wanting Mom's property for himself. That put a new twist on my thinking.

I leaned back in the chair, pushing my hair back out of my face and massaging my temples.

Maybe I should talk to Mr. Coffee and Lori's mother might be helpful. I could pretend it was a condolence call. After all, Mrs. Hopkins had lost her son-in-law. Then I could nose around the hardware store. Surely there was something to be learned there.

I'd get the hang of this. I had to.

As I stood, my foot brushed against something and there

was a soft thump. Oh no, Lori's bag. I'd wanted to see what project she had been working on, and I'd forgotten it was there at my feet all this time. It might be only seconds before Lori returned or the other quilters arrived for class. I ducked my head under the table and reached for the tote bag, but the sound of my students approaching stopped me.

CHAPTER 22

"You always were a magnet for trouble." Gibb stifled a laugh by biting into a crunchy Granny Smith apple. A drip of juice dribbled down his chin, and he wiped it off with the knuckles of the hand holding the apple.

I was a bit offended, always being the butt of the joke, but it was so good to see Gibb smile that I couldn't be mad.

"That's not fair," Lam said. "Stella is doing a great job filling in for Cele. I overheard her students say she was great."

"Really?" I sniffled. I got up from the rocker where we sat on the porch and moved to the railing. With a groan, I rubbed the sore lump on the back of my head and touched the tip of my still-red nose and tender cheek.

In the yard, a roaring camp fire crackled. The students were circled around the flames holding out skewers of stripped maple branches on which they'd impaled marsh-mallows. Every few minutes one would fall and sizzle on the rocks ringing the fire. The women talked and laughed as they sipped warm cider out of canning jars and nibbled their roasted treats.

I was grateful for the breeze blowing smoke our way to fight off the few late-season mosquitoes buzzing around.

"Class did go pretty well." I flipped my hair over my shoulder, but it was too short for that move, and the locks swung back toward my face.

"How'd you pull it off?" Gibb asked.

"I asked for a volunteer to cut samples while I read my notes. We got started on the cutting, but they have to finish up tomorrow."

"See? Sharp," Lam said.

"Not smart enough to follow my instructions to stay out of this investigation." Gibb gave me a stern look as he tossed the apple core into the flower bed beneath the porch railing. "How about throwing some wood on the fire, ol' buddy?" He asked Lam. Evidently, he wanted a private moment with me.

My stomach did a flip. Little brother was really mad. Lam looked at me and waited for me to nod my assent. What did he expect? Did Lam think I'd ask him to stay and protect me from my own sibling? Or that I'd ask him to take sides against his best friend?

"Butt out, Stella," Gibb said once Lam was out of range to overhear his rebuke.

"No," I said, feeling a thrill of excitement at his shocked reaction. Time to stand up for myself.

For a second, we stared at each other. I don't know what was in his mind, but I thought about how thankful I was for my family. Like all kids, Gibb and I had done our share of fighting, but we really loved each other. This would blow over.

I could trust his love.

"Gibb, I need you to run whatever kind of background check you can on two people."

He sputtered, "You're joking. I'm telling you to leave my job to me, and you're giving me marching orders." He slapped his palms onto the arms of the rocking chair. "Stella, you're just like Cele."

"Thanks." I grinned.

"Sheesh." Gibb's head fell forward, and he ran his fingers through his hair, leaving it in disarray. He stood, and my heart thumped in my chest afraid he was going to walk away, but he tugged a small notebook out of his back pants pocket. There was a short pencil stub caught in the wire spiral.

"Okay. Give me the names."

"Sherri Bane and Harley Morgan."

His pencil scratched against the paper. "I'm already checking out your new neighbor. Should have something by morning." He stuffed the pages back into his pocket. "Anything else I can do for you, Agatha?"

I ignored his sarcasm, letting him save face.

"I've come up with an interesting theory. Like you, I was thinking that Tom wanted Mom's business out of Mountaintops, but what if he wanted all of this," I spread my arms wide, "for himself? What if the protest over the business is just the means, the excuse, to accomplish the other?"

"Why?"

"Huh?"

"There would have to be a reason, Sis. Why would a rich man like Tom need Mom's property? He could afford to buy any land on the mountain that he wanted." Gibb fished his finger under his collar, released the button, and loosened his tie.

It was brown, part of the uniform, and the tie tack was a miniature badge. "This place is beautiful, but not the best five hundred acres on the mountain."

"I don't know. I hadn't thought it through," I admitted.

"There's a reason why cops pay attention to motive," Gibb said, sounding too smug.

"The problem is, someone I love has motive, but he won't talk to me about it," I said, digging my heels in for a fight.

"I told you before, Stella, to lay off that subject."

"Lori told me that Tom and Mom had an affair years ago, but Mom denies it. So we know what the truth is."

"You're right. They didn't. Case closed."

"Sure. You and I know Mom wouldn't lie to us, but what's everyone else going to think? How many people has Lori told the story to? Is Lori lying, or did Tom lie to her?"

Gibb shrugged.

"Were Lori and Christine really together the evening of the murder? And for how long?"

"A neighbor of Tom and Lori's was out walking his dog and saw Christine drive by going toward their house right before dark. He saw Christine clearly and says she went up the driveway and then he heard her and Lori talking. Christine and Lori both say they were together for hours. It covers the time Doc believes the murder was committed."

"But we can't be sure when Christine really left."

"I have to have proof otherwise. I'm talking to everyone and asking questions." Gibb moved to stand beside me and dropped an arm over my shoulder. "We both want the same thing—Mom safe and her name cleared."

Laughter erupted from the yard, and I watched as Lam taught Julie a square dance move. The other women forgot their marshmallows and circled the pair, clapping a beat. Lam moved to take the arm of elderly Mrs. Helm and did a do-si-do. She moved well with her skirt flapping as she high-stepped.

"Gibb, I know you're working hard, but maybe you're too close to the problem. You know, too close because of Lori."

"That's what the mayor and city council told me today." Fatigue and irritation edged his voice.

"Are you worried about your job?" I asked, wishing I'd been more sensitive to his problems these last few days.

"Not really. Clearing Mom is more important. Way more important. I'm just glad she's out of jail. I hated seeing her behind bars, but she was safer there. It's not like Sewanee has some kind of FBI safe house I could hide her out in."

"It kept her out of your hair."

Gibb laughed, and some of the worry eased from his features.

"Now I just need to get you to go home. That incident this morning scared the life right out of me. I'd throw you in jail if I could."

I looked away from his gaze.

"You're not going back to Nashville, are you?"

"Nope."

Movement at the edge of the forest caught my eye. A kitten moved cautiously past the party, its black body barely visible against the darkness of the woods.

"Smoky," I said.

"Not so bad now the wind has died down," Gibb said.

Could this little black cat be my neighbor's lost pet? Returning Harley Morgan's missing Smoky would give me an excuse to question him, but I'd bet Gibb would nix the idea if he knew what I wanted to do.

"Oh yeah. It has calmed. Look, Gibb, it's late. Aren't you ready to leave?"

He gave me a suspicious stare. "Are you trying to get rid of me?"

"No. I'm tired. I thought I'd turn in early tonight." I stretched my arms until the shoulder joints popped and then gave a fake yawn.

"It's only seven," Gibb said as he snapped his sleeve back to check his watch.

"Well, it's not every day someone tries to murder me," I said.

"You're taking that awfully well. You even sound cheerful."

"I am cheerful that I'm alive. The problem of finding out who tried to squash me will just have to take a place in line behind other concerns."

I sat tight in my seat until Gibb left after talking for a minute to Lam. The second he was out of sight, I ran to where I'd seen the cat.

"Kitty. Smoky. Here, kitty, kitty."

The cat spit at my outstretched hand and ran under the porch. I scrunched down on my knees and elbows, butt high in the air, and tried to peer through a small gap between the ground and the wooden lattice that decorated the skirt of the porch. The green glow of two eyes stared back from the darkness.

"What are you looking at?" Lam asked.

"A cat, and don't stare at my butt," I said.

"Too late."

"How do I get it to come out?"

"They go under there a lot to get away from Doodle Dog when he gets in a mood."

"No. This isn't one of Mom's cats. It's a kitten. I think maybe it belongs to the new neighbor." I twisted my head so that I could see Lam. "What do you mean Doodle Dog gets in a mood?"

There was a growl off to my left as Doodle came tearing around the corner of the house, bowled Lam off his feet, and then dived under the lattice. Fortunately, the dog didn't fit through the narrow space and was now jammed halfway under the porch. From underneath came the sounds of the kitten howling and spitting in fear.

I could imagine what it looked like from the poor kitten's point of view. A fifty-pound dog, seemingly all teeth, ready to eat him.

Lam rolled to his knees, and we each grasped one of Doodle Dog's hind legs.

"Pull," Lam said.

Doodle Dog wasn't cooperating. For every tug backward he scrambled forward an inch, kicking at our hands and throwing up the loose soil into our faces.

"Doodle! Doodle!" I screamed, spitting out a mouthful of dirt.

"See, this is why the cats hide here. He doesn't fit," Lam said over the noise.

He grunted, gave a final tug, and pulled a growling Doodle Dog free. Lam grasped the struggling dog in a bear hug.

"I'll put him in the garage until he calms down." Lam rose awkwardly with his burden and hurried away before Doodle could escape.

There was a rustling noise from under the porch, and

the kitten shot past the lattice and into my arms, but only because I was blocking the escape route. A collective *aw* sounded from the other women. They'd abandoned the bonfire to watch the show and now stood in a semicircle at my back.

Julie rushed forward. "Oh, he's so cute."

Mrs. Helm said, "Poor thing is scared half to death."

"Look at how he's shaking," Claire said.

The kitten trembled in my arms as it weakly tried to burrow under my sweatshirt.

"I'd better take him home right now." I started off to where my car should have been parked before realizing it was resting in peace at the salvage yard. I glanced at the darkening sky. If I hurried, I'd have just enough time to take the direct route through the woods to the old Abbott cabin before it became too dark to see. I could talk Harley into giving me a ride home. He owed me one anyway.

"Ladies, tell Lam I'll be back in about thirty minutes. I've got to return Smoky to his owner."

I slipped into the woods at the point on the edge of the yard where I remembered the old path began. As kids, Gibb and I had used it often to visit with the grandchildren of Carl and Ida Abbott. We'd played from dawn to dusk there many a time.

There were more branches and brambles than thirty years ago though. After a few minutes of walking, I decided it would be best to turn back and ask Lam to give me a ride. Safer, too. What if Harley Morgan had been at the controls of that dozer this morning? I had no idea who had tried to kill me. Maybe Gibb was right that I was a magnet for trouble. Could it have something to do with making rash decisions?

The kitten stirred in my arms but quieted when I tightened my hug and rubbed the soft fur.

I turned in a circle. Where was the path? The low-growing huckleberry bushes closed in behind me, and the trees, still half full of dying leaves, hid any view of the house. I shuffled my feet through the leaves, trying to find the beaten path by feel.

The light was dying quicker under the cover of the forest, and the cool of evening made me shiver and wish I'd taken time to grab a jacket, but I could feel the warmth from little Smoky's body. It comforted me, given that my fear grew with each passing minute at the thought that I was lost. I moved again in what I hoped was the right direction. If it wasn't, I'd cross a road soon and follow it back home. I realized I could never truly be lost in these woods. I knew them so well. I was only temporarily misplaced as I readjusted to the mountain.

What was that noise?

I spun on my heel. Hoot. Just an owl. Did owls cough? I ran blindly, snagged my sleeve on a branch, and left part of the fabric waving in my wake. Another low-hanging branch swiped my hair into my eyes, leaving me blind.

The forest parted, and I found myself racing across the yard of the old Abbott cabin. Inviting light flowed from the windows, and I kept moving until I was standing on the porch, panting and pounding on the door before I had time to gather my wits.

A yellow light bulb above my head blazed, and then the pine panel swung open.

"Stella?" Harley stood with his mouth open. "Did you have another accident?"

"Accident? What are you talking about?"

"Uh, well, your hair. And your shirt. And, well, dirt." Harley stuttered to a halt and reached out to finger the torn edge of my sweatshirt sleeve.

"Oh." With my free hand I tried to push my hairdo into some semblance of order. A couple of leaves were caught in my hair. I pulled them free, letting them drift to the porch floor.

Harley, out of his church clothes, was dressed in faded jeans, a flannel shirt, and old moccasins. He looked right at home in this log cabin. His look of dismay changed to a smile as he realized I wasn't hurt. I found that I liked the dimples that contrasted with the strong chin.

"I found your cat," I said, hoping to steer the conversation away from my appearance.

"Cat?"

"Smoky." I'd swear the man had forgotten all about his pet.

"Oh, yeah, Smoky." He peeked around the doorframe looking for the animal then stepped back and motioned for me to enter the living room.

I had pulled the hem of my shirt over the kitten to keep him calm. The animal seemed to enjoy the security that co-coon formed in the crook of my arm. I tugged the cover away, and Smoky shrieked. The cat leapt from my arms and landed on Harley's chest. Harley staggered back a step and gave a bellow that terrified the cat even further. In turn, Smoky climbed up his chest and over his shoulder, using that perch to launch across to a shelf on the wall behind Harley.

Three figurines crashed as the cat scurried the length of the ledge and then jumped to cling with unsheathed claws to the curtains. Smoky left a shredded path of destruction all the way to the valance. The kitten came to rest clinging to the mounting bracket.

The poor creature gave a final wail of distress.

"Wow, you really know how to make an entrance, Stella." Harley looked down at his shirt and stretched the plaid away from his chest. It was torn and picked. He smoothed it back in place.

I threw both hands over my mouth in embarrassment, and my breath caught in my throat. All I could get out was a strangled sob.

Harley placed his hands on my shoulders. "Hey, it's okay. I was going to replace the drapes anyway. And, well, the porcelains, antique Hummels, so what. And the shirt, ventilation gives it that comfortable feeling."

"You're not angry?" I asked.

Harley glanced over his shoulder, maybe fearful the cat would attack again. "Why would I be angry?"

When he looked back to me, his face showed a genuine expression of puzzlement. I glanced past my neighbor and surveyed the damage.

My eyes narrowed. "Smoky doesn't seem to recognize you."

"Huh? Oh, I'd just gotten him from the shelter. You know, the same day he ran away."

I glowered probably more now with the realization that I was alone in the man's house. Very alone since no one knew where I was. The ladies could only tell Lam that I'd gone to return the kitten. Then I realized that he would know there was only one house I would walk to. The tension in my shoulders relaxed a bit.

"The kitten's really sweet, I mean, when he's calm," I said.

Harley glanced up at Smoky again but the best he could manage was a wary grimace. He cleared his throat. "Would you like something to drink? I was having a beer."

"Sure," I said, but then quickly realized I was pushing my luck at this point. I didn't want Lam to break down Harley's door when I didn't return quickly. I'd just ask for a ride home and quiz Harley while he drove. "Uh, maybe I'd better get home. I'm pretty tired tonight after, well you know, you were there."

"Quite exciting. How about if we walk through the woods?" He arched an eyebrow waiting on my answer.

"Sure."

CHAPTER 23

I managed for once to wake up with my alarm and wise-ly did not hit the snooze button on my phone. Racing to the shower, I thought about how yesterday had ended much more pleasantly than it had begun. I savored the memory of my walk through the woods with Harley. It had been unde-niably romantic. I'd even forgotten to ask the man any ques-tions about what he was doing here in Sewanee. Mostly, I answered his inquires. Harley had wanted to know all about me.

The memory brought a flush to my cheeks.

After dressing quickly, I found the keys to Lam's Range Rover hanging on the hook by the kitchen door. I snatched them up and left. With any luck, he would never know I'd borrowed his SUV.

I knew the hardware store opened early to accommodate the work hours of farmers and contractors. I should be able to snoop around and ask questions then be back before class started at nine, although I'd probably miss breakfast.

I drove out of Mountaintops and turned onto the two-lane for the short trip to town. If I'd blinked, I would have missed it, being that Sewanee was only four blocks long. First came the *Piggly Wiggly*, the largest building in the downtown, and then a dress shop followed by a jewelry store. There was the tiny furniture outlet and Dr. Clark's office, which he shared with a dentist, and then a few other nondescript stores that each seemed to go out of business at least once a year. The second block sported the fabric store where Mimi also sold used children's clothing. *JoAnn's Café* was next door. The police station ended the real downtown while Tom's hardware business was a spit down the road as the local's described the distance.

Turning off Main Street into the *Feed and Tool* parking lot, I noticed it was almost full, mostly with pickups. I circled to see if Christine's large Mercedes was present. It wasn't. I couldn't resist a sigh of relief.

Once inside the long, low building, I walked up and down the aisles, pretending to look at merchandise. The use for most of the items, jumbled in bins or crowded onto dusty shelves, was beyond my comprehension. I picked up an object and turned it over and over in my hands.

"You need a transformer to go with the ballast?"

I juggled the thingamajig and whirled around toward the voice, which had startled me. The man wore a denim shirt with his name, Presley, embroidered above the pocket.

"Yeah, give me two." I said.

"And two ballasts?"

"Uh, no, only one toilet is leaking." Didn't a toilet tank have a ballast?

"You need a man to install your ballast?" He leered and slicked back dark, obviously dyed, hair. He did it with an unconscious movement, stiff-fingered, only the palms touching his head.

I almost turned and stalked away until I remembered why I was there. "Have you worked here long?" I asked.

"Long enough to know what that is." Presley took the item from my hand, letting his fingers linger against my skin. "How about we meet for a beer after I get off work, sugar?"

"Maybe. I do need some help now though. I was wondering how Christine and Tom Billings were getting along lately? I mean before he died." I leaned forward in what I hoped was a seductive way. The move seemed to be working as Presley's gaze landed on my bust line and didn't budge from the exposed cleavage.

"Fine. That is, if you think a bear and a pole cat enjoy spending time together." He snickered.

"That good? I hear they were co-owners of the business. Do you know who inherited Tom's half?"

Presley edged closer until his arm brushed my breast. His breath smelled of chewing tobacco. He said, "I hear it was the new wife. She's a looker."

"Is she working here now? I mean, like Christine does?"

"Ain't seen her. Why do you want to know all this, sugar?"

"Just curious."

"You're a detective, I bet." He snapped his fingers. "One of them PI types."

"That's right."

He grinned and slicked his coiffure again. The style was one that hadn't been seen for over fifty years. I think it had been called duck tails.

"Was anything weird going on lately?"

He considered the question, rolling his eyes up as he pondered. "Tom'd taken up golf. Used to like hunting, but I think the new wife was trying to civilize ol' Tom."

He scratched his head, mussing the pompadour. "She wouldn't let him wear his overalls when they took the golf lessons. She bought him all kinds of fancy duds in Nashville." He rolled his eyes. "One day ol' Tom came in trying to keep his hands hidden. Had himself a man-a-cure." He drew the word out.

Suddenly, a loud voice cut across the store. "Who parked that skip loader in my parking space?" Christine blazed into the store. "Elvis!"

I jumped, then peered through the rungs of several stacked ladders toward the front of the store. When I looked back to Presley, the man was crouched as if he were trying to hide behind me. The sleazy pick-up artist had morphed into a six-foot kid caught by the teacher. The beady dark eyes were shifting side to side while the piece of hardware he still held twisted in his thick fingers.

"Oh, she's mad." Presley moaned.

"Did you park the skip whatever it is in her spot?"

"Yup, but it wouldn't matter if I was innocent. Mrs. Billings will take it out on whichever one of us guys she catches first. She just likes it to be me."

Christine stalked across the store and men, big and burly, tall and stringy, ran diving for cover.

"Is she really that mean?" I asked, but realized I was talking to air as I caught a fleeting glimpse of Mr. Presley slinking around the end of the row. He duck-walked to prevent his head from rising over the top of the metal shelves where Christine might see him.

I watched the woman's progress while wondering if there would be a way for me to sneak out without her seeing me. It seemed everyone had reason to avoid the woman. I noticed then that someone followed along behind Christine. Harley! Was this chance, or had they arrived together? Harley placed a hand on Christine's shoulder and spoke while leaning close to her ear. Obviously together.

My cheeks burned. Now more than ever I wanted to escape without being seen. The memory of how much I'd enjoyed talking to Harley last night flared up. The man had made me feel downright special plying me with questions about growing up on the plateau. He'd said life on the mountain fascinated him. He'd even flirted, telling me he found me interesting. It hadn't been until Harley had dropped me off at the front door of the cabin that I'd realized I had failed to learn a single scrap of information about the man.

Christine moved closer, and I decided to exit through the door that led to the back storeroom. A sign announced EMPLOYEES ONLY. My escape was only about five feet away, but I had to cross an aisle where I might be seen. As I tried to stand from my awkward squatting position, I lost my balance. My hands flapped, seeking support, and I grabbed at the rung of one of the stacked ladders, causing it to pivot. For a second, it swayed as if unable to decide which direction to fall.

I heard Christine snort and Harley gasp as the extension ladder toppled toward a stack of feed sacks. At least now they seemed so busy watching the show that they weren't looking at me. The soft burlap bags seemed a safe landing spot. The rungs thumped and bounced, causing the top sack to split, and dried corn to go skidding across the concrete floor.

In the confusion, I scurried across the aisle, unseen I hoped, and pushed through one of the double swinging doors. I turned back for a last peek though when I heard a gurgled scream. A farmer had walked in and slipped on the hard kernels. For a second he danced, arms cartwheeling, and then the lanky fellow fell backwards into a display of dog food. The bags at least cushioned his fall.

I ran, leaving the back door swinging in my wake. I crossed the storage space, overflowing with boxes, stacked salt blocks, and pallets of fifty-pound sacks of animal feed, and jumped off the loading dock. It was a quick sprint around the corner of the building to Lam's vehicle.

I didn't think either Christine or Harley saw me. As I sped away, I wondered what my new favorite neighbor was doing meeting with her. Were they friends? Was I just too suspicious of everyone now that my mind was tuned to murder?

Wait a minute. Presley. I'd heard Christine call out Elvis. Hadn't Mom said something about the delivery man having hair that looked as if it had been dyed with shoe polish? Elvis fit the bill, and he happened to work for Christine Billings. I needed to pass that information to Gibb.

Wait another minute. In my haste to leave I had exited the parking lot going the wrong way. I yanked the steering wheel hard and pulled the SUV into a U-turn. The big vehicle couldn't make as tight a turn as my little station wagon, and the outer wheels bounced hard in the ditch, rattling my teeth.

I jerked the tires back onto the asphalt and continued toward Tracy City. That was where Mrs. Bertha Hopkins, Lori's mother, lived, unless she'd moved from the small, run-down country house where she'd raised three children.

I made a quick trip of it. As I rolled down the driveway, which was just bare tracks worn through the scraggly lawn, I realized the house looked far worse than I remembered. Lam's vehicle probably cost more than the home was worth.

It was a small rancher with mossy aluminum siding and crank-out metal-framed windows. One of the steps was missing a board so I had to hop up and over without the aid of the handrail. It looked as if only hope was holding it upright. I forced myself to cross the rickety porch and knocked on the door.

"Thanks, Bertha," I said accepting a seat on a huge blue leather sofa that looked like an off-color elephant in the tiny room. The behemoth barely left space for an old scarred coffee table that nearly touched the giant television hanging on the opposite wall. The Tennessee Morning Show blared, and the host's larger-than-life face blurred at this close distance. His ears looked the size of honey buns. My fingers itched to turn the thing off or at least reduce the volume.

Mrs. Hopkins side-stepped around the furniture to take a seat on the other end of the couch. She dropped her bottom onto the cushion with a sigh.

"Well, what do you think?" she asked.

"Um." To what, I wondered, was she referring? What did I think about her murdered son-in-law? Maybe how did I feel about Mom being the only suspect for that very same murder? But Bertha looked much too cheerful for those topics.

Mrs. Hopkins smiled broadly, showing her dentures and dimples. She waited patiently.

"Go on. Don't be shy, Stella. What do you think?"

I noticed Bertha's hand stroke the supple leather that

stretched between us. The couch was big enough to seat the church choir. Her gaze swung to caress the high-definition screen.

"Oh, hmm, amazing," I said, hoping that would cover the subject.

"It is, isn't it?" She picked up the remote and increased the sound level. "My Lori wanted to buy me all new furniture, but I didn't want to overdo it." Her flip-flop clad foot kicked the coffee table leg, and it wobbled. "I'm a simple country woman. Wouldn't do to put on airs and let my neighbors think I'm a snob."

"Uh, I don't think you have to worry about that, Bertha. I'm sure you've got a lot on your mind right now, I mean, with Tom's death."

"What? Oh, Tom, yeah." Mrs. Hopkins tore her attention from the weatherman's smile. "Him getting killed and all was just like a CSI episode. Only one that's continued. Never did like to be left hanging like that."

"I'm sorry for your loss. I know Lori must be devastated."

"I suppose."

"They were practically newlyweds," I said. "Were they happy?"

Bertha frowned. "You seen their house? There's five TVs. Even got one in the bathroom hanging right over a Jacuzzi with jets. That water shoots every which way but up your nose. Lori let me try it one day." She laughed with the memory that was obviously special to her.

"But her husband's dead."

"Well, I reckon my Lori will be okay. She had to a known he'd go first anyway. His age and all." The woman flashed through the channels, surfing for something interesting as the last show ended.

Shoot. I wished I could sneak a peek at my phone. I was most likely late for class, but so far I hadn't learned anything useful.

"Bertha, what will Lori do now? Do you know?"

"I'm sure she'll be alright. My baby seemed right excited last time I saw her."

"Excited?"

"Said plans were still on track or something like that. You want some popcorn, Stella?"

"No, it's a little too early for me." It was time to be blunt. "What are Lori's plans?"

"Don't rightly know." Bertha laughed. "That girl's always had big dreams. Always talking about the big one. Lord, she sure is taking to decorating and learning that game golf. Never wanted to do all that walking myself."

I stood and edged toward the door. "I've got to go. I'll see you at the funeral."

"Huh? Oh yeah. Reckon. Lori said it should be end of the week. They hung onto the body for an autopsy." She slapped her thigh, gaze glued to the screen. "Don't that beat all."

"Well, see you then, Bertha."

"If it don't rain." She pointed the remote at the TV, already forgetting my presence.

CHAPTER 24

At nine-twenty, I turned the Range Rover into the drive-way and saw that the house had taken on the surreal appearance of a movie set where a mob scene was being filmed. A modern finale of *Frankenstein*. Well, with a smaller mob and no pitch forks, and of course, no burning torches, but a crowd of a dozen or so milled on the stone walkway. These weren't frightened peasants, but judging by how well-dressed they were, I'd guess residents of the Mountaintops community. Lam stood on the top step of the front porch, arms outstretched, palms out, as if to hold them back or part the Red Sea.

From the third story of the house, the students watched with their heads poked out the dormer windows, the women craning their necks and a few leaning precariously over the sills. I thought I saw Mrs. Helm shake her fist at the crowd below, but perhaps she was just waving at my approach.

With my driver's side window down, I heard the sounds of raised voices as I rolled the vehicle to a stop. Before I could step onto the lawn, a shout of "There she is," arose. For a second, I considered running, but I now recognized a few of the faces from the recent homeowners meeting. All were familiar, although there were only two whom I knew beyond chatting about the weather. One of those was Frank Coffee. His stood a head taller than anyone else. He held back, talking to Lam while the group rushed me like ants attacking a picnic. They all talked at once.

"Where is Celestial?"

"Where's your mother?"

"We must speak to Cele."

"She can't hide from her neighbors forever."

"We demand Cele stop or move. Now!"

"Does she think she can make fools of us?"

An ear-splitting whistle from above cut the air and shocked everyone to silence. I looked up to see Julie with two fingers in her mouth ready for another blast if needed. I gave her a thumbs up sign and smiled my thanks.

"Okay, one at a time," I said.

A woman in an expensive cerulean boiled-wool jacket shoved to the front of the pack. "We know Celestial is out of jail, and we want to talk to her. The association is not going to let her expand her business."

"Expand? What are you talking about? Mom's not planning on increasing the size of her business," I said. "Whatever you heard is just a rumor."

One man flapped a magazine in my face to emphasize his words. "You can't deny it any longer now that it is in print."

"What are you people talking about?" I asked, snatching the pages from his hand. I read the title, *Golfing's Best*, printed above a picture of a foursome on the tee. What was it with golf today? This was the third time the topic had come up, and it was still morning.

It had never been a popular sport on the mountain. The townspeople of Sewanee were mostly farmers and tradesmen. They didn't have the time or money for that rich man's game. Only the residents of this upscale subdivision would be interested.

In fact, golf wasn't played on the plateau; there was no course. Most of the land was too steep and rough, except for the very section I was standing on now. The prime land, if someone wanted to lay out eighteen holes, would be right here. Right under my feet. This was the flattest section of Mountaintops, and Cele owned the largest chunk of property.

I flipped the magazine open to where a page had been dog-eared and scanned the caption under the photograph of a man sitting in a golf cart, his sun-weathered face gazing at a distant green, its flag stark white against the lush grass. Seems Bill Bryse was a course designer and developer.

I ran my finger down the column, reading as fast as I could. One question the interviewer asked was what Bryse's next project was to be. His response—Sewanee, Tennessee. The course name *Mountaintop Grand Eighteen*. Golf and luxury homes for the golfers. Rustic luxury homes.

"There isn't a shred of truth to this," I said, my voice starting to sound like a stuck record. I threw the magazine to the ground and gave it a stomp.

"Are you sure, Stella?" asked Mrs. Claymore, who was one of two long-time residents in the crowd. "Maybe Cele's doing this just to make us mad. That's like her."

I remembered that Mom and Mrs. Claymore had never gotten along since her husband had cut down several mature oaks to gain a better view. Mom had spent three days tree-sitting on their property in protest.

"Well, I never. All of you should be ashamed of your-selves." I pushed through the group and hurried to where Frank and Lam stood talking, heads bent together.

"What would Dolly say?" I asked. As usual, my first thought had escaped my lips. I'd always admired the feisty Dolly Parton—maybe too much, if my recent behavior was anything to go by.

"What?" Lam asked, his sandy eyebrows tilting together.

"Stella, I'm sorry for the inconvenience, my dear," Frank said. "I came along in the hopes of keeping things civilized. Looks like I failed." He gave a weary smile and brushed a liver-spotted hand across the bristle of a steel-gray crew cut.

"Frank, what the heck is with these people?"

The tall man linked his arm through mine and drew me several feet away across the grass. He kept our backs to the mob.

"Stella, things have changed at Mountaintops since you've been gone." Frank gazed at the treetops as if the past were laced in the branches, flapping remnants shredded by time and wind. "There are still a few of us around that bought our property from your granddad, but damned few. We have a sense of community. Not these other—" He cleared his throat. "I don't like to speak ill of my neighbors."

"Someone is going to have to explain this to me. Frank, I need to know what's going on so I can help Mom." It might not be fair to the older man to play to his chivalrous nature, but I didn't have a choice. "Cele has always considered you to be one of her best friends."

I watched the war wage in the old soldier's eyes as he decided which side to support.

He chuckled. "You are a lot like your mama, young lady. All right. Mr. Darrington, the stout one, is a big wig from Nashville. Something to do with banking, and he's only lived here two years. He's not opposed to a golf course, but he wants the association to get its cut of any profits. He—everyone here—thinks Cele is trying to pull a fast one. They believe that because she's grandfathered she will make a huge profit, and they're all interested in their share of the pie. Mr. Darrington usually goes down the mountain to play the Manchester Greens."

"When did all this start?"

"About six months ago. Tom Billings blindsided Cele at a meeting and it seems he'd already gotten half the residents on his side. Most of us just ignored her quilting classes all these years. Tom was ready to kick her out that day, but Cele jerked the rug out from under him by saying that she didn't make a profit off the business."

"That's the second time I've heard that, but Mom's never said a word to me. As far as I know, she lives off the income from her teaching."

Frank's shoulders lifted and fell.

"Whatever Cele was trying with that tactic, it slowed them down but hasn't stopped the tide of anger. It's definitely turning against her. Is Cele here?" he asked, looking back at the windows as if trying to catch my mother peeking from behind the curtains.

I placed a hand on his arm. "She really isn't here, Frank.

You know Mom. She'd be out here in the thick of things, not hiding." I wished I could tell Frank where Mom was, but I didn't feel I had the right to reveal her private life to anyone.

"Of course." He nodded. "When will she reappear?"

"She'll be home later today. I'll make sure you're the first person she talks to. I promise." I started to turn away then spun on my heel. "Frank, I think I might have a solution to all this."

"Well, let's hear it, girl. I'm all for fixing this."

"Would the association allow Mom to break this property away from Mountaintops? Since her acreage is on the border of the subdivision, she could put a new drive in from the house to the main road." My hopes fell as I watched Frank frown and shake his head.

"That would probably work except for one tiny problem—Cele's land doesn't actually front the road. The Abbott land stands between here and the road."

"I don't understand. I've seen the map—"

Frank held up a hand to stop me. "You were right up to ten years ago, but that old map has never been updated. There was a little strip of land, between the creek and the road, which was in dispute. To make a long story short, your Grandpa had originally been told by the state to set it aside for an access to a forest service fire road. That was why he didn't actually attach it to either his own or the Abbott's land. But the state never went through with their plans."

"But doesn't Mom own it then?" I asked, watching my brilliant plan fly away.

"Ida had been picking up litter and planting flowers along the roadside for years since Lady Byrd Johnson started the beautification program years ago. Ida asked Cele if she could have it, and your Mother didn't see any reason not to. It was a simple matter of a form at the court house. Because of how the creek runs, it had always seemed more like Ida's front yard anyway."

I sighed. "And Harley Morgan bought Ida out only two months ago?" It was more a comment than a question, but Frank nodded the answer.

As I let the information sink in, I watched Lam work the mob. He charmed the women, one by one, and led them to their cars. By the time he closed a car door on each one, they didn't look quite so determined to burn Cele at the stake—at least not today. Slowly, one BMW, Mercedes, and Lexus at a time, he dispersed the mob. It even appeared Lam could charm men as he and Mr. Darrington shared a hearty hand-shake before he drove off.

I checked my watch. Not even ten. Mom should be back by two. Gibb had offered to drive to Nashville to pick up the newlyweds at the airport. Shue, I was getting a new step-daddy, and I barely knew the man. Of course, I'd known him well enough to ask how he was doing through the years, but I never had a clue that he'd been a big part of Mom's life.

"Frank, do you know Judge Marcum?" I realized I was hungry for some basic information on the man. "Are you friends with him, or have you ever done business with him?"

The older man blushed. "Well, I know him well enough. He and your mama, well, let's say they always did like each other. I expect that's what you're interested in. But truth is they don't get along too well. Different as night and day. Both big personalities that like to butt heads."

He patted me on the arm. "Don't you worry. Mr. Mar-cum's a right good man, but don't be surprised—" Mr.

Coffee smiled broadly, "don't be surprised if that pair doesn't have another spat on the way up to the altar." He cleared his throat in embarrassment. "I, uh, heard the news."

That left my mouth hanging open. Well, I could only hope he was right.

Frank left last. He waved to Lam and me as he backed an older Oldsmobile onto the grass to turn, then pulled back to the gravel drive and disappeared with a final salute.

"He's a gentleman," I said, still thinking over his words. Maybe I had nothing to worry about on that front. I hoped.

Lam didn't appear to be paying any attention to my words. He stared off to where I'd parked his Range Rover.

"Where's my hubcap?" he asked.

Lam turned to loom over me. "You had my SUV for all of an hour, and you already started to dismantle it."

"Uh," I said.

How had this happened? Maybe someone had stolen it while I was in the hardware store. Oh no. I remembered my U-turn and hitting the ditch. I'd have to go back later and look for the hubcap, only I'd have to borrow someone's car to get to town. I hoped the vehicle didn't need an alignment job.

A chorus sounded from above our heads.

"Stella, you're late."

"Let's get class started, Stella."

"Ah, come on, Stella."

"Got to go. Talk to you later, Lam." I bolted up the porch steps and into the house, feeling the man's gaze aimed at my back.

CHAPTER 25

"Uh," I said. "Maybe if we turn this red rectangle this way. Or it looks like this yellow square should be over here."

I shuffled the pieces of fabric again for the twentieth time, sliding them on the slick surface of the Formica tabletop. It seemed that no matter how I tried to arrange the elements of this quilt block it ended up looking like something a three-year-old had planned. Definitely not the work of Celestial Hill, nationally renowned quilt designer.

The students groaned and shifted around the table, each looking for a new vantage point that might provide some enlightenment. We were in the studio, everyone had finished the task of cutting out the pieces of fabric needed to build their mystery quilt, and I was lost. The cotton had finally defeated me. I was incompetent, and my reckoning was just around the corner.

"I kind of liked that last one," Julie said.

"It isn't even a square block." Sherri glared. "You can't have a quilt block with uneven edges."

"Maybe Cele's entering a new phase of design growth. More spiritual, maybe Picasso-like," Jolyn said, hands conducting in the air.

Sherri turned her withering stare from me to Jolyn.

Jolyn sniffed. "Maybe we're not supposed to understand her design elements."

Claire clapped her hands. "It's like a quilting puzzle. A Rubik's Cube even."

"Maybe it's a tessellation." Mrs. Helm bent at the waist to get closer to the block and lifted her glasses slightly so she could gaze through the bifocals.

"A tessel what?" I had no idea what the older woman had just said. "No. I don't think that's it." Whatever Mrs. Helm was talking about, I didn't want to go there.

To avoid Sherri's increasingly questioning stare, I buried my head in the notes I'd taken while in Mom's jail cell. I shuffled the pages again, hoping against hope that the answer would magically appear. Could the page that traveled to Georgia be the one I needed? Or the page Doodle ate?

A bead of sweat rolled slowly down my back, tickling my spine.

Truth be told, I was having trouble concentrating. Harley Morgan's face was, well, in my face. The man kept popping up, like this morning with Christine at the hardware store and at the church in the nick of time and snooping around the yard here the other night. No matter how nice he seemed, and discounting those dimples, Harley turned up too often for it to be coincidence.

That thought reminded me of the kitten. I was pretty sure that cat had never laid eyes on one Harley Morgan, Esq. But Harley had opened a can of tuna to feed the animal before we had left his house. He'd had no pet food in the pantry. Had my neighbor lied to me, or had he really just gotten the animal from the shelter? Part of me wanted to check up on his story, but part of me balked, believing him to be the real thing—a nice guy. Could I be so wrong with my impression of the man?

And Frank had just crushed my hopes for solving one of Mom's problems because of Harley buying the Abbott property. He was literally blocking the road to saving Mom's business.

I felt one of the students move closer to my side.

"I think you should move this here and that one over to this position." Lori's fingers twitched over the fabric. The prints flashed, and when she pulled her slender hands back, the flow of color in her arrangement was pleasing. There was just one problem—the edges were once again uneven. I was pretty sure the result had to be a square. In fact, I remembered Cele saying the blocks were ten-inch squares.

Right now, before the pieces of fabric were sewn to one another, it was larger than the finished result would be. Taking the seams into account though, even I could see that the sides would not be straight. They absolutely had to be straight, and I'd already noticed that there were a couple of extra squares of fabric lying off to the side.

Quilting seams were always a quarter-inch wide. I knew that basic rule and had seen it demonstrated on Mom's videos. Why were quilters so compulsive? If I ever made another quilt, it was going to have nice wide seams. Why not make life easy?

I pushed a print with tiny dots a tad closer to a hot orange print.

"Lori, this can't be right," I said. I looked up at the widow to see tears swimming in her eyes.

"But it looks nice, don't you think? Maybe we could just use what I came up with. All we have to do is cut a half inch off of these pieces." She wiped roughly at her cheeks with the cuff of her sleeve as the tears spilled over.

The other students fell silent.

"I could be a designer like Cele. Or teach like you, Stella. Why doesn't anyone ever take me seriously?" A sob escaped the lips that today were painted with a shade the color of a fresh peony petal. A beautiful china doll playing grown-up.

"I'm sorry, Lori." I couldn't think of how to let her down gently.

Sherri's braying voice cut off my thoughts. "For crying out loud. We're paying good money for the privilege of a real designer's work."

Lori's eyes grew wide as if she'd been slapped. She sprinted from the room.

Julie sighed, and Claire belched a loud humph.

"Well it's true," Sherri said, at least having the decency to look contrite. "I didn't mean to hurt her feelings."

"I'm sorry, ladies. I must still be rattled from that mob this morning." I glanced at my watch. Two-thirty. How much longer could I hold out? Mom would walk through the door any second and save me, wouldn't she? I was just about to use the excuse that I needed to run after Lori so I could delay my downfall when Lam stepped through the doorway.

"Break time." He slid his burden of two carafes and a

plate onto the table and rubbed his hands together. "These cinnamon buns are hot out of the oven. I didn't want y'all to miss this. Decaf and here's regular." He passed paper cups around, but when I reached for one he leaned in and whispered in my ear, "Gibb is in the kitchen. Needs to talk to you." He brushed his lips across my ear lobe.

"Oh." I jumped at his touch. "Is Mom here?"

Lam avoided meeting my eyes and ignored my question.

"No!" I gripped Lam's arm. "Don't tell me she didn't come back with Gibb."

"She didn't come back."

"Aargh. I told you not to tell me." I swiped the pieces of fabric into a pile and shoved them into my pocket. Then I grabbed a sticky pastry off the plate and ran from the room. "Please let this be a joke," I mumbled around a bite of the sweet treat. I'd missed lunch.

When I skidded into the kitchen, Gibb was standing at the back door looking through the screen. From outside I heard a car engine roar to life then fade into the distance. Lori?

"What'd you do to Lori?" Gibb turned, rolled his shoulders under a plaid shirt, and shoved his hands into jeans pockets.

I glanced around the kitchen, but I knew already that this wasn't some cruel joke by Gibb and Lam. Our mother wasn't here. He started to speak, but I held up the cinnamon bun and, with my mouth full, said, "No. Not yet." I flopped onto one of the chairs and finished my dessert. "Get me a glass of milk, Gibb." I licked sugar glaze off my fingers.

He smiled. "Don't you want to hear the story?"

"Not yet. Milk first."

My little brother poured me a full glass and slid it and a napkin in front of me. Gibb sat down at the opposite end of the table, slouching like a teenager.

As I downed half the glass, Lam entered the kitchen and moved to the sink, propping his hip against the soapstone ledge. He grinned and crossed his arms over his chest.

"She's awfully calm. Did you tell her?" Lam asked Gibb.

"She's not ready yet."

I wiped the back of my mouth with my hand, ignoring the paper napkin. "Okay. Now."

"Snow," Gibb said.

"Snow in Las Vegas?" I choked on my second drink of milk.

"No. Snow in Chicago. They had a layover."

"I haven't had time to watch television since I got here. How much snow?" I asked.

Lam replied in a syrupy drawl. "I believe they measure it in feet up North."

I stuck my tongue out. "Did they get married?" For the first time I realized I didn't want my mom to take that step with a man I didn't know and especially without me there. I wanted to be a part of any ceremony so important to her life. I'd always pictured myself as her bridesmaid, just as I wanted her to be mine.

"Nope. She backed out. I have to admit I'm kind of glad," Gibb said. "Judge Marcum is a nice guy, but—" He finished his remark with a shrug.

I shifted my gaze to Lam.

"I'll stay and help out till Cele gets back," he said. "Heck, I said I'm staying until this whole thing is settled, and I meant it."

"I appreciate that, Lam," Gibb said. "I feel better knowing you're here. Sewanee still has a murderer roaming loose."

"And we have no idea when Mom will be back?" I asked.

"The lady at the airline counter said they might be able to start flights out again tomorrow morning."

"You'd think Mom would call me?" I could hear the whine in my voice, and I didn't like it. "Stop it."

Gibb threw his hands up. "I didn't do anything."

"Oh, not you. You either." I glanced at Lam. "It's this stupid quilt."

"How hard can it be?" Gibb asked.

I tried to spear him with a glare. "As hard as finding a murderer."

"Touché," said Lam.

"Alright," Gibb said, "I know this must be tough for you. Mom just makes it look easy."

"My life would be so much shooting better if I could just find that silly sample quilt."

"I know you tore the living room apart looking for it. I saw the results. Mrs. Cabel dragged me in there this morning to complain. I'm supposed to talk to you about your problem or beat you. I'm not sure which."

Mrs. Cabel normally cleaned twice a week, but during camp time she hit the student rooms for half a day every morning. She wasn't happy that I was a tad less neat than Mom.

I sighed.

"I know. She explained yesterday, in great length, how Mom has a place for everything and everything is in its place." My voice took on a sing-song rhythm in a mocking imitation of the woman, which caused Lam to whoop.

"Still haven't found the quilt?" Lam asked, wiping his eyes.

"It's not in this house. I even checked the basement last night." I shivered remembering my venture to the dungeon. With memories of being shoved down the steps still fresh, it hadn't been easy for me, even with every light blazing, Doodle Dog by my side, and a backup flashlight in my hand. "I was going to check the garage this morning before the mob distracted me."

"I don't understand. How could it have just disappeared?" Lam asked. "Do you think one of the students could have stolen it? Maybe it's tucked in someone's suitcase."

Gibb asked, "You want me to get warrants and search everyone's luggage?" His eyes crinkled at the corners.

"I don't think that's the answer. Mom said the little sample was in the office, and it's been locked up tight the whole time." I snapped the stretchy band against my wrist. "I opened the door and let Mrs. Cabel in this morning for an hour, but she's trustworthy. Mom says on her off time she guards the gates of hell."

Both men roared with laughter. When they finally quieted, Lam said, "I agree. It's not Mrs. Cabel."

"Now don't get mad, Gibb," I said. "I know you're working as hard as you can, but we've got to clear Mom's name."

Gibb rubbed the heels of his palms against his eyes and then met my gaze. "I'm not mad. Just frustrated. At this point I'd appreciate all the help you both can give me."

"We've also got to save Mom's business." I told Gibb about the mob that had descended on us this morning.

"Those fools." Gibb's fist thumped the table. "But let's leave worrying about that till later. The murder is what matters."

I didn't want to argue with him. I knew that when he thrust his jaw out in a good imitation of our mother, like he was doing now, that there was no changing his mind. Gibb obviously didn't think there was a connection, but I was convinced of it. The missing sample quilt had become the key to the puzzle. At least in my mind.

"I wish I could talk to Ida Abbott. Poor thing," I said with a sniffle.

"It's not that far off," Gibb said.

"What? You mean the mountain being closer to heaven than the rest of the world?" I asked, wondering why he was talking like a fool.

Gibb shook his head. Had I said something else incredibly stupid?

"She's just down the road," Gibb said.

"Sewanee Cemetery?"

"Sis, that's cruel. It's a nursing home."

I put my hand out, palm toward Gibb. "What? Are you telling me Ida's not dead?"

"Dope, why did you think she'd passed? Nobody said that."

"Shoot. Ida always said she'd never leave the cabin unless she was carried out dead," I said, feeling my cheeks glowing. "I just assumed." I looked from one to the other. "You guys just said she was gone."

Lam said, "She wanted to stay in her own home, but she realized it was getting too hard on her daughter, running back and forth and all to take care of her. Ida's in Sewanee Nursing Home."

I found the phone book and dialed the number. It took several minutes after the receptionist said she'd take a portable phone to Ida's room before a shaky voice said hello.

After identifying myself, I took time to exchange pleasantries. While chatting, I fiddled with the elements of the quilt block and watched Gibb eat a cinnamon bun while Lam passed the time drinking a beer.

"Ida, I'd like to come by and visit with you in a few days." I bit my lip, feeling bad for using an old lady, but I really did plan to stop and see my old neighbor. "I'm curious about something though, Ida. Did you have your cabin on the market for long?"

Ida told me she hadn't even hired a realtor. Someone had come to her with the offer.

"Stella, honey, it was a sign from God that I was supposed to move. Right out of the blue, I tell you. A good price. Right fair. My Alice said it was twice what the place is worth."

"Who was this person, Ida?" I tried to keep my voice calm, despite my hyperventilating.

"It was a funny name. Um. Like that motorcycle. Honda. No. Oh, Harley. Harley Morgan."

CHAPTER 26

"Stella, you're not making any sense." Gibb slammed his car door.

I jerked my hand back when he almost caught my fingers against the frame. Today he was driving his own car, a vintage Mustang, since he had had to drive to Nashville to the airport.

"Quit being a jerk and roll this window down." I banged my fist against the glass. While he turned the crank with jerky strokes, I forced deep breaths through my nose until I was sure I could speak calmly.

"Okay, Brother, you're the sheriff. So you don't think Harley buying Ida's house means anything. I'll accept that." I crossed my arms over my chest, gripping my elbows as if I were staving off a cold wind.

"Did you find out anything interesting with those background checks?" I smiled, remembering all the mornings on the school bus when I had talked Gibb into trading lunch bags with me. He'd never caught on that I had already stashed the dessert in my book bag. Through the years it added up to a lot of oatmeal cookies courtesy of my little brother. No wonder he had remained trim while I still wore his calories.

"I don't know why you're smiling. I don't want to know what's spinning in your head," he said. "Sherri Bane is just what you told me she was. One arrest for drunk driving. Our neighbor Harley is a big-time lawyer. Lives—excuse me— lived in Memphis."

"That's all you got on him? Seriously, Gibb, I think you should talk to that guy Presley who works for Christine. He dyes his hair, and I bet he knows how to drive a dozer." I leaned my hip against the car.

Gibb reached out the window and pushed me away. "Careful of the paint job. Since when did it become suspicious for someone to dye their hair?"

"Mom said the man who delivered the package looked as if his hair had been colored with shoe polish. And Presley is terrified of Christine."

Gibb rolled his eyes. "I wish Mom had thought to tell me that detail. Every one of the guys who works for Christine is scared of the woman. She's a first-class witch. She carries a big broom, at least as far as her employees are concerned."

"That's obvious. But how far would Presley go to keep his job? Would he break the law? Would he try to kill me?" I paused. "But I can't see him killing Tom."

"Me either, but I'll talk to him."

He leaned forward and inserted the key in the ignition, impatient to leave. I rested my hand on his shoulder.

"Gibb, what's going on with you and Lori? Please talk to me.

Both Lam and I have seen you with her. If we have, others will."

A muscle in his jaw bunched. Without a word he turned the engine over. The deep rumble of four-hundred horsepower drowned any chance of my being heard as he pulled away.

I watched the humpback of the old car disappear down the drive with a last flash of sunlight glinting off the polished chrome.

Gibb was nobody's fool. So why was he allowing the widow to play him for one? Was his involvement with her innocent or in the line of duty? Why wouldn't he talk to me?

"Fool," I said, as slipped back into the house letting the screen door bang closed behind me.

Lam looked up from his seat at the table. "Me? What'd I do?"

"Not you. My idiot brother. He refuses to talk to me about Lori." I flopped onto a chair and slid down until my spine gave a pop of protest.

"Um. Maybe it is police business and he can't talk." Lam shuffled the pieces of fabric I'd laid out as if they were a child's puzzle.

"If you can come up with a workable quilt block, I'll—" My voice trailed off when Lam's head jerked up and a wolfish grin spread across his lips.

"You'll what? Don't make empty promises, Stella."

"I'm desperate, Lam. How long do you think those cinnamon buns will hold the ladies?"

He laughed. "They'll be looking for you any second now."

"I've got to make another phone call. Can you hold them off for me?"

"No way." Lam shifted two rectangles in the block. "I've

got an appointment to look at a couple of houses."

"You're going to buy a house?"

"Sure. I've been looking off and on for a few months." Then he added as an afterthought. "Dad's selling his house. He's going to move down to Manchester with lucky soon-to-be Wife Number Six. She has a house from her Ex Number Three."

"Why don't you buy it?" I asked. "I mean your dad's, not the ex's, uh, I mean not the soon-to-be's. He'd give you a good price, wouldn't he?"

"Still too expensive. He's asking around five hundred thousand."

I tried to recall his Dad's house. Hadn't seemed so special that it would go for half a million.

"I'll make this call quick," I said, punching in the number for a friend of mine in Nashville who was a lawyer. Then I casually edged into the dining room for some privacy. I felt uncomfortable asking questions about Harley in front of Lam.

Gail answered, and after I'd asked my question, said, "Morgan? Of course, every litigator east of the Mississippi knows of Harley Morgan. Why are you asking about him?"

"He's my new neighbor," I said.

"Oh, that's interesting, and did you know, Stella, that he's single?"

All my married friends were always trying to introduce me to potential date material. I was the only one in my old circle of friends who wasn't married.

"I'll have to remember that. Tell me more."

"Well, he's never been married, and he has a bit of a reputation as a heartbreaker."

"Gail, I mean his work. Tell me more about him professionally," I sighed.

"Oh. He works out of Memphis. He's got a big firm he took over from his daddy and, get this, his mama. They call her the Southern Barracuda. About a dozen partners and twice as many associates. They mostly handle day-to-day work for companies large enough to have international affairs, but Harley specializes in anything he thinks is interesting that will get him in the news. But I heard just a few days ago he's retiring. All very sudden and mysterious."

"Retiring? He looks way too young for that. Thirty-nine. Forty. "

"That sounds about right. Word is he's tired of the rat race, and anyway the money will continue to roll in from the firm. That's how it works."

I glanced into the kitchen to make sure Lam wasn't paying attention to my conversation. He continued to work on arranging the pieces of the quilt block. The current attempt looked interesting.

"Thanks, Gail," I said.

"Tell me. Is he as good-looking as I've heard? I mean, in person."

I paused. "Yes, definitely." I thought my old friend deserved some tidbit for helping me out. "He has dimples."

"Oh. I'm swooning. Let me know if anything develops." She said. "Catch you later."

Once I'd said good-bye, I placed a hand on Lam's shoulder and leaned over the table. "That's it. That's the pattern! How'd you do that?" I said, my voice raised with excitement. It looked like the same arrangement Lori had made, except the sides were straight, every side lined up to form a neat square.

"Only thing is you'd have to trim about a half inch off

these pieces." Lam lifted the corner on one rectangle to show how he had overlapped the pieces of fabric to achieve a square block.

"Oh well, at this point that sounds like a reasonable solution."

CHAPTER 27

Eugena Colley took a curve so fast the tires squealed, leaving me clinging to the door handle not sure whether it would be safer to remain a passenger in her car or jump from the moving vehicle.

"Eugena, aren't you worried about hitting a deer?" I asked from the back seat after I got my breath back.

"They'll get out of the way." The realtor's laugh would make a mule, or Sherri Bane, envious.

Eugena not only drove too fast but tended to favor the middle of the road. An approaching pick-up, swerving to avoid us, clipped a branch. Anyone who had ever thought I was a bad driver would have to admit I wasn't the worst. But Eugena was a snappy dresser, flaunting a red sequined jacket that I seriously coveted.

"Now, what was I saying?" Eugena lit a cigarette with the car lighter and sucked hard on the filter. "Lam, I'm sure you'll like some of the other houses I can show you. I didn't realize, hon, that you'd won the lottery, so that first place was way too small and simple. I've got several in mind already with a lot more to offer. Granite. Spas. Chef-worthy kitchens. Now we're in a whole new ball game." She jammed the lighter back into the dash, taking her eyes off the road too long for my comfort.

Lam glanced over his shoulder at me and waggled his eyebrows.

A minute ago I'd heard, with my own ears, Lam tell Eugena the biggest whopper I've ever heard. The man actually told her that he'd hit the Millionaire's Raffle and wanted to see bigger houses now that he was rich. I wasn't sure what Lam was up to. This had to have been planned. In fact, Lam had been the one to suggest I call Mimi to ask if she'd come over for an impromptu class on appliqué. Too convenient, but I was curious as to what Lam wanted me to see.

"I believe the Billings place just came on the market yesterday, and I heard Lori might be interested in a quick sale," Lam said. "I looked on one of those real estate sites and saw a nice house for sale on Top o' the Cliff Ave. How about letting me see those two, Eugena?"

I slapped my hand over my mouth at the mention of going into Lori's house. Surely the realtor would think that too strange to allow, but she agreed immediately to Lam's request. Eugena, either unaware or not caring that my mother was the person accused of turning Lori into a widow, whipped the car into a U-turn.

Barely a mile later, she braked hard, guiding the car into a driveway hidden beside a thick stand of rhododendron. Her teased hair never moved.

The car lurched to a stop an inch from one door of a three-car garage. Lam offered his hand to help me from the back seat. I crawled from the depths and stood for a moment swaying on wobbly legs. When I finally looked around, I gasped at my first view of the Billings home.

"This place is a monstrosity." I slapped my hand over my mouth but too late. The insult was out.

Lam hid a laugh by clearing his throat.

Eugena's eyes narrowed to slits. "Now, Stella, this place has loads of extras and endless potential. This way."

The woman strutted up the walk toward the entry of double doors, a look that had been popular in the early seventies. The flat panels were painted black and each had an oversize round brass doorknob in its center.

The primary building material of the structure appeared to be concrete. Slabs of grey, left in an unpainted state, seemed to lean one against the other like a clumsy house of cards. The expanse stretched, long and low, broken only by a few tall, narrow slits of window glass. The house was topped with an almost flat roof of black shingles.

It was certainly an aberration from the rest of the architecture in the Mountaintops subdivision. Over half the homes were log cabins, befitting the heritage of the area. Others were farmhouse styles tending toward natural materials like wood and stone and color schemes that were subtle earth tones.

"Eugena, can you tell me the history of the house?" Lam asked as he watched the realtor first fiddle with her cell phone and then struggle with the lock box hanging from the front door. I guessed she was able to get the combination she'd needed off the Internet.

"Sure, hon. I remember Tom and Christine building this place in seventy-one. It was ol' Tom's wedding gift to his bride." Eugena brayed again as she successfully worked the key in the lock and swung the entry open. "Course, as I understand, Christine designed it. Quite the trendsetter that woman."

"How many square feet?" Lam asked.

He placed his hand on my back and grabbed a handful of shirt, stopping me from following the realtor over the threshold.

"I'll keep Eugena occupied. You look around for clues," Lam whispered in my ear.

"Clues," I said too loudly and peered into the dark interior to see if the woman had overheard.

"Clues, silly. Like the missing quilt," Lam said. "Kind of dark, Eugena. Let's find a light switch." He surged forward and took Eugena's arm, propelling her to the center of the living room.

I entered in time to see Lam follow Eugena through a doorway that probably led to the kitchen. It was just off the area of the open floor plan where a large dining room table sat, hulking brass and glass.

The living room was a flash back in time with an honest-to-goodness conversation pit ringed with steps lined in carpeting. At least the off-white floor covering looked new, and thankfully it wasn't a shag, which I'd guess the original had probably been.

I stumbled down the two steps and dove behind the couch when I heard Eugena and Lam coming back. The realtor's voice filled the room.

"Let's head to the bedrooms, hon. That sunroom looked

brand new." Eugena's next words faded out as the pair moved on in their tour of the house.

I poked my head over the back of the couch. Apparently, Eugena hadn't missed me or didn't care that I wasn't following since Lam was the prospective buyer.

I stood and straightened my shirt, realizing I shouldn't have hidden in the first place. I'd just poke around. Act naïve. Evidently, that was a natural talent of mine.

It was a depressing house, thoroughly dated, and I couldn't picture the new, young bride being satisfied here. It didn't strike me as Lori's style. Why hadn't Lori insisted that they move? What woman would want to live in the previous wife's home anyway?

I scurried across the floor and peeked into the kitchen. Gold-tone appliances and countertops covered in two-inch square ceramic tiles. There was another door from the room opposite an island with a vegetable sink, and I hurried across for a look.

It was a glass-enclosed sunroom and, so far, the only part of the house I thought attractive. Unlike the sterile, enclosed feeling evoked by the entry, this space was light-filled and fashionable: wicker furniture was topped, even over-flowing, with cushions covered in a pink and green floral print. Several dried flower arrangements interwoven with candy-striped ribbons hung between large expanses of glass, bright fabric swags swung across the tops of the windows, adding color without blocking the sun. A lazy ceiling fan stirred the air with paddles of imitation palm fronds.

After taking in the furnishings, I focused on a couple of unfinished needlework projects that were scattered about. Knitting needles and skeins of lavender yarn lay on the coffee table while a needlework frame was positioned near a chair in the corner. The canvas stretched across its rollers showed a seascape in vivid blue shades. Magazines on different decorating and craft subjects lay jumbled on a side table. Two quilts were tossed casually over the back of the couch, and I fingered the binding on one of them. Even with my limited knowledge, these were recognizable as older quilts. Worn at least and definitely not Mom's little class sample. What colors had Lam said were in that quilt? Orange and yellow. Sounded hot.

I gave the space a final glance and moved back to the living room, listening at the hallway for Eugena. She and Lam were in a bedroom on the left, so I entered the doorway on the right. It was a standard white guest bathroom. The next door led to an extra bedroom. The space was so bland, with white walls and a taupe satin bedspread, that I could easily imagine it as a hotel room. The only color was added by a quilt at the foot of the bed.

Again, I didn't need to unfold it to know this wasn't my sample. It was the world's most recognizable quilt pattern—the double wedding ring. The arrangement of soft pastels drew an appreciative gasp from me. This version had obviously been made by an experienced quilter.

"Stella, quit ambling," Eugena said from the doorway. She then whirled around and grasped Lam's arm, propelling him on down the hallway. Before they disappeared, he gave me a smile and slight shrug of his shoulders. Eugena talked as she dragged him along.

"Now, this house is just your style, hon. See, once I get to know someone, I hone in like a laser on what they like."

I started out of the bedroom but paused in front of a

pretty framed needlepoint picture hung near the door. It was a spray of blue pansies with distinctive purple throats against a green screen suggestive of leaves. The initials L. B. were worked into the corner. Lori? If I hadn't been looking carefully, I would have missed that detail since the color shift of the letters against the background was slight.

I took a final look at the room. Two spots of color stood out sharply, the rings of the quilt and the yarn in the handiwork.

Back in the living room, I turned in a full circle while squinting. Each time my gaze encountered color, I stopped for a better look. There was a bright needlepoint pillows on an off-white couch, a cross-stitched banner beside the door that proclaimed welcome, and a quilted table runner.

"Wow," I said.

Eugena peered as if seeing me for the first time today. "I'm glad you've changed your mind about the house, Stella. Are you interested in buying?"

"Maybe," I said. "I am moving back to the mountain."
I swear I could see a sharp glint in Eugena's eyes as she looked me up and down from this new perspective. Was she measuring the size of my wallet?

"Well, Lam says he wants to see that other house, too. Let's go," Eugena said. She hoisted her massive shoulder bag and pulled out her car keys and another cigarette.

If I hadn't thought of her as a source of information, I might not have been brave enough to crawl into the back seat of the car again. I knew Eugena had lived here all her life and started in realty early on.

"Eugena, how come Christine didn't keep the house after the divorce?" I asked. "Uh, I mean, it's such a great place, and she did design it after all."

"Christine's mother had died right before the divorce. Christine had been trying to sell that house for a few months. Way I hear it, Christine thought if she took time and fixed the old place up a bit she could get more money." Eugena took time to light her cigarette. Smoke swirled around her head. "Anyway, Tom stayed on since Christine moved out. That man was pretty tight with a penny. When he remarried, he just moved the new bride in. Lori came and talked to me once about looking at something new, but nothing ever came of it."

So, I'd been right in assuming that a new, young bride would not want to move into the house of the previous wife. I felt a surge of sympathy for Lori. Every turn, each breath, would have reminded her of Christine. I shuddered. But Lori had taken the initiative by contacting a realtor. It must have been the kind of marriage though where Tom made the decisions or controlled the money. Maybe both.

I wished I could ask Lori some questions, but so far I'd gotten little information with the nosy approach.

Thankfully, the trip to the next house was short since it was also in the Mountaintops subdivision. Eugena gunned the engine and raced from Lake Shore Drive to Top o' the Cliff Avenue. She turned into a driveway that headed toward the cliffs of the plateau.

The gravel drive was long, and Eugena accelerated until it was time to slam on the brakes. The car shuddered to a stop in front of a beautiful home styled like an old farmhouse. The house, though not large, rose two stories in a buttercup yellow with white trim and had intricately turned porch posts and a delightful balcony to the left of the entrance.

"Oh, Eugena, this is glorious." I gripped the back of Lam's seat and pulled myself forward for a better look out the windshield.

"Only two years old. The owner is being transferred to Europe. It was featured in an architect's magazine last year," Eugena said, sounding as proud as if she'd built the house with her own hands.

"This is more my style." Lam gave a low whistle. "How much?"

"Now, Lam, it's a tad over your budget, but let's take a look at the view from the back deck before I tell you." Eugena sang out, "Remember the rich can always borrow."

Before Lam could respond, the realtor jumped from the car and trotted along a path leading around to the back of the house. Her suitcase-sized handbag swung wildly with her pace.

Lam drawled, "This is more fun than I expected."

"It sure beats the students watching me sweat. How about you explain what you're up to."

"Give me a few more minutes." Lam sauntered up the path with his hand on the small of my back.

I was having a good time, and I thought it would be truly fun to go house hunting with someone you intended to live with—and loved. Even though Lam walked behind me, I ducked my head to hide my hot cheeks. Was I just getting to an age where I worried I would end up an old maid? Was Lam? Was that behind his sudden flirting and all this touching, which I did like, probably too much.

As we rounded the corner of the house, the view stopped us both in our tracks.

Eugena had already climbed the steps of a back deck. She

waved us forward. "Come on."

"Wow," I said. "This is a view to die for."

The valley, cut by a ribbon of the Tennessee River, stretched eight hundred feet beneath us. In the far distance, the view was rimmed by mountains. The vast expanse, colored by nature, made a soul soar like the hawks flying below the edges of the cliff face.

"It's really something to be looking down on the birds," Lam said. "So how much, Eugena?"

"Okay, okay. One point five," the realtor said.

"One point five what?" I asked.

"Million," Lam answered for her.

"But this is so you, Lam." She waved toward the wall of glass behind us. "I can just picture you there in your living room or better yet in the kitchen." She raised her hand. "Or in your bedroom, waking up to this million-dollar view. It's the ultimate bachelor pad."

"Million and a half," I said.

"Okay, if you must get technical, Stella," she said with a sharp edge of irritation.

"No, that's not what I meant. How can a house in Sewanee be worth that much?" I asked. "Sewanee." My voice climbed another octave.

Eugena spread her arms wide. "Location, location, location."

I cupped my hands around my eyes and pressed my nose to the glass of a French door. The interior was just as darling as the outside, looking like time frozen sixty years in the past. The walls were plaster, and the ceilings rose at least twelve feet. The wooden floors glowed with polish. A person could stand in the fireplace, not that anyone would want to.

I stepped back. "When did this happen?" I asked. When I had left the area the town had been a sleepy, country burg. Back then we bought our clothes at Woolworth's, and an outing to the flea market was considered great shopping.

"Oh, the last seven or eight years," Lam said. "People from Memphis and Nashville and Chattanooga started buying the last few of the lots and building vacation homes. Expensive ones. Like this one."

"Why haven't I heard about this?"

"Well, you've never been in the market to buy a house, and it's not something Cele would have found interesting. When you visited, she didn't mention it. It's not a topic Gibb would think to bring up either," Lam answered.

"It's been a real boon," Eugena said. "There are only five lots available in the whole subdivision, and the last available cliff view sold last year for eight hundred."

"Eight hundred thousand. You mean dollars? Just the land?" I choked on the words.

"Stella," Eugena said, "times change. You need to keep up."

"Why don't the people with these valuable cliff-side lots build more houses?" I looked left and right. These ten-acre lots gave lots of privacy. I couldn't see the neighbors on either side.

"You should know the answer. After all, your granddaddy started all this," Eugena said.

"They can't subdivide because of the original covenants," Lam said. "Every subdivision has pretty much the same rules. It's just that because everything was left wooded here in Mountaintops, with bigger lots, it doesn't seem like the typical subdivision."

I felt a great need to rush back to the cabin. I wanted to take another look at the map on the wall in Mom's office. I knew for sure now that Tom had wanted the property for himself. He hadn't just wanted Mom to get her business out of Mountaintops, and I knew why he wanted the five hundred acres.

One long boundary of Mom's property ran along the cliff edge. I squeezed my eyes closed, trying to remember a detail on the map. Hadn't Grandpa's piece been divided into smaller lots at one time? Wasn't that the original map used by my grandfather? Did I really remember ten or so lots faintly marked along the cliff line?

The story went that Grandpa had started to feel a bit constricted as more and more of the lots sold. He wasn't used to having neighbors and decided to keep a bigger piece of land for the family than he'd originally intended.

"What's ten times eight hundred thousand?" I asked.

"Eight million," Eugena said, without pause.

I looked out over the valley one last time. "To die for."

CHAPTER 28

Eugena stood off a short distance from Lam and me with her cell phone pressed to her ear and her back to us.

"You knew. You agree with me. Right?" I asked Lam. My words came out a hiss as I whispered.

"Stop flapping," Lam grabbed my hands and held them, "you look like a chicken."

"Thanks."

"A lovely, country bird," he said. "I believe you're on the right track. Gibb is wrong to think all this isn't related to the murder. It's too coincidental that Harley Morgan bought Ida's place out of the blue and that it's all that stands between the road and property worth eight million dollars."

Lam released my hands and leaned against the railing to gaze down into the valley. His pale hair lifted slightly from his brow in the breeze that was created by the air lifting up the cliff face. The hawks continued to hitch a free ride on those thermals, and Lam watched them in silence for a moment.

"Why didn't Mom know something was going on, Lam? I can't believe Tom was being that clever. After all, I managed to figure it out," I said.

"Hey." Lam turned. "Cut that out. You're no dummy."

"But what about Mom?"

"She's got her head in the clouds all the time. You know your mom."

"That's for sure. So you remember the map in the office?"

"Yeah, and most people just think Cele is sitting on one big five-hundred-acre piece of land. They would assume it's worth a pretty penny, but not anywhere near the real value if it were subdivided."

"How did Tom figure it out?"

Lam shrugged. "Tom lived here all his life. He's known everybody forever."

"Like you. Did Tom honestly think he could make his sleazy plan work?" I watched Eugena's back. Her free hand gestured wildly.

"I guess when he couldn't, that's when he planned the break-in. He was maybe getting desperate. He probably figured that she would rather leave the cabin than quit her business. Actually, who knew what the man was thinking?"

Suddenly, I couldn't stand to see Lam so close to the drop off of the cliff. The deck of the house actually jutted over the ledge and left us secured only by the rail he leaned on. I grabbed his hand and tugged him the couple of steps toward me. Lam took it to mean that I wanted him closer.

I continued our conversation to distract myself from having him so close. "But Tom would need Ida's lot, too, and

Harley's got it."

"Who is this Harley Morgan?"

"No one here knows him, so he didn't arouse suspicion when he bought Ida's place." I didn't want to add that I'd been doing my homework on the man.

"Right," Lam said.

"But why Harley?" I asked more to myself than to Lam.

Lam placed his hands on my arms. "This was fun, wasn't it? Hey, I really liked that first house. All cozy and in my real price range. What did you think about it?"

I was grateful not to have to answer when Eugena, closing her cell, surged forward and grasped Lam's arm. "Lam, hon, how 'bout we schedule some more time for house hunting tomorrow?"

"I'm going to be busy for a few days, Eugena. I'll give you a call next week," Lam said.

Eugena looked disappointed but turned as we seated ourselves in her car. "Well, how about you, Stella? What kind of place do you want?" she asked over her shoulder.

"Wow. I don't know. Wait. Something fun. I want a fun house."

Eugena frowned as she braked at the end of the driveway before pulling out onto the two-lane. She politely offered to drop me at Mom's before taking Lam back to pick up his vehicle at her office. It was only two minutes out of the way. I agreed, knowing the realtor wanted extra time alone to try and talk Lam into another session with her. I would rather have dithered away another hour, but I really did need to get back to the house.

Just as Eugena slowed her car at the gates to the cabin, Esther's Toyota barreled out of the driveway, nearly causing a head-on collision. The old car rocked to a halt, and the transmission whined as Esther backed up.

"Is that you, Stella?" Esther called out her open window. "I was just looking for you. Come on. We've got to go." Esther gestured to hurry me along.

"Is something wrong? Is Mom alright?" I asked, feeling my heart jump into my throat as I shoved open the back door.

"Fine. Everything's fine, but come on. No time to waste."

I told Lam I'd be back to the house as soon as possible. He started to protest, but I pretended I didn't hear as I crossed the road.

"Esther, I haven't seen you this excited since you spotted Randy Travis at the gas station," I said, sliding into the passenger seat.

"I wish it was good news, sweetie. Betty May called me. Seems the association council is holding a secret meeting. They're planning to vote to start legal proceedings to kick Cele out of Mountaintops."

"This is crazy. Can they do this without her being here to stick up for herself?"

"Sure can. Ain't right, but they're doing it."

Esther accelerated so quickly that the tires squealed, and I'd bet she left rubber behind. The older woman didn't slow until she turned into the parking lot at the lakeside clubhouse. She parked beside a large white Mercedes.

Christine. My stomach did a flip, and I tried to convince myself I wasn't afraid of the woman. Yeah, when pigs took wing.

I slammed my car door then turned back, wanting to help Esther pull her crutches from the back seat.

"No. You go on. Stop them." She waved me off. "Hope we're not too late."

I jogged up the walk, but once I got to the door, I paused for a second to try and control my breathing. I'd never been good at talking in front of groups, and now I was going to have to fight for Mom. As I walked in, the door clanged shut behind me, and eight people stopped talking and stared. So much for sneaking in.

"Lordy," I said.

I glanced at each face to see exactly who was on this council. Sitting at the center of the table was Frank Coffee. Distress etched furrows on his features as he gave me a weak smile.

To his left, Christine met my gaze with a fierce stare and a smile that was far from reassuring. By her side Lori looked exhausted and dazed. As I watched, Christine placed a hand on Lori's arm, and I saw her give a squeeze. Did Lori flinch in pain or was it my imagination?

To see their faces, it was almost as if the two women had switched ages. The circles under Lori's eyes, the sagging shoulders, and gray cast to the complexion added at least twenty years. Beside her, Christine beamed with power. The shoulders were thrown back, and her jaw thrust forward as the eyes glinted. Her vigor and good health peeled the birthdays away.

It struck me that Christine was once again dressed in white—a soft, fuzzy sweater and short hair held back with a scarf tied around her head—while Lori was still in the chenille jacket she'd been wearing earlier at the cabin. The rainbow of colors brightened next to Christine.

I pulled my gaze from the pair with an effort. Next, I saw

three women whose faces I remembered from the last meeting. One was Andrea Hudson. I didn't know the other two. Seated on the other side of Frank was Mr. Darrington. His eyes darted around the room as the man refused to acknowledge my presence.

Off to the side, sitting back from the table, was Harley. He was pushed back in a folding chair with arms crossed over his chest and long legs stretched straight out, one ankle over the other. Today, he wore a white dress shirt and expensive-looking charcoal slacks. When he saw me, he jerked upright and knocked over a half-empty bottle of water by his side onto the floor. The splash darkened tasseled loafers. He ducked and set the bottle upright, but when Harley leaned back in the chair, he also refused to look at me.

Was that a blush on his cheeks?

I rubbed my palms against my thighs, remembering that the pants I wore weren't the most flattering in my wardrobe. They added five pounds, and the waistband rolled and pinched. I marveled that I could worry about something so trivial at this moment. I scuffed one cowboy boot against the other.

The door slammed behind me, and I breathed a sigh of relief when I heard the clatter and shuffle of Esther's awkward approach. I felt braver with her by my side. The older woman's arrival broke the silence.

"This is a private meeting of the elected council," Christine said.

"And I don't give a skunk's rump. I'm staying."

I wished I could say I'd said those words, but it was Esther's voice that had sung out loud and clear. Her words were followed by a snort of mirth from Harley's side of the room.

Christine blanched.

"Anything y'all plan on doing, you can do in front of this old woman." Esther continued forward toward a chair and dropped into it with a sigh so big it was clear she wasn't leaving any time soon.

I said, "And I'm staying too." I cleared my throat. "I have a very good memory, and I plan to let Mom know every word that's said. And who said it."

"If your mother—excuse me, if Cele Hill—would have talked to us, this might have been avoided," said one of the trio of women.

"She's been rather, uh, indisposed." My face flushed.

"But we shouldn't have to wait," Andrea said.

"Don't try to blame Mom with a flimsy excuse like that. This isn't some kind of national emergency," I said, my voice bursting loudly with anger. I cleared my throat and stepped up to edge of the table where the council members were lined up, seated on the opposite side.

"Mom is your neighbor, and you, all of you, should be treating her as such. You should be ashamed of yourselves." I wagged a finger.

"Amen," Esther said.

I glanced at Harley. This time he looked me in the eye, and I thought I saw him flash me a thumb's up, but then his hand went to his ear and gave a slight tug on the earlobe.

What was he doing here? He certainly wasn't on the council. The man had only moved in a few weeks ago. How had he known about the meeting? From Christine? Was he here with her today?

Mr. Darrington said, "But that's exactly the point. Cele is our neighbor, and this is a residential neighborhood. It's not zoned for a business. The covenants expressly forbid the running of a business within the community." The man punctuated his comment with a humph.

"Mom isn't running a business." I wasn't much of an actress, but I hoped I could project an appearance of confidence backing my words. I had no idea what kind of game my mom was playing when she'd told the council the same thing before. I just needed to delay them.

"Ms. Hill has already told us that," one of the women said, sounding less confident than Mr. Darrington, "but that meeting was interrupted."

"This is ridiculous." Christine snorted. "Cele has customers coming and going all year, and these camps are by far the worst of it. We're not going to put up with this flagrant violation of the homeowners association rules."

"But shouldn't we hear Ms. Hill's explanation?" said one woman, leaning around Lori to speak to Christine. She twisted a gold necklace around and around her finger.

Christine slammed her palm against the tabletop. Everyone except Harley jumped, and Lori looked as if she might collapse face-forward onto the table.

I said to Mr. Darrington, "You said you thought Mom was going to expand her business. That's absolutely not true." I figured I might as well carry on with my bluff.

"Perhaps we should wait until Cele can speak before the council," the unsure woman said.

"No," Christine said. "We need to get on with this."

Frank Coffee, sensing the tide had turned, said, "Let's go ahead and put the previous motion to a vote. I vote no. No to taking any action against Cele Hill at this time."

"I vote yes." Christine's voice rang loud and clear.

"I agree with Christine," said Andrea. She turned and dug her elbow into the side of the woman sitting beside of her.

"No. We should wait."

"I say no." This came from the other lady who had already expressed her doubts.

Christine scowled. "What about you, Lori? How do you vote?"

The young woman wiped the back of one hand across her eyes. "Yes."

"What was that?" Frank asked.

I wasn't sure if he hadn't heard the faint voice or if he couldn't believe the vote was now evenly divided three to three. Everyone turned to watch Mr. Darrington. My throat tightened. His earlier comments left little doubt in my mind which way he would vote.

Mr. Darrington opened and closed his mouth, and then I saw him sneak a quick sideways glance at Harley. "I think in all fairness Mrs. Hill should be given a chance to respond." The man dabbed at a bead of sweat that rolled down his forehead.

Christine shoved her chair back and grasped Lori by the arm. "Let's go, Lori. I'll give you a ride home."

Lori nodded but with vacant eyes. She followed the older woman without a word.

I dropped onto a chair to watch the pair go out the door, followed by Harley.

Why had I expected Harley to stay and talk to me?

Frank walked up to me. "That was too close, Stella. Is Cele back yet?"

"No. There was a problem with her flight home. Hope-fully tomorrow."

"I'm afraid we've only delayed things. I don't understand why Christine has taken up Tom's silly vendetta."

"I don't see why Mr. Darrington voted no," Esther said, having struggled out of her chair.

"Frank, let me ask a question," I said. "What if Mom wanted to subdivide her property and build more houses? Could she do that?"

"Lord no, child. Only the original developer could do that. The subsequent owner doesn't have the same rights— even if she is the developer's daughter."

Esther looked surprised. "Cele wouldn't do that anyway, sweetie. If she had her way, no one on this mountain would ever cut down another tree."

"Were you thinking that was what Mr. Darrington meant when he said Cele was going to expand her business?" Frank asked.

I didn't want to explain my true fears, so I merely nodded.

"Esther's right. You don't have to worry about that, Stella," Frank said.

CHAPTER 29

"You okay, little Stella?" Esther asked as she slowed the car at a curve on the road on the way back to Mom's.

"Sure," I said, and then realized I'd sounded so distracted that my answer probably hadn't done much to ease the old woman's worry. "I'm fine. Really." I patted her hand on the steering wheel.

"Seems like getting the vote to go Cele's way should have made you happier."

"Oh, it has. I just wish Mom would get her butt home. I miss her. I need her."

"Myself, I'm glad she didn't marry the judge. He's a right nice fella, but I've always wanted to make the wedding cakes for you and her when you both get hitched. Gibb too, of course," Esther said.

"That'd be great, and I'm also glad that they canceled the wedding. We've sure been through a lot in what? Only five days."

As I counted the days in my head I could hardly believe I'd been through so much in such a short time. I'd lost my job and was moving back home. My mother had been in the slammer, and here I was chasing after a murderer who had tried to kill me, too. Someone, anyway, had made that attempt. Not to mention that an old friend was flirting deliciously with me. Then, there was Harley. I found myself attracted to this man that I hardly knew and worried might be a killer.

Boy, flirting with danger seemed to come naturally to me.

Esther jogged me out of my reverie.

"Time flies when you're having fun," Esther said. "Seriously, hon, Betty May told me something else earlier when she called about the meeting. She's the biggest gossip in Tennessee. She saw Lori and Gibb together. They were sitting in Lori's car in front of the police department."

"Shoot, I told Gibb this was going to happen."

"Do you know what's going on with them?" Esther asked.

"No. Little brother won't spill the beans."

"I told Betty it was police business, but I know her. She'll still spread it all over town."

We were now within less than a half mile of Mom's house, and I said, "Esther, let me out here, please."

"Whatever for?"

"I just feel like stretching my legs before hitting the classroom again." I groaned.

Esther laughed and stopped the car. "It is a nice afternoon." Before she pulled away, Esther called out her window, "You have your mom call me soon as she gets back."

"Take a number," I said to the retreating Toyota.

I powerwalked a few feet down the shoulder of the gravel road until Esther's car disappeared over a hill, and then I darted into the woods. I wanted, while there was still good daylight, to walk to the cliffs on Mom's property. It had probably been a good five years since I had been along the edge of the plateau—that is, until this morning's house-hunting excursion.

When Gibb and I were young, Mom had made us swear a blood oath not to play in that area of the property. I mean an oath with real blood. She'd taken a big needle and pricked our fingers as well as her own. She had chanted this long, impressive litany she'd made up about honesty and honor. Funny thing was that Gibb had obeyed better than I had.

By the time I was thirteen, I'd regularly scoot through the woods to a special place I'd selected for reading and writing in my journal. It was a broad, flat rock near, but not too close to, the drop off. It was private, away from the prying eyes of a little brother.

Truth is, I'm scared of heights, and I never get close to a dangerous drop. In my apartment, I make the super perform any chores that require more than a stool. At the state fair, I stick to the merry-go-round and the scrambler no matter how hard my friends laugh.

I stepped over a fallen log and skirted a thick patch of broad-leaf rhododendron. When two pheasants flushed from the underbrush, I let out a screech that any owl would envy. I allowed myself a moment to catch my breath, leaning back against a tree and patting my chest as if to get my heart started again.

I moved on, thinking that I had forgotten, despite the fright I'd just endured, how much I loved walking in the forest. In the good old days, Cele frequently led Gibb and me on nature walks. I could still identify every tree in any season. I could pick mushrooms and berries without fear of poisoning myself, and I could tell you which animal had passed through by the droppings they left behind. During our wilderness treks, Mom would cry out "Poop!" when she spotted droppings. Then she would pick one of us to make the identification.

I had no doubt that if I were ever stranded in the woods, I would survive and not lose a pound.

The trees, without warning, gave way to the rocky edge of the plateau, and I stopped in my tracks. One minute the woods enveloped the land, and the next the world dropped off without warning. Here in front of me there were ten feet of broad rocks sloping gently downward and scrubbed clean of topsoil from the wind blowing at the cliff edge. Then there was a whole lot of nothing.

The view Eugena had shown Lam and me this morning had nothing over Mom's property. I watched a barge far below on the Tennessee River. It was so small that I could barely see it from this height. I gazed at the horizon, wondering how far I could see. Six or seven miles surely. Even though I wasn't anywhere near where the rocks began their steep descent, my head started to spin. I squeezed my eyes closed to calm the dizziness.

"No. I'm not going to let this get the better of me." My whisper was picked up and carried away on the stiff breeze.
I forced my eyes open and shuffled three steps forward. I took a half step. I leaned forward at the waist. I got to within two feet of the cliff's edge, and then my knees sagged. I dipped down to my knees.

"Stella," a voice called from behind. The wind made it unrecognizable.

I jerked upright and turned in time to see somebody rushing toward me. It happened so quickly, the face was a blur. The memory of the basement door slamming in my face popped into my head and, in fear, I took a step backward.

Uh-oh. Big mistake.

The loose pebbles and grit rolled under my slick-soled cowboy boots. My arms cartwheeled, and I spun backward.

There wasn't even time to scream as I fell.

A wide ledge about seven feet below the cliff's lip broke my descent.

My wits settled back slowly. I was on my back, spread eagled, but unhurt other than having had the breath knocked out of my lungs. I was quite comfortable, really, since the surface here was sandier than rocky and warm from the sun. I heard a hawk squawk, and I opened my eyes in time to see the bird swoop down to check me out. He came close enough for me to count his feathers. Evidently, the predator decided I was too large to carry off and wheeled away into the wide, blue yonder—that empty space I was trying not to think about.

"Stella!"

A strangled cry from above broke through my daze.

Harley's face appeared above me, peeking over the ledge.

"Stella, you scared the fire out of me. This isn't funny. What are you doing?" His face was red, and his hair fell forward around his face. He pushed it roughly back.

I didn't move. "What do you mean, what am I doing? You tried to push me over the cliff."

"What? What?" He sputtered. "It looked like you were sick or hurt. I was coming to help you. I was afraid you were going to fall, and then you jumped. I thought you were dead," he said, his words breaking into gasps at the end.

Harley leaned farther over the edge until I could see his shoulders. He looked left and right, surveying the terrain. "There's no way for me to get down."

"Believe me, you don't want down here. I want up there."

"Are you hurt? Sounds like you've got a concussion."

"Don't be daft!"

"Aren't you scared?" he asked. "You seem so calm."

"Do I?" I realized I had yet to move a muscle except for those needed to talk and open my eyes, though I had them squeezed tightly closed again. I lay with my head closest to the cliff edge, and I had no intention of looking in that direction.

"Stella, don't move back toward the edge."

"You're kidding, right? You think I need that bulletin?"

"Can you stand?"

Harley graciously ignored my rudeness. I'd have to keep in mind that this man was my only hope of getting back up to the top. If Harley Morgan decided to walk away, no one would ever find me. Talk about the ultimate diet.

"Ultimate diet," I said.

"What? You are hurt. You've obviously got brain damage."

My eyes popped open in time to see Harley's head disappear, and I shrieked, "Don't you dare leave me!"

"I'm not leaving you, you ninny. I'm taking off my belt."

"Ninny. That's what Gibb calls me." A tear squeezed from under my eyelid.

"Smart man."

Harley was now lying flat on the ground with his shoulders extended past the rock lip and both arms stretched as far as he could reach. He held his leather belt by the tip end. The buckle dangled.

"Stella, stand up and grab the belt."

"I can't."

"Why not?"

"I'm afraid of heights."

Harley snorted. "So was jumping off the cliff some kind of aversion therapy?"

"Hardly." I squared my shoulders as best I could from where I rested flat on my back in the dirt.

"Seriously, Stella. You're going to have to stand up and grab the end of my belt. I'll pull you up."

"Are you strong enough? I don't know if you noticed that I'm not exactly a skinny-minny. I'm not sure I like this plan. I knew I should have started my diet before this."

"It's either this or I leave you to get help."

"No!" My voice started as a whine and grew like a siren.

"Calm down. I'm afraid of heights too, but you don't see me crying like a baby."

I looked at him. "Easy for you to say from up there."

At least this situation proved, or I supposed it did, that Harley wasn't trying to kill me. Had he really thought I was sick and tried to help me? I had no choice but to trust the man.

I scooted crablike as close to the cliff face as I could before rolling to my knees. I pressed my face so hard to the rock that I could feel the rough surface scraping my cheek as I clambered to my feet. Without looking, I let my fingers walk up the wall, searching blindly for the leather strap.

"It's not long enough," I said.

"It's plenty long. Just look."

"No."

"Okay. I understand. Just reach to the right. Sorry, it'd be your left."

I inched my hand over and felt the belt brush my wrist.

I grasped the lifeline.

"No. Wrap it around your palm and then hold your other hand over it too."

"Sounds as if you do this for a living." I let a quick sob out.

"Nothing to it. It's only two feet."

I did as he instructed and then felt the tension on the belt as Harley pulled. For a second I almost released my grip, but I forced my hands into tight fists. The buckle bit into my palm. When my feet left the ground, another more strangled sob escaped my lips. There was a jerk, but before I could react, Harley's hand grasped my wrist. He'd just been shifting his grip from the belt to me. I also let go with one hand and grabbed his forearm.

"Okay. We're doing great. See, it wasn't so far. Really only about a foot above where you could have reached," he said, breathing hard. Then Harley gave a muffled grunt.

The man's hand went slack, and the end of the belt he'd been holding fell past my face. If it hadn't been for my grip on Harley's arm, I would have fallen. Now I dangled by one hand. If I fell, I might get lucky and hit the ledge again or I might bounce and fall off the cliff edge. Flying lessons.

I let the belt fall from my hand and clutched Harley's arm.

"Harley," I said. "You can pull me up now."

No answer.

"Harley. This isn't funny."

He groaned.

"What's the matter?"

No answer.

"Shoot," I said, my voice cracking.

What was wrong? I had no idea, but I was going to have to get myself up.

Fortunately he had on a suede jacket that gave me a good grip. I stretched and gained a few inches, but then I realized that I'd actually just pulled Harley forward a bit.

Not good.

So far, all I'd seen were the rocks, but now I tipped my head back. I breathed a sigh of relief when I saw that I was now close enough to grab the ledge. I felt along the rock and found a good handhold. My fingers dug in and, despite the fact I could feel my fingernails snapping, I clawed my way to safety.

Harley ended up draped a few inches closer to falling, but we were both safe now.

"Harley?"

I flipped from my stomach onto my side and found myself gazing at his face. The man's features were slack, eyes closed as if he'd decided to take an inopportune nap. When I leaned over him, I could see blood on the back of his head.

There was a stout broken branch lying near the man. It couldn't have fallen from any tree at the edge of the woods, not in any way that would strike him hard enough to cut his head and knock him unconscious. The tree line was simply too far from where we lay.

I glanced around. There was no one to be seen. I listened but could only hear the wind and Harley's soft breathing. He sighed, and his eyelids flickered open.

"Did I save you?" he asked.

"Yes, you sure did. You're my hero." I leaned over and kissed him on the forehead.

CHAPTER 30

"**O**uch."

Yowl.

Smoky gave a sympathy yowl every time Harley yelped as I dabbed antiseptic on the cut on the back of his head. The man and the cat had become a team.

"Don't be such a baby. It's barely a scratch," I said, scattering band aids as I rifled the first aid kit Harley had pulled from a cabinet.

We sat at a Formica-topped kitchen table in Harley's little cabin. The table was an honest-to-God antique with the red laminate and chrome gleaming in the glow of the late afternoon sun slanting through the window over the sink. The matching chrome chairs sported overstuffed, red vinyl seats.

It had taken us a good twenty minutes to walk through the woods to his home. Harley, arm draped over my shoulders, had leaned heavily on me during the trek, refusing my suggestion that we go to Mom's, which was closer.

"I still think you should have let me take you to the hospital," I said.

Harley stroked the black kitten as Smoky nuzzled his neck in return. "You just said it's barely scratched. Make up your mind."

"I'm not talking about the gash. You might have brain damage," I said, trying to get back at him for his earlier remark about my mental state.

Harley laughed so hard that Smoky jumped from his lap to the table top. The cat walked around, sniffing the rim of a coffee cup and a plate—Fiestaware no less—with the remains of what I supposed had been breakfast.

"Don't you put your dirty dishes in the sink and rinse them?" I asked.

"It's just crumbs. What are you, the housekeeping police?"

I sighed, thinking this was my kind of guy.

"Who would want to kill you?" I asked, giving up on my search for a bandage that might work on the back of someone's head. I didn't think Harley would let me shave part of his hair, and he wouldn't wear a gauze turban. He'd just have to be careful and sleep on his side for a few nights. I'd spent the last fifteen minutes cleaning the cut and running my fingers through Harley's wavy black hair. I hoped he hadn't noticed that I had enjoyed playing nurse.

"Why did you think I was trying to kill you?" Harley asked with a grimace when he twisted his neck to look over his shoulder at me.

"I asked first."

"But you made a pretty serious accusation."

"But you pushed me off a cliff."

"Darn it, woman! I'm the one who got bashed in the head. Why won't you let me win the argument?" Harley stood, glaring at me with his fists on his hips.

"Did I win?" I smiled. It felt nice to ease the tension in my body, and usually I never won arguments. I thought I had been pretty brave for a woman who had almost taken an eight-hundred-foot swan dive, but my hands were still shaking.

"Okay. I'll let you win," I said. "I thought you might have tried to kill me because three days ago someone deliberately slammed the basement door in my face just in time to shove me down the steps. I could have been killed." I pulled my sweater sleeve up past my elbow. "See the bruises? And, of course, you had a close-up of the dozer."

"Was the basement incident how you got the scratch on the end of your nose?" Harley reached out.

His fingertip on the end of my nose seemed to pass an electric shock into my body.

"Uh, no. That happened when Lam hit me with the screen door."

"Was that when you got this bruise on your cheek?"

Harley rubbed the back of his knuckles across the side of my face.

"Well, no. That was when Lam hit me with his elbow."

"That does it!" Harley exploded. "I'm going to beat the blond right off that gigolo." He whirled and jerked his suede jacket from the back of the kitchen chair.

"Whoa, cowboy! It wasn't Lam's fault. I'm kind of clumsy." I took the coat from his hands.

Harley moved to the refrigerator and took out a beer.

"You want one?"

"Sure."

"Let's go sit somewhere more comfortable. Grab the cat."

Harley wobbled a little as he walked to the living room, and then he flopped onto the couch with a half sigh, half groan.

I choose the matching chair opposite the sofa where I could see the man's face and settled back, giving my weak knees a break. Smoky immediately jumped from my arms to the back of the overstuffed chair.

"Oops. Do you let him on the furniture?"

Harley gave me a puzzled look. "Why wouldn't I? You should get over this obsession you have with being clean and orderly."

I took a deep and satisfying pull from the cold bottle. No pouring beer into glasses in this house. "It's your turn to testify, Harley. Who would want to kill you?"

"I don't know." He gazed into the empty fireplace.

When I started to protest, Harley held up his hand and shushed me. We sat for a few minutes sipping our beer in companionable silence. It felt so homey that I wanted to whisper that we shouldn't even talk, just enjoy the quiet.

Finally, he said, "Do you really think I look like a cowboy?"

"Harley, stay on the trail here."

"Okay. I've been a trial lawyer for so long I've earned my share of enemies."

"So, you think that's it?" I snorted.

"No, although that might be better. I just haven't figured out which of the two of them did it."

"Who two?" I asked, although I was sure I knew what he

meant without asking the question. I was pretty sure that Harley was smart.

"Lori or Christine," he said.

"So you don't think Mom did it?"

"No. Never did," Harley said. "She's been too neatly framed."

"How can we find out who bonked you?"

"By learning the truth about Tom's death."

I rubbed the itchy, healing tip of my nose.

Harley asked, "Tell me again why you think I might try and kill you?"

"I had no idea who you were."

"I am somewhat famous, at least in this state." He puffed his chest out in cartoon fashion and then let it deflate.

"Big-shot lawyer."

Harley pulled a long face.

"What's the matter?" I asked.

"I hate being a lawyer." He laughed. "Well, I don't have to worry about that anymore. I'm retired."

"Harley, how did you get involved with this? You are mixed up in it, aren't you?" My voice carried my surety that this man wasn't here, in this cabin, by chance.

Harley ducked his head, hunching his shoulders. "Uh, I'm—well I was—Tom's last blood relative. His nephew."

"But that's not all."

"Okay, Miss Smarty Jeans. Tom called me a couple of months ago and asked if I'd do him a favor. He wanted me to buy this piece of property for him. He told me he just needed the deal to go through while staying anonymous."

"Didn't that make you suspicious?"

"Not at all. It happens frequently in business."

"You had no idea Tom was trying to get my mother's property by hook or crook?"

"No idea." He held his hand up in a three-fingered boy scout's salute.

"So, you had no idea what was going on?"

"No, Stella, I really didn't. But when Tom was killed I decided to stick around to see that his killer was caught." Harley's voice took on a steely note. "To make sure of it."

I could easily picture Harley commanding a courtroom with his strong presence.

He said, "Plus, I suddenly owned this property without having Tom alive to pass it to him. Usually in these anonymous deals I'd just have been the buying agent, but my uncle insisted that I actually make the purchase. Said he was going to buy it from me in a short while. Then when I got stuck with it, I had this overwhelming urge to retire."

I stood and paced a path in front of the coffee table. For the first time, I took in the whole of the room. Harley had been slowly and steadily decorating. The funky antique kitchen furnishings didn't stand alone. The living room was definitely kitschy. I wasn't sure if that was even a word, but it described the look.

Everything was retro fifties. The sofa and chair wore floral slipcovers. I bent down and peeked under the ruffled skirt. An expensive beige fabric. I glanced next at the lamps. Funky. Oh, Harley definitely had style.

The only glaring note of bad taste was a cat condo standing in the corner. It was the deluxe model with three boxes for hiding, one at floor level, one halfway up the thick pole, and the other balanced at the top, which was about head-height. Carpeting and twists of hemp rope made it climber friendly, and there were a couple of dangly feather toys for Smoky's entertainment.

As if the cat sensed my thoughts, he jumped down from the chair, skittered across the hardwood floors, and proceeded to put on a show of his gymnastics skills.

Definitely homey.

I noticed that a glass jar on the side table held licorice. It was one of my favorite sweet treats, and my mouth began to water. I realized I'd missed lunch. I lifted the lid, whipped one of the rubbery ropes from the container, and bit off a good portion of the end.

"Oh, sassafras. The best flavor," I said around the mouthful.

I glanced at Harley to find him staring with a horrified look on his features. Well, that would teach me to talk with my mouth full.

"Stella. I had those out in a dish earlier, and I think Smoky might, uh, have taken a lick. Or two." A furious blush spread across his cheeks. "I should have thrown it out, but you see, sassafras is my favorite flavor, and it's hard to find. I was going to wash each piece before—"

I grinned and took another big bite.

"Say, Harley, how come Mr. Darrington voted for Mom?" Something about how Mr. Darrington had looked at Harley before he voted made me suspicious. That man had been too nervous.

"Uh. Well, he was a client of mine about a year ago." Harley stared, sighed, and said, "Ah, Stella. I blackmailed him."

CHAPTER 31

"Whewwwee. Wheeeewww." I puckered my lips and blew again and again, trying to whistle. I had never mastered the skill, but Harley's car made me want to whistle, or sing, or dance, or do something fun. It was a fantastic 1954 Ford Fairlane painted in aqua and cream. As I guided it down the gravel road, hands gripping the big bone-colored steering wheel with a chrome horn ring, it seemed to float. It steered like a boat.

Best of all, his radio was tuned to a country station. I couldn't believe he'd offered to let me drive the antique. Of course, I'd refused to let him drive me home in his condition since that would have left him returning to his cabin alone. My offer to walk home through the woods drew outrage and revolt. The loaner had been his idea. Guess he hadn't heard about my driving skills.

I was practically giddy with relief that Harley wasn't a murderer. It was good to know he was as nice as he seemed.

I was still worried about Harley or rather, for his health. He should have gone to the hospital, but he'd been adamant in his refusal. He said he was going to kick back and rest, that he just needed peace and quiet. I agreed to leave him alone only when he promised to limit the drinking to the one beer and to allow me to call later in the evening to check on him. Harley had even given me a spare key to his front door, saying he'd intended to ask Cele to keep one for him anyway.

We both knew that calling Gibb was the next order of business, but I said I'd take care of the chore before the day ended. I wasn't looking forward to the tongue-lashing I knew I was going to get from the Sheriff. He would say that the time delay might mean lost evidence, but before Harley and I had left the cliff, I'd walked around looking for footprints or any item left behind. There had been nothing to see on the rocks. Could fingerprints be lifted from the bark of a tree limb? I doubted it.

So, where did that leave my investigation?

I had been right that Tom wanted Mom's property, cabin and all, for himself. He'd probably planned to develop the lots originally surveyed on the five-hundred-acre parcel. According to Frank though, that couldn't be right. Was Grandpa, the original developer, the only one who could subdivide? Frank had sounded so sure of himself, shue. Well, I'd think it over tonight, see if I could come up with some new angle.

There was the nagging thought that Harley might not have been the object of the attack. Anyone could see that stopping him left me hanging—literally. I'd asked Harley who might have known he was going to take a walk to the cliff. He'd told me no one. He'd decided on the spur of the moment after leaving the meeting—just as I had done.

Harley had explained how he'd found me. He'd heard my scream when I'd flushed the two pheasants from the under-brush. He had actually been heading toward a different part of the cliff. If I hadn't screamed, he would never have found me. No one would have. I shivered.

I docked the car in front of Mom's garage, and when I hopped out, the door closed with a solid thunk that hasn't been duplicated since the middle of the last century.

I jerked the screen door open but stopped short. The back door was locked, unusual for the cabin before bedtime. I had to fish through my tote looking for my spare key. In the yel-low light of the bug bulb over the porch, it was difficult to see, but I finally found it in a zippered pocket.

Once in the kitchen, I saw that there was a note on the table held in place with a can of baking powder. Lam's scrawl advised me that Mom had called and he was driving to Mem-phis to pick her up. He intended to layover along the way at a hotel for a few hours of sleep and be at the airport for her nine o'clock arrival tomorrow. Evidently, Mom and the judge had decided to travel home along different paths.

I sighed. Memphis was about a five-hour drive. Even with Mom's arrival in the state in the morning, they wouldn't make it back to Sewanee until tomorrow afternoon. Another day in charge of the quilt camp.

I read the last lines of the note. The gals had all taken off to a square dance at the town hall. Now that was a good idea. I'd change quickly and join them. Once there, I would call Gibb and have him meet me at the gathering. He couldn't yell too loudly in front of a crowd.

Changing only took a few minutes. Earlier I'd been able to finally run the washing machine and now had my choice of clean clothes. I selected a red plaid long-sleeved shirt with faux pearl snaps instead of buttons and a denim skirt to go with my boots. After changing socks, I scrubbed a shoe brush over the leather to rub out a few of the scuff marks from my scramble over the rocks.

Thinking about it brought goosebumps to my skin and made my breath catch in my throat. After a splash of warm water on my face and a swipe of powder on my cheeks and nose, I was revived and ready to join the fun. Besides, I'd feel safer with others around me, too.

Back in the Fairlane with the doors locked, I sighed with relief as the car glided down the road on its big balloon-like white walls. The smell and feel of the car and the music made me feel like a kid riding back home with Grandpa and Grandma after church on Sunday.

Yes, even with everything bad going on, coming back to the mountain made me happy.

The trip to the heart of Sewanee took only ten minutes. I cruised the square and pulled into the last angled parking space available in front of the old town hall built from big hand-cut blocks of limestone. I smiled when I saw a hay wagon on the lawn with a sloppily painted sign propped in the back. The sign proclaimed square dancing with the great Wailin' Willy as the caller and the Four Plucked Angels playing.

I knew the group. The Cahill twins played fiddle. Jim Dorton wielded a mean bass fiddle. Eighty-four-year-old Norma Gill played the mandolin.

My pace quickened when halfway up the front steps my ears picked up the first twangs. I threaded past a few couples standing on the stoop nursing cigarettes and sipping from paper cups. Several people called out greetings as I crossed the lobby. I waved as I trotted past, but then I did a double-take and stopped so fast my boot heels slid on the marble floor.

"Whoa. Is that you, Abby? Abby Fry?" I called out to a woman waddling toward me. She looked to be about twelve months pregnant. A man held her elbow, helping her as they dodged other guests.

She noticed me and squealed. "Ohhhh! Stella Hill! I swear you're the last person on earth I expected to see tonight." She gave me a one-armed hug. "And it's Abby Renhouse now." She hitched her thumb at the man beside her. "Tommy, meet my best friend from high school."

He gave a wave.

"You look like a hippopotamus," I said without thought. "I'm sorry. What an awful thing to say." My face must have been glowing like a neon sign after blurting out my first thought.

She laughed. "That's my old Stella. Tommy, this girl has a problem with saying the first thing she thinks. Don't worry, Stella. I feel like a hippo. Twins." She pointed to the T-shirt she wore. The words, stretched tight, read, TWINS: TWICE THE SPIT UP.

"I'm just surprised. Remember you were voted most likely to never marry?"

"Didn't the yearbook predict you'd be the first woman on the moon? Hey, if you're in town for long, come by and see me at work. I'm the bookkeeper at the *Piggly Wiggly*."

"Well, you always did have a head for numbers."

"And I can sneak ice cream out of the freezer," she laughed.

Tommy leaned around his wife and said, "Make it early next week. Abby's going to explode any second now, and she won't be back to work. I got her to promise to quit." He grinned at his wife.

Abby started to say something when her eyes grew wide. "Oh boy. I think the fireworks are about to begin."

"Are they having fireworks tonight?" I asked, clapping my hands together.

Abby reached out and clutched my arm in a grip that could have crushed my bones. "No, silly," she panted, "the babies. Tommy, do something!"

"Really? This is it. Hey, everybody," Tommy shouted. "This is it! Uh, where's the hospital?"

A couple of guys laughed and said, "Come on, Tom. We'd better drive. You might end up at the vet's."

I watched the group hustle out the door and settle Abby into the back seat of a car.

With a sigh, I realized my time back in Sewanee had given me a major case of home-sickness. I'd definitely visit Abby next week and take two baby gifts.

I started again to work my way through the crowded entryway and into a large room. This was really the county courtroom with the wooden pew-style seats pushed against the back wall. The band stood on the judge's dais at the far end of the room with Willy teetering on a hay bale while clutching a microphone in hands twisted by arthritis. His nasal voice cut the strands of music, talk, and laughter.

"Swing your partner. Now do-si-do. Been to church. Turn the ladies." Willy's voice set the rhythm for the dance.

"Stella!"

A shrill call caught my attention. I peered through the

spectators and saw Julie standing with several of the other ladies. They were all clapping to the music and laughing. She waved for me to join them.

"This is terrific. Look at Mrs. Helm go!" Claire pointed toward the dance floor.

Elderly Mrs. Helm was indeed kicking up her heels. She was doing a lovely country waltz on the arm of a young man who looked all of eighteen. He also appeared winded from trying to keep up with her. She was definitely making good use of Lam's dancing lessons.

Leann cupped her hands around her mouth and leaned close to my ear. "Stella, Gibb is coming this way." She pointed.

With an involuntary twitch, I ducked my head as if I was expecting him to box my ears before I'd even confessed.

"Hey, Sis. Glad you could make it." He grinned like a little boy with a secret or a frog in his pocket.

"What's up with you?" I asked.

"You made quite the impression on ol' Presley. He wanted to know if you'd go out with him. Was mighty disappointed when I told him you probably wouldn't."

"Funny man. Did you ask him if he delivered a package to Mom?"

"I did, and he says no, but he got awfully jittery. I think he's lying, and you might be onto something. I'll go back tomorrow and pick him up after he's stewed all night. When we take them to the jail to ask questions, it turns the pressure up. Riding in the back of the squad car tends to scare people."

"Told you so," I chanted and then realized that if I were more gracious, I could smooth the news I had to tell. "Uh, great job, Gibb. I always knew you were good at your job."

"Oh, a compliment! What kind of trouble did you get into today? Should I put you in jail?" He pulled a long frown. "You're worse than Mom."

"I had a spot of trouble this afternoon."

As I replayed the events, Gibb's face reddened. He even tugged at the collar of the sweater he was wearing, and I half expected to see steam spurt out.

"Any evidence has to wait overnight. Animals, the wind," he said and then looked down at this feet. "Are you okay, Stella?"

I punched him in the arm. "I'm fine. Thanks for asking. I really am sorry, but it was almost dark by the time the rescue was over. And it was dark when I got Harley back to his cabin. Helping him came first."

Gibb nodded. He looked distracted, as if he wanted to ask a million questions but couldn't decide where to start. His reverie was broken by a loud cry from the dance floor.

"Yippeeee!"

Everyone stopped, mouths gaping, as Sherri Bane took her partner, a small elderly man, and swung him a little too vigorously. Despite the horrified expression on the man's face, I recognized Rev. Dumfries, the retired Baptist minister. He was pushing his late seventies and was lucky if he weighed in at one hundred and twenty pounds. My student easily outweighed him by as much as a fifty-pound feed sack.

Sherri's grip failed, and Mr. Dumfries flew like he'd been ejected from the scrambler ride at the carnival. Fortunately, a couple of farmers standing off at the edge of the dance action caught him. The overall-clad fellows steadied the preacher, dusted him off, and gave him a nudge toward the refreshment table.

"I think there might be a little more than Coke being distributed," Gibb said. "I heard Frankie Williams squeezed off a batch of moonshine this morning."

We both watched Sherri weave her way through the couples, tapping women on the shoulders, trying to get one of them to give up their man to dance with her.

"I think you'd better take Ms. Bane back to the cabin, Stella."

"Me? You're the Sheriff."

"Yeah, but I'm going to go talk to Harley Morgan. Something I could have done an hour ago if some ninny had called me. Oh, since Lam's on the road, I'll be over to sleep at the cabin tonight." He gave a grin that showed all his teeth and turned on the heel of his boot.

I stomped to the middle of the floor and started following Sherri, but she didn't see me and couldn't hear me, so she continued on her mission of finding a dance partner. Every time I got close and reached out, she flitted just out of reach. I figured we looked ridiculous with me following closely on the butt of the drunken woman.

Someone came up behind me and grasped me by the hips. I looked over my shoulder to see that a conga line had formed. Is this what people had thought we were doing?

The band switched into a twangy Latin rhythm.

I tried to shake off the hands but was unsuccessful as the kicking and shifting side-to-side just about pulled me off my feet. Sherri pranced out of sight through the crowd, which was now clapping along.

By the time I'd led the line twice around the room trying to find Sherri, I was out of breath and had a serious stitch in my side. I finally spotted her guzzling from a red and white paper cup at the refreshment table.

I peeled the fingers from my hip bones one at a time and broke away.

"Say! Hi, Stella!" Sherri said.

I leaned over the plastic tablecloth, palms down, gasping for air after that dance.

"Here. This'll revive ya." Sherri shoved her cup under my nose.

The hundred-proof fumes hit my sinuses and gagged me.

"Geez, Sherri, what is that stuff? Paint stripper?" I asked, jerking back out of range of the odor.

"Don't know, but want more."

"That smells lethal."

"Die happy." She swayed.

"Okay," I said, "I got something even better. Let's go get some."

"See, you're not as goody-two-shoes as you act, Stella." Sherri wagged her finger in my face as her words slipped and slid around each other.

I linked my arm through Sherri's and started jerking her along. She bumped into a few people along the way, but I didn't slow.

"Hey," she yelled, "let's do that again!"

I hung on tightly as I hauled the woman down the steps. I hoped we wouldn't take a tumble. It'd be a shame to live through my earlier scare only to be crushed under Sherri.

At the car, I let go for a moment to fish the keys out of my denim skirt pocket, a procedure that took both hands. When the key surfaced, Sherri was nowhere to be found. Where could she have gotten to in those few seconds? I unlocked the car door and left it open before turning around in a complete circle. There was a noise beyond a low yew hedge opposite the sidewalk.

I peered over and found Sherri face down on the grass. Loud snores erupted when I tried to get her up.

"Sherri, we're almost there. You want another drink, don't you?"

"Sure nuf." Sherri sprang to her feet with renewed vigor.

All I had to do was point her in the right direction, and the woman dived into the car. I hauled her upright and buckled the seat belt across her waistline. She slapped at my hands the whole time, but I finally heard the snap of the buckle.

A loud burp rumbled from the passenger seat. Lord, please don't let Sherri be sick in Harley's car.

Sherri said, "Great dance, but not enough guys." Another belch.

I gunned the engine, and the car lurched back from the parking space. I shifted into first and cranked the window down at the same time. I shifted through second and third and fourth, increasing speed down Main Street. Unlike newer models with five or even six gears, the antique Ford stopped at four. Back in the good old days, Americans hadn't minded being gas guzzlers. Speaking of guzzlers, Sherri was still talking, describing her ideal man. It was frighteningly reminiscent of Gibb. I made a mental note to alert my brother, just to be safe.

I held my hair back from my eyes with one hand as the wind whipped it around my head. The wind was colder than whiz, but if I could just get my drunken passenger home without incident, I'd make myself some hot chocolate.

The Mountaintops guard shack was dark and empty, and the automatic security gate took its sweet time lifting.

I roared down the gravel road at a pace I'd never used before in the woods at night. I lived in fear of nighttime driving because of the thought of cute, furry creatures out foraging. One minute they're nibbling at the Ditch and Highway salad bar, and the next—well, I just wouldn't think about it.

Fortunately Sherri didn't erupt, I didn't feel any bumps under the tires, and the driveway of the cabin was in sight. I made the turn and stopped the car, killing the engine. Then I leaned over Sherri and popped open her door.

"You won't remember a thing. I promise," I said, releasing her seatbelt. I shoved the woman out of the car and wondered if maybe I'd enjoyed it too much.

"Ouch! You're mean, Stella."

I thought about leaving Sherri on the ground rather than attempting to wrestle her to the cabin, but good Southern manners prevailed. It only took thirty minutes and six falls to half-drag, half-walk Sherri to the dorm room. Before leaving her to sleep it off on her twin bunk, I made sure she was face up on the bed.

CHAPTER 32

This was the coldest evening so far this fall. As I crossed the yard back to Harley's car, I rubbed my hands briskly up and down my arms, causing the cotton fabric of the sleeves to rustle. I was lucky to have remembered that I'd left the car open. I would have hated to return his classic car with opossum prints on the seat covers or, worse yet, a little surprise left behind.

As I slammed the door shut, a light from the sewing studio on the third floor caught my eye, and I stopped on the damp grass to gaze upward. The ladies must have left it on. I hurried into the kitchen and filled the tea pot with tap water for my hot chocolate, but I didn't turn on the burner just yet. There was something I'd been meaning to check, but it had slipped my mind earlier when I'd come home after nursing Harley. Lam's note had distracted me.

I set the full kettle on the table and trotted through the

house to the office. I pulled the stretchy band on my wrist far enough to unlock the door and eased it back without snapping the skin. I'd done just that one too many times.

I stood in front of the framed map of Mountaintops. With my finger I traced the road from the front entrance to the east edge where these five-hundred acres were located at the far edge of the development. I had remembered correctly. There were dashed lines dividing the big block of Hill property into several smaller lots. I counted twelve, nine along the cliffs and three interior.

My finger glided to where a small black-and-white photograph was tucked in the corner under the glass of the plain wooden frame. It showed the smiling trio of Grandpa, Gran, and a twelve-year-old Cele looking as happy as a kid could. They all smiled for the camera. I wished I knew who had taken the picture, but I didn't. I practically pressed my nose to the glass trying to glean some bit of information that might help unravel the puzzle. A man had been murdered in this room because of this property. Not only did Gibb and I have to clear Mom's name, but Tom deserved justice, even if he had been plotting against her.

Beneath the photograph, but mostly hidden by it, was something I had failed to notice before. I could see Mom's signature, Margaret Hill, in youthful script. The first three letters were buried under the photo, but it was obviously her name, and I recognized her writing even though the ink was faded from years of sunlight. Above Mom's name, and almost completely blocked, appeared to be Grandma's spidery writing.

I lifted the frame off its hook and laid it face down on the desk top. With a nail file I found in the center desk drawer, I pried up the metal clips holding a piece of thin cardboard backing to the map. I tossed that onto the ironing board, causing dust to billow. Next I used my fingernail to lift a corner of the brittle paper only to have it crumble from the stress. It was stuck tightly to the glass.

I'd need to be more careful. I slid the nail file under the edge of the photographic paper, loosening it from the map. Next I speared the back of the photo with the point of the file and slipped it to the edge of the frame where I could grab a corner and pull it free. I flipped the map back over. Signatures.

Grandpa.

Grandma.

Mom.

A fourth scrawl. Oh Lord. Thomas Billings.

Why had they all signed the map?

I immediately saw the answer to my question. Grandpa had penned a message above the signatures. It said, "The proud developers of Mountaintops." Gramps had included his wife and daughter and Thomas Billings. Grandpa and the young Tom, who would have been about nineteen or twenty, must have been friends. So Frank was wrong. Mom could sell the lots and make a fortune if she wanted. Even as I realized the truth, I knew she never would. But Tom would have.

Through the years, no one in the family, when talking about Mountaintops, had ever phrased it so that I understood that Mom was legally one of the developers. It had probably been a whim on Grandpa's part, and Mom, at that age, maybe thought of it as a game.

A door slammed somewhere upstairs. For a moment, I held my breath, but the house was now silent. This was too creepy for me after the events of the last few days. I felt sure Sherri would still be sleeping it off in the first-floor dorm and not wandering the cabin.

I scooted across the plank floor and eased open the closet door. I shoved my arm between coats and sweaters and passed my fingers along the wall. Cold steel. Wrapping my hand around the double barrels of Mom's twelve-gauge shotgun, I tugged it through the coats, which snared on the metal sight at the end of the long gun. This gun was the real reason my mother kept the office locked when students were in the house.

Once freed, I thumbed the lever that broke open the weapon to expose the breech. Both barrels held a shell. Thankful that Grandpa had taught me to shoot in my early teens, I snapped the gun closed as quietly as possible. For the first time during this visit, I left the office door unlocked when I left the room. I moved to the foot of the staircase, stopping to listen. Nothing.

To my left in the living room, a single lamp burned. With light glowing dimly in the foyer, I moved up the steps. It was a slow process with my back pressed to the wall and my tip-toe pace. I made it to the top of the staircase at the second floor without hearing another sound, but halfway down the hall a soft sobbing reached my ears.

The level of noise increased as I moved toward the stairs to the third-floor loft and the sewing studio. I gripped the gun tighter, thinking about calling for help, and then realized I was armed and someone was crying. It seemed as if I had the upper hand.

Once on the third floor, I pushed open the door to the studio. Lori sat at Mom's sewing table. It was almost as if she had collapsed over the antique sewing machine. Except for the sobbing, she was limp.

"Lori?"

The young woman raised her head, but unfocused eyes

stared at the wall rather than acknowledging my presence.

"Lori, are you all right?" I bit my lip for asking such a stupid question.

"I tried, Stella." She still watched a spot on the wall. "I tried to love Tom. He was an okay man, but he lied." Her hands balled into fists.

I expected to see her bang the table, but Lori started beating herself, pounding her chest and then slapping her own face. She was like a marionette, awkward and without any power behind the movements. I propped the shotgun against the doorframe and rushed to her. It wasn't that I was afraid she'd hurt herself; rather, it was hard to witness such raw despair. I grasped her wrists and worried she might lash out at me, but the fighting ceased immediately.

"Lori, it can't be this bad," I said without thought.

Another inane comment. Of course, it could be worse than I imagined. Just a few hours ago, Harley and I had been speculating that this woman had killed her husband.

Lori didn't seem like a murderess.

"I killed him, Stella. I killed my own husband." The wail released more tears, and Lori's shoulders shook violently with a spasm of grief.

Oh boy. I hadn't even had to ask and I'd been so wrong. The more I'd learned over the last few days, my vote for murderess had gone to Christine. How could I have been so far off track?

"Lori," I said, glancing around to see if scissors or other sharp objects were within her reach, "What happened? That night, I mean?"

"Tom said he wanted Cele's property. He'd been telling me for months. I thought he wanted us to live here." Her hand stroked the sewing machine. "I thought he wanted the best place in Mountaintops for me. I wanted to move out of that awful house." She shuddered at the words.

Lori turned to look at me now, seeming to recognize me finally, as she went on with the story. I was glad not to have to prompt a confession.

"But he lied. He planned to sell all the lots. Did you know Cele could break this place up and make a fortune?"

"Yes." I cringed at the thought of how close Mom had come to losing everything. I thought about how money didn't matter to her. Mom cared about the right things in life—home, family, work, and living an honest life. "Could Tom really sell the lots?"

"He helped your grandfather in the beginning. Invested some small inheritance he'd gotten and did the surveying. Tom sold out early on when he needed money to start the feed business, but he was still one of the original investors. He said all that mattered was how the covenants were worded. Tom wanted to turn the cabin into a clubhouse, not a home for us." Tears dripped off her chin.

"How did the two of you get into the office, Lori?"

"Tom got stupid Presley to help. He unlocked the window, and we snuck in. Tom didn't want me to come, but I did." Lori grasped my hand. "I love Cele like my own Mama. I didn't mean to hurt her. Really I didn't, but she's had so much for so long. I never had anything good. I tried with Gibb, but he didn't want me." She choked on a sob.

"Why did you kill Tom?" I asked.

"He'd lied. It wasn't until we got to the office that I saw the map, and I finally understood everything. When I asked Tom if we were going to live here, he laughed at me."

Lori's lips curled back in a snarl, and I drew back. She clung tighter to my hand.

"Oh Lord, Stella, don't be afraid of me. I didn't mean to kill him, but when he laughed, I got so mad. I hit him, and he pushed me away. Tom was so big. He swatted me like a gnat. He hurt me. Then he turned his back on me like I was nothing. A dirty, stinking nothing."

"What was he looking for? The business books?"

Lori nodded, causing the tears to fly. "He was trying to find more evidence to get people on his side. He had a lot of neighbors mad at your mama."

"Tell me, what happened after he turned his back on you?"

"Cele's scissors were on the ironing board. I was just so angry. Everybody's always treated me like I'm nothing. I picked them up without thinking. I stabbed him. I didn't even know he was hurt that bad. He stumbled around the room. It was awful. The scissors fell to the floor. He sat down in the chair, and he looked like he was going to kill me when he got able. I was afraid of him, Stella. He would have broken my neck."

"What did you do?" I could feel Lori's fear from that night. It glowed in her eyes. It was there in the shaking of her hands, the gasping breath.

"I ran. But—but I stole something. I want to give it back. Make things right. I'm not a thief."

I could hardly believe my ears. The woman had killed a man, and she was worried about being called a thief.

Lori reached into her tote bag and pulled out a bundle of muslin. She flipped back the corner to reveal, hidden in that cover, more fabric—reds, yellows, and blues.

"Oh, it's beautiful," I said.

Lori shook out the little sample quilt, flicking the edges until it was spread over the table. It was maybe forty inches square. There were beautiful stars scattered across the fabric that seemed to twist and turn, dancing to some stellar music.

"It's so pretty I couldn't resist." Lori collapsed, falling from her seat.

I grabbed her and at least kept the woman from hitting her head on the floor. Her skin felt icy cold as I helped her back up onto a folding chair while she moaned.

"I can't take anymore," she said.

I knew I had to get help for Lori, but I was afraid she might hurt herself if I let her out of my sight.

"Lori, let's go down to the kitchen. I'll make you a nice cup of tea." Silently I added that I would call Gibb. I needed professional help.

He could sort this out. Had Lori told me the truth? No one would confess to murder if it wasn't true and not with all those details.

"Let's go, Lori."

She let me slip my arm under hers, and I helped Lori to her feet. It wasn't until I led her unwieldy body around the table that I realized there was someone standing in the doorway.

Christine.

I wondered why she was here, but with the thought of asking, my mouth went dry.

Lori looked up, saw Christine, and went completely limp. Her dead weight was too much for me. The best I could do was lower her again to the floor. The chair was out of the question—she would have slid right off.

"So, she confessed," Christine said.

She wasn't asking, so I didn't answer. "I need to get help for her."

"I'll watch Lori," Christine said. "You should probably call Gibb."

I watched her gaze flicker to the shotgun leaning against the doorframe. The look caused a chill to run down my spine.

"Don't worry, Stella. I won't let Lori get the gun. She needs to be in a hospital. Maybe restrained."

"You're right, Christine."

"You thought I did it, didn't you, Stella?" Christine laughed.

I wish I had said no quickly, but instead I felt my cheeks flare. It was all the answer Christine needed.

"Oh, it's all right. In fact, I think I liked that you believed me capable of murder. But I loved Tom. Obviously more than she did."

Something came to mind.

"But you said you were with Lori. That it couldn't have been her."

Christine shrugged, and the white sweater tied around her shoulders slipped. She tugged the knot tighter.

"I guess I had the time wrong. Sorry, she must have already killed him by the time I got to her house. My house."

"Maybe we should take Lori downstairs. We can manage if we both take an arm," I said. For some reason I hated to leave Lori with Mrs. Billings Number One. There was no love lost between the women.

"No. That would take too long. Sorry I don't have my cell phone with me."

Christine crossed to Lori, dropped to one knee, and felt for the pulse on the wrist.

"It's weak. Fluttery. Hurry, Stella! You know how to find Gibb, and I don't."

She was right. I grabbed the shotgun and hurried out of the room. If I offended Christine by not trusting her with the gun, that was okay by me. By the time I slipped the shotgun back into the office closet and snatched up the phone, I was out of breath. The first time I tried to dial Gibb's cell number my hand was shaking so badly that I dropped the receiver. I picked it up, but instead of dialing again, I clutched the phone to my chest.

"Think, ninny. Something isn't right."

What had Lori said? Tom hadn't seemed to be badly hurt. He walked around the room. The scissors fell from the wound.

Shoot. Gibb had told me Tom was found in the office, lying on the floor with the weapon buried in his back. What a horrible image, but when Lori left the office, Tom was sitting in the chair. Probably still alive.

I believed Lori.

Someone else had stabbed the man a second time.

I wondered why Christine was here. Why had she come to the cabin?

I dialed the jail house instead of Gibb's phone. When Deputy Mullins answered, I told him it was an emergency, but I was babbling and hardly making sense of the story.

"Just get Gibb out to his mom's. It's bad." I slammed the phone down and started back to the studio, trying to hold my fear at bay. I wasn't sure what scene I would find when I got back to the third floor.

CHAPTER 33

I took the steps two at a time, stopping only to grab the shotgun again. When I skidded around the door frame of the studio, Christine was still kneeling beside the sick woman, except now they were struggling. Lori had Christine by the wrists and was making a weak attempt to push the older woman back.

Christine looked up. "She's out of her head."

"Help is on the way. Let's get Lori downstairs." I hoped if I sounded commanding that Christine would follow my lead.

Kneeling, I managed to half drag Lori to her feet. Christine's effort was mostly show or at least it seemed as if I were lifting a hundred pounds by myself. I grunted with the effort. When our trio shuffled out the door of the sewing studio, I breathed a sigh of relief. The shotgun was difficult to drag along with Lori, but I was terrified that I might need it.

Christine didn't give it a glance, and Lori, even though her eyes were open, didn't seem to be seeing anything.

After supporting the woman down two flights of stairs, I didn't have an ounce of energy left in my body. I dropped Lori onto a kitchen chair and flopped down on a chair beside her while propping my weapon against the table. Christine remained standing. She hadn't broken a sweat and looked cool and collected in her white slacks and sweater set with the cardigan still knotted around her shoulders.

"Ugh. Ugh, wait. I, uh—" I sucked in a huge gulp of air and mopped sweat off my brow.

Lori took that moment to fall face forward onto the table. At least she didn't slip to the floor, but I reached a hand out to steady her just the same.

When I looked back to Christine, a pistol had appeared in the woman's hand, and she was pointing it at me.

"Uh, Christine, that's a gun."

"Why, yes it is, Stella." Christine gave the weapon an exaggerated look as if she were surprised to find it there. "I believe it's the same gun Lori and I were fighting over while you called Gibb. Which reminds me, I don't have much time."

She circled around the table and grabbed the shotgun.

"What are you going to do?"

"I do believe I'll just kill you both."

"No need to get snide."

Christine laughed. Genuine mirth this time. "I'm going to miss you, Stella, and I never thought I'd say that. You've been a thorn in my side these last few days. Too bad you didn't go all the way down when you jumped off the cliff. I thought you were going to do yourself in and save me the job. After all, I missed dumping your car on top of you. Yes, I lied a bit about the time I was at the store. I figured I could get away with fudging a few minutes."

"What have you been waiting on? If you'd planned all along to kill Lori, why didn't you do it that night?" I wondered if I could stall this mad woman long enough for Gibb to get here. Would that save Lori and me? It would only take a second for her to pull the trigger. Somehow I felt Christine wouldn't hesitate.

"I know what you're trying to do. Let's go, Stella. I'll indulge you with answers after you get Lori into my car."

"But, please, just tell me: was Tom going to come back to you?"

Christine's face darkened like a thundercloud had passed over it. "Seems like he'd moved onto someone else. Someone entirely new." She waved the gun to show that she wanted me to get Lori to her feet.

"I'm too tired."

"You really should work out. You're looking more and more like a baked potato."

Now that was too much.

I grabbed the handle of the enamel teapot I'd left on the table earlier and threw it with all my might. Filled with water, it made a dangerous weapon.

Images of pitching to Gibb on lazy summer afternoons flashed in my mind as I watched the teakettle fly through the air in what seemed like slow motion. My little brother had, for two years, aspirations of being a professional ball player. Good thing he'd wanted to be right fielder, leaving me to throw to him for practice.

My aim was true, and Christine took the kettle square in the face.

She gave a yelp, and the gun fell to the floor with a clatter. Unfortunately, as Christine dropped like a rag doll, her foot sent the pistol flying across the room, and she landed on the shotgun. She seemed to be unconscious, but I was afraid to take the chance of grabbing either of the weapons.

I picked Lori's head up by her hair and slapped her harder even than I meant to.

"Wake up! Geez, Lori." I swatted my hand back and forth across her high cheekbones a little more gently.

"Stop, Stella!" Lori covered her face with both hands. "I was pretending. Christine is crazy."

When she realized I wasn't going to hit her again, Lori peeked between her fingers at Christine lying flat on the floor. Blood covered the older woman's face from the gash on her forehead. Christine moaned and stirred, and Lori and I screeched in unison and took off for the back door. It was two-stooge pandemonium when we tried to squeeze through the opening at the same time.

Finally, we burst onto the porch, and Lori sprinted across the lawn.

"Lori, this way!" I called as I ran toward Harley's car. I heard a loud pop and saw Lori duck.

A glance over my shoulder showed that Christine had recovered enough to stand swaying on the porch. She pointed the pistol at Lori, but the barrel rose and fell with her unsteadiness.

"Come on. The car!" I yelled.

This time Lori listened and followed me toward the old Fairlane. I worked to dig the keys from my pocket as I ran. Because I limped along with one hand stuck in my pocket, Lori beat me and jerked open the back door. She dived to the floor.

I jumped behind the wheel but couldn't find the ignition. I kept jabbing the key on the steering column until I remembered old cars were different. The key went in the dash.

"I don't have my tote bag." My voice cracked at the same time the back window did.

"That maniac is shooting at us, and you're worried about driving without a license?" Lori's voice was two octaves higher than normal.

I managed to turn the engine over and rev it until I remembered this wasn't an automatic. At that moment Christine's face appeared in my window, and my door flew open.

Her growl was great incentive to find the clutch. I think I stomped it and the gas at the same time and pulled the gear shift down. The big car threw chunks of sod into the air and then found its purchase to leap backward, slamming into Christine's Mercedes.

"Aargh! Why'd she park there?" I couldn't believe it. Harley had loaned me this fantastic car, an antique no less, and I'd managed to have a fender bender in less than two hours. Oh, and the back window had been shot out.

"Stella!" Lori's scream was muffled from the floor of the back seat.

The car bucked. Christine, now behind the wheel of her car, had rammed us. She was trying to disable the Fairlane, and if she did, we would be easy targets.

"Do something!" Lori said. Her pale face appeared over the back of the seat.

I pushed the shift stick up. The car must have been in third gear instead of first because the engine roared, and I think we did a wheelie, if that's possible in a car. Maybe I clipped the corner of the garage as we lurched forward, but I wasn't sure.

The car turned in a big arc around the lawn as I pointed it toward the driveway. The tires skidded on the grass, and I reversed the direction of the turn to correct, but the old car didn't have power steering. We went from a skid to spinning in circles on the dew-wet grass.

Christine's bloody face glowed red for a second in the Fairlane's headlights as the Mercedes sped ahead to block the driveway. She turned her car so that it completely filled the gravel path between the stone gateposts.

I finally got the spinning of the Fairlane under control by slamming on the brakes, but now there was no way past the danger. The car shuddered to a stop and idled with a rumble of power. How long had it been since I'd called the jail? Would Gibb get here in time?

"Stella, do something!" Lori shouted again, banging me on the shoulder with her fist.

"Stop that!" I flapped my hands at her.

"Drive! Look!"

"Make up your mind!" I said, then looked to where Lori pointed.

We watched as Christine got out of her car and took a stance like a TV cop. She fired in our direction.

"She's shooting at the tires, Stella." Lori started swatting at my head, completely hysterical now.

I jammed the gas pedal to the floor and put the car back in gear—first this time. I twisted the steering wheel back and forth to confuse Christine as I shifted through the gears. We shot past the house and around to the back, but there was no place to go where Christine couldn't get to us. At the edge of the lawn, I twisted the wheel.

"What's she doing?" I asked Lori as I circled past the side

of the cabin where Sherri was sleeping.

"She's chasing us again. Oh—"

The Mercedes rammed the Fairlane.

My forehead banged against the steering wheel from the force of the impact. I risked a look over my shoulder to see if Lori was okay. She'd been thrown to the floor.

"Stay down," I said as I saw in the rearview mirror the Mercedes surge forward for another attack.

I circled the cabin again, seeing Sherri's face gazing open-mouthed from one of the windows. After two circuits, I couldn't shake Christine.

"No, no, no! I can't get away."

Now the Fairlane was pointed toward the woods, Christine was less than a car length behind us, and I had no place else to go. At the last second, before the car plowed into the forest, I threw my arms over my face. I wished I'd taken time to fasten my seat belt.

I braced myself for an impact, but the car didn't hit any trees. The jolting and banging against the undercarriage told me we'd run over a few saplings, though. When I realized we were okay, I opened my eyes and pressed the gas pedal back to the floorboard. I steered a crooked path between the trees.

"Oh, Harley's not going to like this."

"What?" Lori's face popped above the back seat again. When she saw where we were, tree limbs slapping the windshield, she howled.

I screamed too when I saw headlights following us. Christine would have a smoother trip because the Fairlane had blazed a trail.

"You're crazy." Lori dove for the floor.

We bumped through a clump of laurel, and for a second

the tires spun as something on the undercarriage caught on the rope-like twisted trunks. Then the car shot forward like it had been released from a giant slingshot.

That's when the Fairlane's lights went out.

Just as I mumbled a prayer that I wouldn't hit any critters, the car broke through the forest onto the lawn of Harley's property.

"We're safe. Lori, it's okay. Harley will help us."

I could see his log cabin just ahead in the moonlight and a glance behind showed Christine was no longer following us. I pressed the brake pedal.

Nothing.

I pumped the pedal.

Nothing.

The car had slowed some since I'd taken my foot off the gas but momentum carried us on. The grille plunged into the cabin with a huge thump. The logs were strong, but the seventy-year-old chinking gave way, and the long hood of the antique car burst through the wall, finally coming to a stop atop a double bed.

I took my first breath in what seemed like a decade. The car door was jammed, but I was able to get it open by pressing with my shoulder. When I crawled off the seat, my legs were wobbly, but they held.

The door to the bedroom banged open, and Harley stood staring wide-eyed.

"Stella, next time use the front door."

CHAPTER 34

"Ah, that's good." I licked a bite of ice cream off the spoon and, eyes closed, savored the rich chocolately flavor. Then, I nipped off the tip of a slice of pizza. Sausage and mushroom. My favorite.

"Honey, do you know what that kind of food does to you?" Cele asked.

"Mmmm, yes. Yes. Yes!"

Mom eyed me like the fellow diners watching Meg Ryan in *When Harry Met Sally*.

We were in the kitchen while Cele prepared lunch for herself and the class. Lam had picked Mom up at the airport, and the pair had arrived home yesterday afternoon, missing all the fun of the previous evening. She'd immediately jumped into her duties as teacher and gotten the class back on track. I'd thought I might have the nervous breakdown I was overdue for, but I'd surprised myself by spending the afternoon getting things squared away—like giving a deposition to Gibb. I'd finally gotten him to explain why he had been seen by so many people with the widow. My brother had been putting pressure on her, trying to get a confession. If Lori wasn't guilty, he figured she knew more than she was saying.

Mom was home, no one was trying to kill me, and I was no longer the teacher. So life had returned to normal. Well, not exactly normal. I'd told Mom that I'd had to quit my job or be fired and that I planned to stay in Sewanee. She was happy and supportive.

Now the students were upstairs in the studio, chain-piecing. Whatever that was.

It was kind of funny. Lam was moving out as Harley carried Smoky's cat condo across the yard. Mom had offered Harley a place to stay until the bedroom of his cabin could be rebuilt. It was the least we could do for the man. He'd been in a room at Jim's Motor Lodge for the last two nights, but who'd want to live there for long?

Unfortunately for Harley—and me—the Fairlane was totaled. Evidently the brake line had snagged and broken on some underbrush or a tree root during my wild ride. That's why I'd been unable to stop the car. Really, it wasn't my fault I'd hit the cabin.

He came in the door with his arms full and a cowboy hat on his head. He said, "Be right back down, ladies."

"Mmmm," I said, watching him walk through to the dining room. The door slapped shut behind him.

"That man is fine looking," Cele said.

"Hey, hand's off, Mom." I straightened in my chair to find my mother, hands on hips, staring down at me, a smile on her pretty features.

"Just testing you. I'm not interested. I wondered if you were."

"No. Yes. Oh, I have no idea, Mom."

She kissed me just above the bandaid on my forehead. "Don't worry. You have plenty of time to figure it out and while you do, we're going to have so much fun quilting."

Lam breezed into the kitchen carrying a duffle bag. "That's it. I'm packed."

He dropped the bag onto the floor next to Doodle Dog and himself into the chair opposite. His brow furrowed when he looked at the food in front of me. "Maybe I should have left those shorts for you, Stella. You're going to need to keep up with the jogging."

"Very funny. As a matter of fact, I am going to start running and biking and, well, lots of new things. Whatever I want." I scraped up the last bite of melting ice cream.

"And quilting," Cele added.

"I'm not sure I want to do any quilting for a while, Mom." I pushed the bowl out of my way and scooted the pizza box closer. "I've never been so relieved in my life as I am to get the responsibility of quilt camp off my hands. But I don't know. Maybe I do want to start again." I really had enjoyed learning more about quilting.

"Only two more days of class, Stella," Cele said. "Extending the session was the least I could do. I'm glad all the students were able to stay over."

"Oh, I don't think anyone wanted to miss the next installment," Lam said.

She moved back to the stove and stirred the contents of a large stockpot sitting over a burner. It was almost lunch time. The class—minus Lori, who was on her way from the Sewanee jail to the hospital ward in Nashville's larger, better equipped one—would be down in minutes.

"What's that smell?" Lam asked, his nose wrinkling.

"An okra soup for lunch. Last out of the garden for this year. I think I'll thaw some of the tofu fettuccini for supper. Unless you already served it, Lam, while I was gone." Cele's long peasant skirt whirled around her calves as she turned.

Lam and I shared a look and burst out laughing. When he'd gotten himself under control, he said, "No, ma'am. There's plenty left."

Mom wagged a ladle at Lam. "Mark my words. You're going to miss out on my rice cakes with bean curd sauce. They're the side dish with the soup."

"Well, I am going to miss you. You too, Stella."

The sound of someone coming down the stairs stopped our conversation.

"Don't mean to interrupt. About that offer of lunch," Harley said, popping around the corner.

"Perfect timing," Cele said, moving toward the cabinet to retrieve another bowl. "Soup's ready."

This time it was Lam and I responding together as we shouted, "No!"

"Uh, how about some pizza, Harley?" I asked.

Harley sniffed the air while trying to pretend he wasn't. "Great, Stella. My favorite." Anybody would have to admit the man was a quick thinker. He sat between Lam and me and placed his obviously new hat down on the table out of the way. He reached into the box for a slice, taking a bite of the crust first.

"I'm being falsely accused. At least try my sun tea," Cele said and poured a glass without waiting for an answer. "How's the room going to do you?"

"It's great. Thanks for the offer to stay during the repairs. I wasn't looking forward to all that banging" He swallowed and winked at me. "Smoky's getting himself acquainted right now."

"Nice hat," Lam said, tracing a finger around the brim of the cowboy hat.

"Thanks, Lam. Someone I admire recommended the look," Harley said.

I blushed, and Lam glanced back and forth between Harley and me.

"Did you rent a car?" I asked to change the subject, though it made me shiver to think about the Fairlane again. The destruction of his home hadn't bothered the man nearly as much as seeing his prized car demolished.

Harley breathed a deep sigh, maybe counting to ten, and nodded yes.

Cele paused in loading a tray with glasses of ice and a pitcher of tea. "You know, Stella, I think it's a new record for you. Two cars to the junkyard in two days."

She continued working, unaware that her remark had upset me. Mom was nearly ready to serve lunch to the class and was busy getting out spoons and napkins.

Lam said, "How many does that make for you now?"

"I've lost track, thank you," I said, then sputtered when I realized how my remark had sounded.

"As your lawyer, Stella, I recommend you plead the fifth," Harley said.

Not trusting myself to reply, I stuffed another bite of pizza into my mouth.

"Cele, might I ask a question?" Harley asked.

"Sure, shoot! Uh, go ahead," she said.

"You still have a problem with the association wanting your business out of Mountaintops. Have you thought about how to handle it?"

"I'm letting Stella figure that out for me."

"Mom, that reminds me. What were you doing telling the council that you don't make a profit with the business?" Mom and I had been so busy over the hours she'd been home that I'd forgotten to ask.

"Ah. I knew that cat was out of the bag." Cele sat on the remaining chair. "It was partly a lie, which makes me feel awful. My quilts are well known now, especially in Japan, and I sell quite a few. That income has allowed me to donate quite a bit of my business profits to charity. I know that all this is still a business, and it's still profit, but I was trying to confuse the issue to buy time."

Lam, Harley, and I sat speechless for a few seconds until Lam said, "That's great you've been able to do that."

"Yep." She rose and gathered the tray and started for the dining room, padding on bare feet. Over her shoulder she said, "I swear people care too much about money." She disappeared through the doorway.

Mom didn't own a computer and had probably never experienced the Internet. She really did think love of money was the root of all evil. She'd have loved it if the hippie movement and communes had lasted. People living in harmony with the land. Loving and sharing. It probably embarrassed her to make more money than she needed to live. I could just picture her sending letters and photographs back and forth to another country. I'd bring her into the twenty-first century, and I'd bet I could double her sales.

"Try to talk her into hiring a money manager," Harley said. "I don't think the fact she's giving away her profit is going to dissuade Cele's neighbors. She's right that it's still really a business."

"Shue, ol' biddies should mind their own business," I said.

Harley and I both grabbed for the last slice of pizza, and he won.

"I have an idea though," Harley said, grinning like he'd invented bread. "I think we could persuade the residents to let Cele break her property away from the subdivision. I'll give her the strip of land she needs to make her own road out to the highway. After all, you've already blazed the trail." He grinned.

"Hey, Stella," Lam said, "He's stolen your—"

"Great idea, Harley. You're a genius." I carried the pizza box and our napkins to the trash can and stuffed it all in.

"I'll make a few calls to residents, and you can start campaigning, too," Harley said. "We've got nearly a month before the next association meeting."

Lam pushed up from his chair, grabbing his bag as he did. "Get Esther to help."

"Great idea. Lam, I really do hate to see you go. Thanks for sticking with me." I hugged him and included a quick peck on the cheek.

Before I could step back, Lam threw one arm around me. He gazed into my eyes, seemed to come to some decision, and then gave me a real kiss.

"Wouldn't have missed it, and I'll be around. See you, Harley, and be careful." Lam let the screened door slam and then said through the mesh, "Don't forget you owe me a hubcap, Stella."

"What'd he mean by that?" Harley asked, as Lam walked away.

"Who knows?" I wasn't sure if Harley was asking about the hubcap or the kiss. "Harley, I really am sorry about your car. You know that, don't you?" I asked to change the subject.

My stomach twisted into a knot. So far I'd apologized a dozen times, but it seemed Harley was having difficulty with the loss of the classic automobile.

I added, "I mean, you save my life, and I wreck your Fairlane. Some trade."

He mulled over my latest apology and finally said, "Hey, I got a cat out of the deal."

My eyes narrowed. "You mean, you got Smoky back. Right?" I asked. The way he'd phrased his reply brought up my old doubts about the man.

"Uh. Stella, I don't like to lie. I'd never seen the kitten until you came over and threw the little wildcat at me. I was snooping that night."

I jumped to my feet. "I knew it. What were you looking for?"

"At that point, anything. Remember, I was literally in the dark. I'd just moved here, my uncle had been killed, and unfortunately, the only person I really knew was Christine."

At the mention of her name, I shuddered. Christine couldn't hurt me now. When the electrical wiring on the Fairlane had failed and she couldn't see to follow anymore, Christine had driven her car into a tree. She'd been pretty woozy from being beaned with the tea kettle. Gibb was happy to help her and take the woman straight to jail.

Harley stood and stepped close. "I know. She always scared me, too. Christine was never the kind of aunt a kid could love.

Not that I saw her and Tom that much. My Dad and Tom never got along well, so we didn't visit often from Memphis."

"Do you know if Tom was really going back to Christine? She told me he was seeing a new woman."

"Tom never said a word about any of that to me though I don't think he was too happy with Lori. He'd thrown himself into this idea of getting the cliff lots, turning this cabin into a clubhouse, and building a golf course."

Harley stroked a strand of my hair back from my cheek, causing me to shiver. I rubbed my hands up and down my arms to get the blood flowing. "Did you know his plans from the start?" I held my breath, waiting on his response.

"Not really, Stella. I swear. He talked vaguely about developing a golf course when he asked me to buy the Abbott property." He gripped my shoulders. "It wasn't until I started questioning Christine, following her around, and generally making a pest of myself that I realized what was going on. Who the players were."

"Is that how you knew about the secret council meeting? I mean, from following Christine?"

"Yes. I realized my presence might make the difference since Darrington owed me one. That's the truth of it."

Cele sailed back into the kitchen followed by the sounds of the students laughing and talking as they sorted themselves around the dining table. Harley dropped his hands with a guilty look.

"The truth of what?" she asked.

"How Harley saved the vote of the council when they wanted to kick you out, Mom."

"Ol' biddies. They should mind their own business," she said.

Harley and I laughed. Maybe I was a lot more like my mother than I'd ever thought. If I was, that fact made me proud. Mom didn't ask what we found so amusing, just picked up her tray of soup bowls and left the kitchen.

From the next room could be heard cries of "Okra soup!" I snickered. Lam would be missed by all.

"Harley," I asked, "Do you think it was Lori or Christine who tried to shove me down the stairs? Christine confessed to trying to squash me with my own car and bonking you on the head, but who slammed the basement door on me?"

"My bet's on Christine. She was pretty vicious. That day at the cliff I think she was probably coming to my house to give me an earful for messing up the council vote. She must have seen me walking off into the woods and followed." He moved around the kitchen, looking at the architecture of the big logs with the rough chinking between the wood. He ran a finger in the groove. He stepped over to the soapstone sink and rubbed his hand over the front edge with its deeply worn lip. "Lori must have been terrified of the woman."

Mom stomped back into the kitchen and stopped, fists on her hips. "I swear. All they can talk about is Lam's biscuits. Lam's fried chicken. It seems Lam is a great cook and no one likes okra." She strode to the basement door. "Humph. Well, I'm still thawing tofu for supper. It's good for them." Her last words faded as she stomped down the steps heading to the extra freezer.

Doodle Dog got to his feet and walked to where Cele had left the basement door open. He moved around behind the wooden panel and, with the top of his head, pushed the door closed. The dog ambled to the back door, pushed the screen door open, and settled himself on the porch.

Had I almost been done in by a dog?

I said, "Lori told Gibb she helped Tom break into Mom's office. She really thought Tom wanted rid of Mom so they could have the cabin to live in. I don't think she meant to kill her husband, but she truly thought she had. Lori told me after the car chase that she stayed in the quilting retreat because she thought it might be helpful, that she might have the chance at some point to throw Gibb off the scent of who the murderer was."

"I agree that she never really meant to hurt Tom. We'll never know, but Christine had probably followed them," Harley said.

"I disagree. I bet Tom had told her the plan. I think she was the lookout. But, you're right, we'll never know for sure. Lori just didn't know someone had seen her lose her cool and pick up Mom's scissors. Christine crawled in the window after Lori fled. She took advantage of the situation." I shivered. "Ugh. What an awful woman. Lori was depending on the alibi that Christine offered. She didn't realize Christine really murdered Tom and would probably have killed her before very long.

"It came at such a price. Christine needed Lori, but Lori needed her more." Harley returned to his seat. "Tom's half of the business went to Lori."

"Do you think Christine was trying to get it from Lori?"

"I don't doubt it. After that, the young woman's life wouldn't have been worth a penny."

"That was stupid of Tom to will the store to Lori with Christine still involved."

Movement outside the window caught my eye. The ladies were skulking across the yard heading toward their cars. They piled into two vehicles and raced down the driveway. I'd bet they were going for burgers. Poor Mom.

Harley looked puzzled. "Tom died without a will. That's why everything went to Lori. She was rich. What made you think he had a will?"

"He made Lori sign a pre-nup. I just figured he'd have a will too."

Harley said, "Tom got all his legal work from me for free because he was cheap. As far as I know, there was no premarital agreement."

"I guess Lori lied to me at almost every turn. I swear I hate game playing. I'm never going to lie again in my life."

Harley turned to face me, a grin on his face. "You're not? Say, is there something going on between you and that fellow Lam?"

I dipped my head not at all sure how to respond. "Well, we've known each other for a long time." I cleared my throat. "I honestly don't know how to answer your question, Harley."

"Sounds like you're open to negotiations." Harley brushed his lips across my cheek until they found my mouth. The kiss was sweet and not at all pushy. Then he whispered in my ear, "See you tonight. I've got to go and talk to a contractor. I do believe I'm going to like living here."

I spent the next hours pleasantly enough, reading on the porch while Mom was holed away with the students in the studio for hours. After forty pages, two glasses of iced tea, and a moonpie—I'd written Mom an IOU—I was ready for some company besides Carly. She'd graciously allowed me to rub her back with my foot while I rocked. I sauntered up to the studio. All the students were gathered around a table. I worked my way in beside Julie who gave me a beaming smile.

"Look," she said.

Mom's small sample lay across the tabletop.

"Mom, your quilt is so beautiful." I leaned farther down to better examine the class sample quilt spread across a table in the studio.

"Thanks, Stella," Cele said, running her hand over the top of the small orange and blue sampler as if to stir the colors.

I examined the seams in the Twisting Stars quilt. The sharp intersections of the colors gave the fabric a sense of movement—definitely twisting, rotating around the center of each star block. How had I not noticed this the first time I'd seen the quilt? Oh yeah, Lori had just confessed murder.

I fingered the quilt top one of the faster students had completed under my tutelage. It looked nice to me, but I had to admit the instructions I'd eventually given the students had resulted in something much different from Mom's Twisting Stars pattern.

"Your design is nice, Stella," Mom said. "I think you have potential to be a designer. Why did you decide on this pattern?"

"Between one page driving to Georgia, one getting eaten by Doodle, and, ah, I just liked this, Mom. Your quilt is nice, too."

Julie slipped up beside us and said, "Cele, could you help me for a second? I'm having trouble with a seam. I think the bias stretched."

"Of course. Julie, you have to treat the cloth with respect."

"Of course." I threw my hands up in the air.

THE END

Enjoy These and More from the AQS

AQS Publishing brings the latest in quilt topics to satisfy the traditiona
to modern quilter. Interesting techniques, vivid color, and clear
directions make these books your one-stop for quilt design and
instruction. With its leading Quilt-Fiction series, mystery,
relationsip, and community all merge as stories are
pieced together to keep you spell-bound.

#10279

#7274

#1697

#7313

#1692

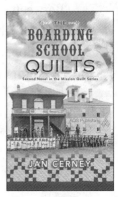

1645

Whether Quilt-Instruction or Quilt-Fiction, pick one up
from AQS today.

AQS publications are available nationwide.
Call or visit AQS
www.shopAQS.com
1-800-626-5420